Cocaine

Cocaine

A Novel

Phil Strongman

ABACUS

An *Abacus* Book

First published in Great Britain
in 1997 by Abacus

Copyright © 1997 by Phil Strongman

FAB lyrics copyright © 1994 by Stuart Kelling.
All rights reserved. Reproduced by kind permission.

A CIP catalogue record for this book
is available from the British Library.

ISBN: 0 349 10957 5

Typeset by M Rules in Sabon
Printed and bound in Great Britain
by Clays Ltd, St Ives plc

Abacus
A Division of
Little, Brown and Company (UK)
Brettenham House
Lancaster Place
London WC2E 7EN

For Jay Strongman, Andrew Gordon, Phil and Claire,
Paul A., Stuart the K., Steve, Martin, D. Leman and Bob D.
. . . and anyone else who's ever walked down
Wardour Street at dawn.

Cocaine

I Live Alone And I Give The Orders

I had jumped the gun. I had, in fact, been just a bit too hasty. I'd promised Jerry that a piece about his friend's trip-hop band, the Space Age Nomads, was definitely going to appear in the next issue of *Groove* magazine. It wasn't a feature really, more like a re-written press release, but it still read okay and the Space Agers' single still sounded pretty good. Good enough to justify me putting them in the mag's Floor-Fillers chart, anyway. It helped that a few club DJs really had been playing it – though not enough to justify me charting it – but quality wasn't really the issue here. The problem was my promise. Although ninety per cent of what I churned out usually ended up in print, I couldn't guarantee it. And Jerry, who'd got me into a lig or two over the years, was desperate that the Space Age Nomads got plugged in the next *Groove*. Not that plugging was his job. I didn't know *what* Jerry did for a living, come to think of it, though he always seemed to have money to burn and parties to go to. Which must have been where I met him, once. Either there or where we were now, propping up the bar in The Coach & Horses. 'Park Life' was playing.

'It's not Vee's single, it's just on his label. He's gotta new label,' Jerry said, staring at his glass of Jack Daniel's. I was supposed to know Vee, but I didn't. Vee was something of a big-shot, that much I was aware of.

'Is that sorted? Definite?' Jerry went on, looking around me as he tugged on his designer lapels. It was kind of sorted. Pretty much. I'd seen the next issue at the office, on computer. It was in the bag. But, like I said before, it wasn't definite. His eyes returned to me.

'Oh yeah,' I lied.

'Good,' he went on, ''cos he's depending on it. He'll be here in a minute.'

'Who will?'

'The lad hisself. Vee, ma main man.' Jerry must have caught my mental twitch as he spoke because he quickly added, 'Don't worry, you'll love him, he's cherry, he's cool, down with everyone, not heavy at all. Not when you consider what a big noise he is.'

'Yeah?' I said. 'I can't work out why we haven't met before.'

'Well, these big noises always are very quiet, aren't they?' he answered with a cheesy grin. 'Vee's a diamond geezer, though, a diamond geezer. He'll sort you out. With a drink, like.'

'Cheers.'

'Yeah,' Jerry said, accepting my thanks with his usual ligger's catch-phrase, 'Put me on the door, put me on the tour . . .'

Before I could ask anything else, Vee walked in. I knew it was him straight away. He was medium-to-tall, dark hair, good looks enhanced by a touch of scar tissue, blue Paul Smith shirt, colourful, undone at the neck. In his late twenties, I guessed. Jerry went over, the perfect courtier, and whispered something to him – about me? – as they approached.

'Hi, Pete. How's it going?' Sarf London accent. Vee's eyes swept around the room, taking it all in – the empty tables, the two lovers necking in a corner, the deserted bar counter. As he did this we shook hands, a move which he used to pass something on to me. I hesitated, then pocketed the plastic packet. A good size bag too.

'What you been doing, Vee?'

'This and that. Caning it . . . Wanna drink?'

'Vodka and it, cheers.'

'Vodka and it, twice,' he said to the Aussie barman. Vee grinned. He was friendly, personable. A London lad. I went to the toilet. Checked the bag – it was white powder, at least a dozen grams. *A dozen grams!* I tasted it and my top gum went numb within seconds. Joy powder, Bolivian marching powder, charlie, coke, cream, gear, terry, tinkle, tink, toot, snoot, sherbet, snow and bu – the latter pronounced like the first two letters of bugle, which was yet another pet name . . . they changed all the time, the names; once one had appeared in the newspapers someone would use another and everyone followed suit. Only the dictionary remained constant: 'Cocaine; a narcotic in the form of an energising powder synthesised from the paste of the South American coca leaf. Seen pre-war as an adult tonic it has been illegal in the United Kingdom since . . .'

I still couldn't believe it though: a dozen grams, what was that worth? The cops would say it's a grand's worth *on the street* – but that would have to be a street in Mayfair. Still, it must have been worth at least six hundred pounds. What to do? Was a dozen grams enough to get the Law casting you as a dealer? Yeah, must be, seven or more grams could do that. I was looking at two years inside, maybe three if I got caught with such an amount. And all of it was on me then. All of it. Guilty as charged and burning a hole in my pocket.

The sensation in the whole top half of my mouth faded fast. The numbness spread though, taking my throat off the list of active organisms. This was strong stuff. Far purer than anything I'd ever taken before – not that I'd taken that much before. How pure was it? Thirty per cent? Thirty-five? Maybe even forty per cent pure? That put its value up to nearer a grand. But getting sentenced to three years inside . . . or would it be four? The paranoia grew, soaring with the high as if it was the high's evil shadow. Every cloud has a tin-foil lining. My heart thumped faster and faster. Shit, I just wanted some humble grass, m'lud, don't jail me . . .

My face was shining so I splashed it with some lukewarm water as I wondered why none of the hot taps ever worked in any London bar. I walked out of the toilet, trying to look legitimate and business-like. The bar was completely deserted now. Even the lovers had gone. And Jerry and Vee were nowhere to be seen, of course. Great, that was all I needed. Maybe they'd just been busted and we were all due to appear on *News at Ten* with blankets over our heads . . . I couldn't help noticing the sunlight as it picked out the lazy dust floating in the air, just like the chalk-dust in a summer class-room as school died.

'Can I get you anything, sir?' The barman returned, grinning blankly, like he knew something. Or someone. I was going to ask where Vee and Jerry had gone but I stopped myself, mid-thought, on the grounds that it might incriminate me. I definitely couldn't give the stuff back now. *Let's just take another dab*, I thought, *and kick the rest under a table, eh?* But what if some plain-clothes copper came in a few seconds later? I could imagine the conversation.

'And who was standing there then, barman?'

'It was a tall bloke, officer – look, that's him outside now!'

The absolute certainty of getting busted was growing on me by the second. Couldn't leave the stuff. Couldn't keep it. Stuck in the middle with you. Great. I should have known better. Always look a gift horse in the mouth.

I had to get out. Get out and get home. I knocked back the dregs of my drink and stumbled outside. Vee and Jerry were not, of course, struggling with a police patrol on the pavement outside. Not that the absence of cops calmed me down. I still felt like I was in the judicial spotlight. *Look inconspicuous!* I silently screamed at myself. I thought about getting a cab, but it was tourist city out there. No chance. A Number 19 bus swung past then got caught at a red light. I jumped on it. Went upstairs. Went to the front. I was unseen. That was good. The vodka I'd taken was combining with the bu now, was kicking in something chronic, so I took another dab, just a little – why not? – as the bus lurched over a bump in the road. *Hey, this soaring nothing feeling is really a great adventure!* I tried to keep it down, tried to feel ironic and distant. I failed.

I was getting careless. Some powder – half a gram, a gram, more! – floated down on to the floor. Shit. I used my boot to grind the powder into the chewing-gum dirt as I bundled the cling-film plastic together again, and thought about getting off the bus. My jaw was buzzing now. Deciding to take a chance, I got off in New Oxford Street and ducked into Denmark Street, which was where I bumped into Chas from the Hot Import record shop. He was there with a couple of baggy rave characters with silly hats – E17 rejects wearing hats with ears. They were all covered with 'Love' logos and acted like they wanted to dish out a good kicking.

'He's back and now he's wack. Just the man I was looking for. Pete here owes me some dosher, doncha now?' said Chas.

'How'd you figure that one?' I fronted it out with a smile.

''Cos the last lotta booties you give me was all domestic. Well dodgy. So you owe me some wonga, doncha?'

Which was true, kind of. Except that he'd ripped me off before, like every single time he'd ever bought off me, like all buyers in a buyer's market. And it's always a buyer's market. But . . . let's not quibble.

I wasn't a part-time shoe-salesman, by the way. Booties means bootlegs, for the uninitiated. Illegal recordings that DJs would kill for because all the turntable wannabes couldn't get hold of them in Woollies. You can buy them from basements in Covent Garden or Camden. Or even from Chas if you really want to get ripped off. They're usually from America, sounds that haven't been or won't be released, rare mixes, mistakes, copyright problems. I was sometimes in possession of one or two . . .

I could have turned on my heel and walked away from Chas and all that – I might have got a bottle over my head, though I seriously doubted it – but if I did walk away would I have closed off yet another of my limited outlets? Yes and no.

'Do I? Don't recall that, Chas . . .'

'He don't "recall that". You kill me, man, you kill me, doncha?'

No, I thought, *but I'd like to, right at this minute.*

'No,' I actually said, 'you just did me a favour, didn't you?'

'You,' he shook his head sadly as if this was part of some huge tragedy which moved him greatly, 'you used to be down with everyone, dincha, Pete? Way you're going on nah you're gonna end up on the rock'n'roll, encha?'

Rock'n'roll – dole. Unemployed and unemployable. Yes, it *was* possible. More than possible. I'd never gone to college or anything. I know that sounds weird, especially now when every other Scout hut has the word 'university' blue-tacked outside, but that's how it happened. I'd left school a year before the second Summer of Love (copyright EMI records 1988, all rights reserved) so I joined in that scene instead. University of life – well, Soho. A full-time course. Running clubs, doing artwork, working for nothing half the time and making thousands the rest. And writing about it all too, convinced there was some bigger, higher meaning to it all as we raced the cops to the next rave road-block while screaming '*Acieeeed! Acieeed!*' It all ended up as big business, of course, being run by people with double-barrelled names or double-barrelled shotguns. I should have grovelled my way back into college then, back into the loop, but I didn't. Too busy partying. I couldn't complain – I'd had a lot of fun – but here I was, a decade on, free of all qualifications, on every credit blacklist going, existing as a freelance music hack. I say 'existing' because it sure as hell wasn't a real living . . .

Chas grunted louder, I'd ignored him too long.

'Said you're gonna end up on the rock'n'roll, encha?' he repeated with emphasis. I shrugged in reply. It seemed the sensible thing to do while he was playing the disillusioned big brother.

'So,' he went on, 'whatcha bin doin' then, boy?' He screwed his eyes up. He wanted an answer. What *had* I been doing? Specifically, what had I been doing to pay him off? Chas and his droogies still looked like they might turn nasty. This was getting crazy, I decided. I couldn't owe him more than a few quid, just peanuts . . . Then again, I've known bouncers that would break your jaw for a twenty. And they knew crack-heads who would do it for ten. So what was the deal? I leaned forward, all confidential. *You're in on this too now, Chas baby. Have a favour back.*

'Fancy a dab of something?' I offered.

'What you got? I don't want no speed.'

'No, no. It's faster than that. Only the best for my mate Chas.'

'Sound.'

'Sorted.' The gang chipped in like the idiot chorus they were.

'Solid—'

'Safe—'

'Smooth—'

Chas grinned mirthlessly. We strolled down the tiny alley that separates the guitar shops on Denmark. He took a huge dab, his boys less so, they were lairy of anything that wasn't beer. Chas pulled out a matchbox – this was all so blatant – before he gave me a questioning look, like I was the big boss-man now. And, suddenly, I could see the attraction of dealing gear. Forget the profits, forget the easy access. The biggest bonus was being in demand. Girls suddenly attracted to you. People forming a line at parties. Chas changing moods like the wind. Not that I wanted to become a dealer. I'd spent a few weekends in the cells for various things – usually for being at some pay party that had been raided – and I didn't ever want to extend the experience. But that didn't stop me nodding in reply, granting a favour to Chas as I cleared my debt. He emptied the last few matches from the box and I tipped a gram or so in there and closed the bag. I was probably three grams lighter then, all told – does that make a difference, m'lud? Chas licked his lips. I was forgiven. In fact he now owed me one. I toyed with the idea of giving it all to him, the lot, and forgetting all about it, but something at the back of my brain stopped me. Something definitely stopped me. I dunno what . . . cocaine, probably.

I got a cab home. The ansafone light flickered. It was Jerry's voice.

'Pete baby, this is Jezza. Me an' Vee had to go. Things to do an' that. But you got the stuff, right? That gear is so pukka you can cut it fifty-fifty. You'll make a fortune, my son. Just make sure that feature goes in, eh? Just make sure it's locked. Ring you later.'

That last line made an idea leap from the back of my brain to the front. *Let's be logical*, I thought, *let's be straight ahead logical*. Vee, the coke baron, now expected a feature and/or review. A review of his trip-hop mob. He'd given me nearly a thousand pounds' worth of pure cocaine for just that very purpose. If the feature didn't go in, he'd figure I owed him a grand in return. Maybe much more than a grand, since he probably needed a good review in the next issue far more than he needed the cash. He probably had posters and ads lined up – timing was all.

I didn't just owe Jerry a favour if the review didn't run. If it all went wrong I now owed Vee. I should have checked before I opened my big mouth. I couldn't actually guarantee that the review would go in – a last minute advert paying cash, a mistake at the printers, a rush-release on a Prince album, anything could happen and usually did. As a free-loading freelancer I didn't have that much influence. Any definite was a definite maybe. Nothing was definite unless you were an editor. Or a sub-editor. And sub-editors usually become editors. Although many subs are undoubtedly talented, the main reason for their rapid rise through the ranks is that, like production staff, they are actually in the office all day. Now this is what they are paid for, but the suits in charge of things never seem to quite twig this and think, instead, that this daily attendance shows some extraordinary beyond-the-pale dedication. Freelancers are, with a bit of justification, consid-ered dangerous flakes, and the staff writers, if there are any left, are seen as drunks – and they're always out doing silly things like covering stories – while the very word art, as in art director, is enough to terrify any *bona fide* member of the board. No top spot for them then. So, if you're a magazine writer or freelancer, it always pays to stay in with your subs. Even when they take out, as they usually will, the key para-graph that explains everything – or the punch-line that made others laugh out loud – you can't freak out at 'em because they're more important than you in the grand scheme of things. They were, or would be, in charge. And being in charge was something I most certainly was not.

That was why I'd kept the coke – in case my plug for Vee's mob got spiked and I had to sell some. At least that's what I told myself. I had toyed with the idea of just giving it straight back to Vee, but I knew he wouldn't want the goods back, not now. He'd want their wholesale worth – at least – and in cash. I dialled Jerry's number, thinking that I must find out more about Vee. Jerry's ansafone was on and I decided I wasn't well enough to leave a message.

I took another tiny dab of coke as I sorted through my mail, feeling hyper but strangely confident. Why not be on an upper? The review would probably go in and, even if it didn't, there was always the plug in the Floor-Fillers chart to keep Vee happy. So what was I worrying about? Nothing, as usual . . . The hi-fi automatically flicked through the capital's radio stations. There was Jules Someone playing House on Kiss FM and Capital Radio was playing House and Pete Someone on Radio 1 was playing – guess what? – House . . . The House mafia, live and in full effect on all channels. I figured I was lucky to be alive in such a wonderful age of diversity.

I ripped open the last envelope. There was a lig on. There was always a lig on. This one was at the Happy House. Tonight. My name had been put on the door.

A lig, as you surely know, is a launch party – for some CD or band or book or club or boutique or whatever – wherein copious amounts of free drink are served up to a host of trendies, hacks, paparazzi and various other hangers-on. These party-goers are usually known as liggers. A true ligger won't actually write or photograph anything that will mention the event that he's just ruined – in fact, a true ligger won't even have been officially invited – and this is implicitly understood by most organisers. They pretended to love the product and we pretended we'd write about it – or, at the very least, spread the word.

I hoped Jeff would be there, but it was pretty unlikely. He hated the Happy House – it had been littered with junkies the first time he went and he hadn't been back since. Jeff is my half-brother, a 'top-notch club DJ' as they say in the Sunday supplements. He wasn't ultra-fashionable any more, but he'd still been on air a few times and he still made a living and enjoyed his role. He played whatever he liked, whenever he liked and there weren't that many DJs in clubs who could do that, let alone on the airwaves. As I said, he wasn't that trendy, but trendy had become something of a devalued term. It usually didn't mean trend-*setting* any more. It just meant reading, and getting all your ideas from, certain magazines and/or buying into 'yoof' TV and MTV. And anyone and everyone could buy into that. 'Anastasia only wears grey, has nipple-clamps, a face tattoo of Himmler and her ambition is to date her dad! Big-up respect, yeah! Jungle in the House! And, after the break, we've got some close-ups of a testicle operation!'

No word-of-mouth was required. No special talents. No suss. Therefore everyone was hip. And if everyone was hip, then no one was. So being unhip was hip. And how hip you were depends on how unhip you could be, see? This meant that, in some niteries, the Simon Park Orchestra, the 1910 Fruitgum Company and the cha-cha-cha were the coming thing, while Gilbert O'Sullivan was now the Godfather of Punk. Clever, huh?

2

Having So Much Fun

The Happy House entrance lights were too bright, making the scene – a girl in a pink painter's smock being gingerly searched by the security – look like something out of a movie. Thirty seconds after being searched and going on in, she returned, saying to the staff that she'd left her fags in the car and could she please get them and come back in? Please? *Pretty please?* They said yes, of course, though it was really only an old trick that small-time dealers sometimes used, girls especially. They would get frisked, get the all-clear, then nip out and return, loaded down with E's and whizz, and the bouncers would then nod them straight through because, well, they've already been searched, haven't they? Yeah, yeah, yeah . . .

I spied Jerry inside the sunken foyer. He was wearing an oversized powder-blue mac, and I sought him out like an Exocet.

'Jerry, wha' happen, man? What's going on?'

'Everything – come here, I want you to meet some designers.'

That's all I needed. I wanted to find out more about Vee,

11

vis-à-vis my chances of being crippled, and Jezza wanted to introduce me to a couple of art students.

'You'll love 'em, they're really fit, cherry man not wack—'

'Great, whatever you want, but we gotta talk about Vee—'

Jerry stopped dead in his tracks, stepping over a sneering girl in a half T-shirt and silver jeans. He licked his lips as he turned slowly and spoke, his eyes everywhere.

'*Vee?* Is he here?'

'I dunno, Jezza, that's why I'm asking you.'

'Course he's not here,' said Jerry, relaxing and walking on. 'I would know.'

'Thought you said he wasn't heavy . . .'

'He's not, not really.'

'So why d'you look so worried then?'

'Me? Worried? Pete, baby, you're losing it.'

'No, I'm not,' I breezed. 'And you *are* worried. Come on, tell Uncle Pete everything . . . you know what they say, a trouble shared is a rumour started.'

'Nah . . . I jus' owe him a few quid. I was s'posed to give it to him this afternoon, or take it round tonight. But he can wait. He don't mind. Me and Vee are like that.' He showed me his two crossed fingers.

'And which one's on top then?'

'Pete, man, there's no longer any top or bottom,' he philosophised. 'Not anywhere, not with anyone. Now there's just deals. You know? Deals? That's all there is. And the people you trust are the people you deal with, see? And I trust Vee. He's a diamond, man, a fuckin' diamond.'

'So he doesn't knee-cap people then?' I said, my fading paranoia still seeking reassurance.

'Knee-cap? You're crazy, man. You've been caning it too much. Vee might do *someone*, somewhere, maybe, if they pushed their luck. But he'd never do you, 'cos you know me, see? He's gonna be the godfather of me kids. So, lighten up . . . Are you staying out late? What time did you come out tonight?' he asked, trying to change the subject.

'I came out at nine.'

'Still working nine to five then?' He smirked a big, sloppy smirk.

'Why do you always say that?' I asked before he laughed at his own feeble joke.

'Well, I dunno. Why do you always ask me why?'

'Because, Jerry, I'm trying to offer you some solid stability in a ruthless world of change—'

'Bollocks . . . have you seen this?' he said, slapping a magazine into my hands. It was the colour supplement of the *Chronicle*, folded open on a page that featured a big colour splash of the kids' latest heroes, The Scallies, a rock'n'roll band who were fast becoming superstars. One of the hangers-on in the main picture was Jerry, leaning on The Scallies' guitarist.

'Sweet,' I nodded. 'You look good.' And he did look good.

'Yeah, I might be going on their world tour.'

'Friend of the stars, eh?'

'That's it, son,' he said as he slowed to a halt before two girls. 'Pete, meet Desdemona and . . . Georgina, isn't it?'

'Geraldine.' Geraldine, a skinny brunette, corrected Jerry with a tricksy smile. Desdemona was darker, Asian. Both of them *seemed* like sweet young things. They tolerated Jerry and me anyway. A closer look revealed that they had big bright eyes that were flat, and even flatter stomachs with two rings stuck in each belly button. Two. Overkill. You could tell they were designers. They must have been all of eighteen years old. Maybe seventeen. It was no big deal, though. I'd seen girls of fourteen in clubs before now. Geraldine and Desdemona were from Bournemouth, just up for the weekend they said, at which Jerry winked at me. We talked aimlessly about fashion and music, and when things slowed down Jerry showed them the *Chronicle* supplement featuring himself, telling them that I wrote for the *Chronicle* – which was true, I'd get maybe four pieces a year – but the girls were dying to blurt out what they were really after. Jerry, who fancied himself as a remixer that week, was talking about people faking it in music.

'These days,' I mumbled, trying to be profound, 'almost everyone is faking it everywhere.'

'I've never faked it in my life,' pouted Desdemona.

'You haven't been taking the right drugs, then,' giggled Geraldine in a Dorset/London hybrid accent before adding, 'speaking of gear . . .'

Here it was. The pay-off. The inevitable question. *Do you score here often?*

'You boys got any stuff? Any coke?' It was all so predictable that I almost wanted them to go away, but after another ten seconds of contemplating their figures I began to wish I had brought some of my coke with me. I hadn't dated anyone for months, and even my last inglorious one-night-stand had been a week or two ago. Giving these two coke would have been a bit of a bribe, but didn't all relationships involve some kind of bribery? Not that you could call it a relationship.

I shouldn't have worried – Jerry had some charlie on him. Naturally. And that's the way the conversation began to veer. *I'm a journo and he's got more charlie than Chaplin. We can help you, girls, we can help you.* It was sickening, really, but that's the way things were. Twenty seconds later the girls were licking some spilt powder off Jerry's cuff, acting like demented kittens. All four of us were crammed into one cubicle of the gents' toilet, eyes bumping off each other like magnets. They sniffed a line apiece and then it was Jerry's turn. He chopped up his gear on the cistern, sniffed it through a rolled-up tenner and then I took half a line and made a dab at the rest. Jerry finished a third line off as I wondered if my wet finger, just off the cistern lid, was going to give me jaundice later. Jaundice or Hepatitis B. Or both. Or were they the same? I made a mental note to get some vodka – if I swilled it around and gargled it enough it would surely kill all known germs. Either vodka or brandy would do it. A brandy will settle your stomach too. Brandy will settle most things, if you drink enough of it . . .

Things began to go sour when the girls began to act like they were addicts or something. Not that they wouldn't be

14

friendly later, they would probably even put out, but only if we gave them some more toot. If we wanted them. Bittersweet young things that they were.

'There's a party up west. Near the Hangover.' Jerry whispered in my ear when we were back on the stairs.

'Are we taking these two?' I asked as quietly as I could.

'Maybe, if you want to . . . Girls, there's a party on. You up for it?'

Their faces revolved around to ours again. Their big bright eyes were even flatter now, pupils tiny. Germ warfare victims with no emotion. Close up, they'd almost look like aliens. Pretty, but alien. Had I ever looked like that? I might have done once or twice, which was a frightening thought. Maybe they'd scored some coke before they'd even met us.

'Oh yeah, when's it happenin' then? This party?'

'Now. Do you wanna wait outside for us?'

'Outside?' They were genuinely horrified. One minute they were being given Class A drugs in a top London niterie as they hung out with friends of The Scallies, and now they were being asked to wait outside. Outside! Them! Designers! Outside! Them!

'Yeah, just for five minutes, girls, just for five, I gotta get invites y'know. I'll just be five.'

They sulkily strutted up the steps and lingered on the edge of the foyer's pool of light. Jerry said something to the guy with the guest-list and pocketed a couple of crumpled tickets. I looked outside. The designer-clad designer girls outside were chatting to some Essex lads in mod shirts – *we wanna go to Camden!* – as Jerry swept up to me, the mac twirling around his ankles.

'There's someone outside who can give us a lift. We just gotta wait a couple of minutes.'

A few moments later a DJ in duffle-coat and goatee run-walked up to Jerry. Although by then it was jammed tight, we still managed to get through the exit easily enough, but Desdemona and co. were nowhere to be seen. They'd probably had a better offer and taken it. The rest of us piled in a white mini-cab which screamed off like some getaway car. The Yugoslav driver was nineteen or twenty years young and several laws unto himself – he didn't go through a single green light the entire journey – but we were all too high to care. As I glanced back I saw the designer girls outside the club, emerging from behind one of the stone pillars. One of them waved frantically and I nudged Jerry – he had the tickets, after all – but he silently shook his head and the Happy House soon disappeared into the background. They'd find what they were looking for anyway. A trendy-wendy guy with a fuck-off-and-die coke stash. Their knight in shining Armani, some cat with all the cream . . .

'We're running out of toot,' Jerry moaned as the mini-cab neared the West End. By now, I was too much in the swing of things to slow down, so I opened my mouth and gave the game away.

'Make him go via my place. I've got some gear there,' I heard myself saying. The mini-cab radio was blaring out 'Everything Is Gonna Blow' and I thought yeah, that's how I feel.

The party venue was a former restaurant, now a kind of wine-bar-type club with stupid empty picture frames and driftwood thrown on the walls at random. But the floor below almost looked like a night-club when the lights were low. In my hyper state I was totally drug-conscious, aware of all the deals – the tables at the back looked like a hip chess tournament played at high speed. Under flickering lights. Once your eyes – and your mind – had adjusted to the gloom, you saw it all. If you knew what to look for – lots of little hand moves, cash and powder going back and forth over, under and around tables. Amid much back-slapping and side-tapping. As if they were great friends. Young journos and trendies getting loaded. Getting blasted. Almost everyone was, if the truth be known. Virtually every single one of the media crowd was doing something illegal at some point during the week.

There was free booze at the bar to celebrate the launch of

some new vodka mixer, so people were knocking back the Russian spirit like there was no tomorrow. Consequently they were all talking more than normal. There were some time-servers from admin, accounting and ad departments present, too, all of them trying to act like real human beings. Top button undone, bri-nylon tie loosened, kissy-kissy! *Love your suit!*

I talked to Eye, Eye being a bottle-blonde PR for Fried Funk records. Eye, as she'd always be the first to tell you, is a good fun person. 'Good fun people' are usually like good fun entertainment, being neither good nor funny, but Eye's actually both. When she's not being miserable, of course. By the time you finish reading this sentence she'll have been promoted or sacked.

That night Eye was the only person there, Jerry aside, that I knew. The rest was a storm of strangers, and Eye was the eye. We talked about today's drug fetish and I repeated what Jeff had said about trip-hop – the discs are okay but you have to be stoned to really love them. Stoned music usually made by stoned people and probably aimed at stoned people. Unlistenable and depressing without chemical stimulants.

'Everyone's on drugs these days,' I said, 'especially the teens, 'cos there's no real jobs for most of 'em and no one thinks they can change anything any more. If you think you can't do anything to *that* out there, you just settle for seriously damaging *this* up here.'

'That's an amazing theory,' Eye said. 'What are you on?'

One of her pals rolled a huge spliff of skunk – liberally sprinkled with Moroccan Black – even as she agreed with me. I took the joint, damned as I was, and inhaled greedily. Even the joint didn't do much to slow me down, my heart was beginning to roar like a lion. Everyone was starting to annoy me by speaking in slow-motion. I'd had too much coke. *And*, I thought, *you are talking too slowly! Far too slowly! Get on with it! Faster! Faster!* Cut to the chase! *Cut to the chase!*

Someone offered me some toffee. *Sweeties and school-age innocence*, I thought, so I took it. And then discovered that by 'toffee' he meant the chewy Manchester thing that's full of speed. I got kicked into overdrive. Double-time. But good. Which was too bad. Everything got very hectic, very fast. I lost Eye – and her pals – and Jerry in the crowd. I found myself with the hostess of the place. She was called Gina. She was an overgrown wild child, a kind of no-nothing twentysomething. She contributed to the *Telegraph*'s fashion pages – or was it *The Times*? – and was operating on the wrong side of twenty-five. Like me. But she also had unlimited credit, and she was supposed to be that week's It person. Unlike me.

'It's all this stupidly fast techno crap that brings me down,' I said as the ruthless soundtrack of bass booms thudded around me.

'If it's too fast, you're too old,' she sniggered. As if she was still seventeen.

'Yeah, yeah, yeah.'

'You're really pre-digital, aren't you?' she lisped sympathetically, her eyes a touch worried as if the dinosaur before her might crumble away before her very eyes. Mind you, the way I felt, total disintegration wasn't a complete impossibility.

'If that stuff can't be about human rhythms, it should at least be about love or hate or Bosnia or something,' I rambled as I felt my left eye start to twitch.

'If you really, really wanna know about love, Pete, you should pop an E—'

'Huh?' I grunted back as my hand desperately smoothed my flickering eye to a standstill. Afterwards I noticed my hand was trembling slightly.

'And as for Bosnia,' she went on, 'we really should leave those ethnic-cleansing things to the government. They do have a plan, you know. A long-term thingy. And I'm *sure* it's clever—'

'Oh yeah, so clever it's fuckin' stupid.'

'No, I really think we should leave it to them—'

'We've done that for years now,' I said, 'and what have you got? TB and rickets are back, the UN's a joke and the Serbs have got away with locking people up in concentration camps and starving 'em—'

'Starving 'em!' she scoffed. 'They should be so bloody lucky! I've been on a diet for months.'

'That's not really that funny, you know? Not really.'

But, I must admit, her idiot views had only been part of my problem with her. Most of it was because she spoke so damned slowly. It felt like time for more vodka – gotta fight that jaundice. Medical paranoia. By 1 a.m., though, it was all even worse. I was seriously worried. I'd only done the odd few lines of coke – was it a few? I couldn't remember – but I was still getting that heart-strain. Pulse flickering! Too fast! Too fast! *Too fast!* Palpitations. Heart-beat stuttering. That awful *I could die tonight* feeling swirled around me like a shroud. *Maybe I could die now*, I thought gloomily. Cocaine and vodka wasn't an ideal combination, not in large amounts. The bass notes that boomed from the sound system merged into one continuous threatening rumble. The bass drum thumped into my chest, doing a nasty rubber imitation of the heart-beat with the added complication of echoes shooting up into my jaw and reverberating deep down into my stomach. Now it was worse. Non-stop. I hated that feeling. I hated that feeling almost as much as I feared it.

I hit the soft drinks like there was no tomorrow as I hung on to the arm of Marie-Ann, an elfin-looking record company girl. She seemed sweet. She talked sympathetically about the evils of drugs, the many deaths she had known. *Cheer me up, why doncha?* I thought. But even her doomy chat was better than nothing. Marie-Ann was there, after all. She cared, apparently. A witness. But even this port-in-a-storm was doomed.

'Don't leave me. Stay at the bar,' I heard myself plead.

'Don't worry, I'll be back. Are you gonna be here?'

'Yes and no . . . Yes, I mean, I'm not going anywhere.'

'You can say that again.'

'Huh?'

'Well, look at you. A typical music hack! You're off your face . . . doing bad shit. Too much of it. Too much, too soon.'

'I'm trying to chill,' I tried to pacify her, anxious that she should stay. 'You're right. I am in a bad way . . . and I don't mean to be flippant.'

'Okay, I just gotta speak to my boss,' Marie-Ann insisted. 'But don't worry, I'll be back in a second.'

'You will come back?' I sounded like a child pleading. She smiled as she nodded in the affirmative but she then slipped away and didn't look back. The seconds turned into minutes. Of course she wasn't coming back. What kind of fool was I? What was in it for her?

I notice she'd left her business card on the bar. Terrific. Even when you're dying someone's networking you. I drank more orange and mineral water and slowly started to revive. I'd been trying to work a drug evening – going up-down-up-down. Dope then coke then weed then speed then drinks. That way, if you got it right, you could take off while always remaining in control. Unfortunately I'd overdone all the ingredients and my flight had crashed just after take-off. No casualties though, apart from the Captain . . .

After an hour of terror, things started to get better. I hadn't seriously embarrassed myself – I still remembered the whispered giggles that had occurred when the publisher of *Bloated!* magazine had first taken speed. 'Call an ambulance!' she'd screamed over and over again. 'Someone's trying to kill me! Kill me! They are!'

My own feeling of doom started to slink back into its little black box. Maybe I was gonna live – if I could just slow my heart-beat down a little. I blagged my way into the DJ's box and took a few tokes of someone else's joint. Started to feel a little better. Bit by bit. Another joint, another half-pint of mineral water, another inch off the accelerator . . .

At 2.30 a.m. I was definitely alive. I staggered out into the cold night air, all my troubles washed away. Paul, the *Groove* art editor, was outside, leaning on a lamp-post, looking like a French fashion photo – why did he always seem to be in black and white? He was looking for a taxi. I hadn't seen him in there at all – how stoned had I been?

'Hey stranger, long time no see,' he smiled, a little bit wasted, before adding, 'or hear.'

'Well, lad . . . I have phoned a few times.'

'Were you in there?' he jerked a thumb back at the wine-bar club as his eyes sought out a cab.

'I dunno. Probably. Were you?'

'Yeah . . . You should come into the office soon. There's been some changes. The next issue's totally screwed.'

'Screwed?' I felt my voice rising as panic gripped me again. 'Whatcha mean screwed? Are there many changes?'

Paul smiled lazily.

'No. Not many but often.' He thought about what he'd said, smiled at it then laughed. 'Not many but often. No, seriously, there *have* been some problems.'

A cab pulled up at his waved command.

'Problems?' I echoed him weakly like some dying comedian.

'Yeah,' he slammed the cab door behind him and pulled the window down, 'yeah, the dance pages have been halved. We lost the features and the Floor-Fillers. Drop in soon and I'll try and get you some more work.'

The cab sped away before I could ask any more. The dance section was cut in half. The features, the Floor-Fillers chart had gone. I would still get a kill-fee, but kill-fee had taken on an ugly new meaning in the last few hours. And Jerry's reassurances hadn't reassured him, let alone me. *Hey, Vee! Big noise! I didn't get the story in, despite all my promises . . . So there you have it, Mister Master Criminal, I ripped you off – whatcha gonna do about it?*

3

Cat-Sitting For
Iggy Pop

I wandered into DPC's Dee-Pee House, the home of *Groove*, feeling worse than worse. A real bad coke come-down. I couldn't even be bothered to chat up the receptionists. A real downer. All bleached out. No hope, no glory. What was the point? It was funny how chemicals always made your hangover worse. God knows what they did to you internally, but whatever they did you can bet it wasn't a natural process. To give you an example of what I mean, Jake, an old mate, once worked at some small zoo in the country. He loved it – he'd clean up after the tourists had gone and then smoke a few spliffs in the quiet of this empty zoo – well, it was empty apart from the animals, who, incidentally, he really got on with. Anyhow, one day some rave comes to the small town and Jake goes and does E, three lines of coke and a couple of acid tabs. Chemicals. And so when he goes to work the next day the mammals in the menagerie go ape, go completely crazy – not one creature would take food off him. They sensed something was different. Jake got the sack in the end, finishing his idyllic lifestyle. I thought that was bull when I first heard it but I've been told some similar tales since. Weird shit, chemicals . . .

Things were exactly as promised at *Groove*. Crap. Even for me. Especially for me. Nearly everything had gone from the dance section. Everything of mine, anyway. And now it was at the printers. What was left of it.

'Don't worry about it,' said Paul, 'we'll just run 'em next month.'

But they probably wouldn't. They never did. And besides, next month would be too late, the feature would be well past its sell-by date. I'd been relying on *Groove* too much, I decided. I should really have kept in contact with more mags. But that wasn't the biggest difficulty before me. I had precisely eight days before the next *Groove* hit the news-stands. Eight days before Vee found out the worst. The very worst. I nipped next door into *Muzak* magazine, thinking I could squeeze something in there.

'Is Stan around?'

'Stan the New Man's out now, man. He might come back for a meeting. Try ringing in an hour.'

Stan the New Man, named after being caught baby-sitting, is the head man at *Muzak* as well as being an old *Soho News* acquaintance from way back. I rang back in an hour. Someone else said he was in conference, phone back later. If I'd been dumb enough to phone back later they'd have said that he'd suddenly been called to an out-of-town meeting – and half an hour after that you'd have seen him drinking in Mezzo. He'll get right back to you – yeah, yeah, yeah . . .

It was a humid day and I suddenly felt very hot, forehead sweating, top lip itching. Too much of that snow white. My nose irritated the hell out of me. Probably some charlie still lingering in my sinuses. I rubbed it but the heat got worse. Some day-old powder was finally filtering through, the seventh cavalry arriving way too late, putting one foot back on the roller-coaster. I didn't wanna take any more. Not that day. But the need to chill was becoming urgent. Undoubtedly. The need to get away from that hopeless feeling of emptiness.

Point zero, my very own tropical hell-hole. I called brother Jeff but he was out, and his flatmate had nothing to smoke either. Jeff's flatmate suggested I call Barry.

Barry is a mixer. He plays with sound in studios nowadays, although in the dim and distant past – i.e. three years ago – he wrote a few dozen classics himself. Pop songs, rock songs. Nothing that ever seriously sold. Most of which didn't even get released. He has no special gimmick and even getting a minor hit in northern Spain didn't help much. A massive unknown talent. So now he fixes studio equipment and mixes other people's tracks. And they're usually tracks that are nowhere near as good as his own. What fills studios these days? Idiot techno or banal ad themes – or sixties-style bands, you know the ones, the Oasis Beatles Sixties, Ocean Colour Sixties, Kula Sixties . . . All of which drives him crazy, as you can understand. Those whom the gods wish to destroy they first make bland. Except that our Barry is not going quietly. And, as is obligatory with a lot of musicians, he gets completely out of it for a few days every other week. And I had phoned him at the right time.

I took the pipe from Barry, inhaled the hash smoke and held it in for ten or twelve seconds. A dozen seconds doesn't sound that long but it feels like years and years when you're dealing with scalding hot smoke. But the high seemed to start immediately, and I could feel waves of pleasure coming out of any part of my body I cared to think about. My knee joint, then my ankle, then my face, all tingled, making me aware of the incredibly complex network of nerves in each limb. They were like a fine fog, illuminated by my awareness the way a lighthouse lights up the fog at sea . . .

My body hummed pleasantly. It was a 'pure' high that time, completely non-sexual. Benevolent. Every time the loins twitched during a cough, like the coughs that doctors demand during school medicals, the feeling intensified massively. I tried deep, internal breathing to copy this. Again it was sensational and, again, so intense. So very *intense*. The triumph of dope over experience. Like you'd been breathing through a bong for an hour. A bong lung, the ultimate artificial lung. My limbs were still tingling. It was like that feeling when you were getting it on with someone you were really into – when that was happening there was nothing else in the entire world, what you were feeling was everything, every single thing.

I went out on Barry's balcony. We'd had a few laughs on the balcony – me, Barry and Jake. A few laughs . . . It overlooks London and all the city's buildings. They look like 3-D toys from up there. But you don't look at details like buildings when you're buzzing as much as I was that day. The sky outside was nearing sunset. And viewed from a third-floor flat on a hill it was, quite simply, fantastic. Awe-inspiring. A vast expanse of luminous blue framed by huge sun-crested rolling clouds. On the left the sun's rays were shooting down, their stardust made visible by some misty cloud-spray, while in the centre there were some subtle creamy-white smudges. The whole thing was bisected by a couple of jet trails that emphasised just how vast and incredible it all was. That was one of the good things about dope, it could stun you back into childhood, make you once again appreciate all the simple wonders around you. The taste of this, the look of that. The fantastic nature of nature. All the things that life's knocks, life's cycle, had made commonplace were revealed to you as being mind-blowing again. You could see why Rasta priests smoked grass to get closer to heaven . . .

There are, of course, a couple of drawbacks to draw. One is the smoking element, which can't be that good for you – though you can always put it in coffee or cakes or whatever. The second is more problematic, like when your child-like obsession goes off-beam – since very young children don't normally make their own dinner, nor do they seriously think about sex. And so, if you're not careful, you can end up eating an entire loaf of Hovis or discovering that you've just made your girlfriend's fifteen-year-old sister pregnant. If you're not too careful. But the up-side is dazzling sometimes, the levels of consciousness that hit you when you take it. It's passé too, of course, now that everyone raves about Ecstasy and coke instead. I never went for E in a big way, not even back in '88. There is something insidious about E, or rather about some of the people who take it. Most are okay, but some are ruthless bastards who take E to become a nice weekend human being – *let's hug, let's hug* – before going back into the office on Monday, batteries recharged and all ready, once again, to bitch, bawl, lie and fire. There were a few I knew who worked as attack dogs for Maurie More, the editor of the *Chronicle* newspaper. It was said that they even had lists of 'E friends', who were considered several rungs lower than 'real' friends. I could already imagine exactly how their phone-calls must have gone: 'Umm yes, it is . . . Who is this exactly? . . . Oh, right . . . Er, did I meet you on E?'

Also, the media yuppies always get the best stuff. The cut-to-shit crap that most of the teens take – the stuff that just might put you in a coma – never comes near the up-market ravers. The advice they give out – 'get on one' – is like some toff drinking ten-year-old malt whiskies then recommending that perhaps us ordinary folk might just care to try something similar – like meths.

I found myself inside Barry's flat again. I stared in his round mirror with my Persol wraparounds on – a hundred nicker for a pair of bleedin' sunglasses? You were done, my son – the two darkened lenses immaculately reflected Barry's big round lampshade, the white paper thing that hung behind me. Now there was one big round white shade looming in each of the two front lenses of my shades. It made it look like I'd got completely exposed eye-balls beyond these glasses. No eye-lids. Like some X-ray vision horror movie. Naturally unreal. And yet real. Another great natural FX shot from the unshootable film of our misshapen lives.

Barry stopped picking fluff off his sweatshirt and showed me a letter he'd written to some best-selling writer. He'd written it backwards, completely backwards – you needed a mirror to read it. Maybe him being one of those left-handed geniuses helped. '*I could be,*' he'd written, '*a character in a sub-plot of your next novel. I wouldn't mind. In fact, I would consider it a bit of an honour.'* He's unique is our Barry, completely unique. Then he was talking about some ex-flatmate musician he'd known. Some girl who was trying to get a record deal. Join the queue, sucker.

'Don't tell me,' I said. 'I had to interview A & R men all last week, one was at this gig—'

'And when you asked him about the band he said, "Nice tight little band, they just need a few more gigs . . ."'

I couldn't help laughing, because that was exactly what the A & R idiot had said, albeit with a bit more chin-stroking solemnity.

'How many A & R men does it take to change a light-bulb?' Barry asked, warming to his theme. 'None! We're not changing light-bulbs this year!'

'Yeah,' I smirked.

'And most of them are just so fucking—'

'A bit shallow?'

'A bit? You can drown when you're that shallow.'

'Really shallow.'

'Deeply shallow.'

'That's deep,' I said. 'And that depth and ninety pence will buy you one king-sized cup of coffee.'

'It's the day of creation, right? And this rabbit says to a snake, "What do I look like? What am I?" And this snake mentions the long ears, big teeth and fluffy tail and the rabbit says, "Wow! I must be a bunny-rabbit!" And this snake says, "What about me? What do I look like?" And the rabbit says, "Well, you're slimy, you've got a forked poisonous tongue and no ears whatsoever." And the snake says, "Oh no! I must be an A & R man!"'

'So where is she now then?'

'My old flatmate? She's back in the States. I got her some work out there. Couldn't get myself much work Stateside but I managed to get her some.'

'Have a good time out there?'

'Yeah, crazy . . . One night, we were totally stoned, we're driving along some dark country road and there, in the middle of this tiny traffic island, is this very small, very dead deer—'

'Who killed Bambi?'

'Exactly. And the girls ask what happened and I said that he'd been hit by some car, obviously, and they said, "Oh no, it might have been something else." So I said, "What? What do you think did it? Do you think it was suicide? Do you think he crawled over there and then slit his own hooves?"'

Slit his own hooves. Is that insane or what?

'So what work did you get 'em? In the States?' I asked, interrupting Barry while I could still speak.

'Oh that, yeah . . . Cat-sitting.'

'Huh?'

'Yeah, cat-sitting for Iggy Pop. Mr Osterberg always has someone in to look after his cats when he's away on tour. And he was really impressed with Za-za. The way she handled his cats.'

Now I really had heard it all. *I could be a character in your next novel.* Damn right. What's the strangest job you've ever had? Slitting deers' hooves . . . or cat-sitting for Iggy Pop?

4

A Collapsible Tongue For America

The heatwave was still clinging on – but it was 'only' 90 degrees, down four, as I wandered into Nathaniel's office complex in Camden. The latter turned out to be a hot, airless room within the Circle company's office complex. I was looking, confidentially, for work. Any kind of writing work – agents, copywriting, ads, promotions, toilet walls . . . preferably something that paid in cold hard cash. Because the debts were slowly mounting again and *Groove* wasn't helping out as much as it used to. But I bided my time with Nathaniel, a dance promoter, as he told me all about Circle, a big promo company. Apparently you have to pay them real money if you want them to 'work' your band.

'They've been having big problems with their agents,' Nathaniel told me as I innocently thought, *Wow! And I thought Circle were agents*.

Nathaniel said to go ahead to the bar as he'd got a few more phone-calls to make. I went on to the agreed rendezvous, which was Luke's, just up the road from the office. Not quite the Good Mixer of legendary Camden Mafia fame, but near enough. Luke's, I was told, was about to spend three hundred thousand pounds doing it all up. How can you spend a third of a million doing up a bar? What were they gonna use on the walls? Gold fucking leaf?

There was a group of Camden types gathered around an inside table. Nathaniel identified them as being important though I already knew that instinctively, from their attitude, the way they lounged around, their body language airily declaring that they'd definitely won the big battle of the pop playground . . .

'You should speak to him, there,' he pointed, 'he's looking for someone that can turn out good copy . . . and him there. His label have—'

Nathaniel reeled off a string of trendy-wendy Sleeper-Bleeper-Wheezer-type groups. I kept thinking that he was right, I should schmooze on over, but the idea got drunk away in the laziness of the late afternoon. I could see the opportunity accelerating away, fading like the sunlight, and yet I couldn't fight it. I wasn't very good at cold selling myself, to tell you the truth. I was a bit too shy, you see, on the quiet – yeah, I know every stripper and chat-show host says that too, live on prime-time, but in my case it happens to be true. I couldn't even handle someone's party unless I was a bit wasted, and as for cold-calling, all that 'Hi! I'm Mandy, fly me!' stuff really did my head in.

Then some girl – a publicist? agent? – told Nathaniel that a group she was working for, Collapsible Tongue, had managed to get some deal in the States. The band name seemed so completely ridiculous that I couldn't help grinning like an idiot as Nathaniel congratulated her. And that's when I began to take on board how vast the music biz really was. Really is. Bands and clubs and PRs you've never ever heard of. I usually told a little white lie if asked about some unknown band – 'Hitler's Dick? Yeah, know 'em well, great little band' – since white lies often led to white lines.

Everyone must do it. The Music Biz, Camden branch, would alone run to several phone directories. Who could know them all? And who'd want to? There's so many folk who have taken expensive courses on it and are now experts at turning someone else's music into a living wage. Or even a fortune. There are no handicaps, and if the raw material's crap, so what? So's everything else. This is business, man. A flyer on the table said, 'You'll survive in '95 to get your kicks in '96.' Some fucking hope.

The Camden big wheels rolled out of Luke's – *there it goes*, I thought, *that big, big deal* – and me and Nathaniel were joined by the Circle boss. He was messy-looking, though friendlier than most. But then, it always is easier when you're the boss. As two of his assistants turned up the drinks flowed again, and, at one point, the subject of The Scallies came up.

'Jerry's a big pal of theirs, isn't he?' I said as the barmaid came over.

'Yeah,' said someone ruefully, 'that'll all come out one day . . .'

'Yeah,' I replied as I thought: *All what will come out one day?*

I should have spoken up and asked the obvious banal question, it would have saved me a lot of time if I had, but our table had struck up a conversation with the barmaid, who was collecting glasses, and I forgot all about it. I'd thought she was some Spanish aristo down on her luck, she had that kind of look, but she turned out to be Yugoslavian, if that term exists any more. We chatted away merrily, though I soon realised she wasn't available. Her stepfather was a Serb and mum was a Croat, so they'd got shot at by both sides. A bomb blast a thousand miles away hurt someone here. Sarajevo in Camden. And somehow the music biz fitted into my view of all this: the UK has a scratch-card economy so everyone's clutching at straws – and not always to sniff through either. Some kid in darkest Wales has no chance of being a coal-miner or steel-worker so why not try and be a rock star or rapper? At least it's theoretically possible. Unlike a mining job. The music biz has stayed big – it's the real world that's got small.

At the next table some suit was going crazy at a young

photographer. The latter, a would-be paparazzo, had snapped some actress but not, it seems, to the satisfaction of the Supreme One sitting opposite.

'This is all pretty-pretty *shit!* I want it raw!' screamed the suit. 'Off-hand, unprepared – a complete mess! I told you – I want that bitch to look like a dog!' And with that, the suit freshened her lipstick and made for the door.

I thought I'd had a quiet day, but then I added it all up and realised that I'd consumed half a bottle of wine at noon and three large vodkas shortly after. And two lines of charlie. But so what? I dug in my pocket, deciding to drink down to my last tenner. Then I realised that the solitary note in my pocket *was* my last tenner. There had to be some cheques clearing, somewhere. I hoped. Just like The Who in the mid-Sixties, I was running at a loss. But unlike The Who I didn't have a major record label behind me. I wasn't *that* worried, not yet. Not as worried as I should have been. After all, I did have a tiger at home – a white powder tiger. A cocaine tiger. As long as you've got coke, you've got possibilities, right? Right?

I left Luke's with the promise of two hundred quid's worth of work from Nathaniel – but not for a week or two. Everything still unresolved. As I reached Camden tube three street-dealers tried to rustle up some trade. '*Dope? Coke? Rocks? Wanna buy? Wanna buy?*' Almost like Times Square in New York in the good ol' days – all that was missing from the rotten Big Apple illusion was a Moonie preacher and two seventy-year-old women in hot-pants. The latter should ideally be wearing too much rouge and looking not unlike the living dead. No one in New York ever gave up on the American dream. Not even when it was dead. Not even when they themselves were dead.

At home I checked the invites I'd been sent, plugging a rap fusion gig that was on the next night at the Astoria. As I thought it over, I could see the drawer containing the coke, sitting in a corner, glowing slightly like Superman's Kryptonite. It was tempting, but I forced myself to do something else instead – I found a blunt by the bed and slowly smoked that. After three phone-calls I managed to raise a companion for the gig. She was Caledonia, an acquaintance who was a 'video compiler'. Whatever that is. She was from sunny Scotland and was usually quite friendly unless she was off her face. It didn't matter though, she was up for the gig. I have to admit that I heaved a sigh of relief. I had done too many solo in the recent past. There's nothing worse than being alone in some packed night-club.

I'd also been sent a Thomas Dolby greatest-hits disc, which I didn't fancy playing, but after a few tokes of the blunt it began to sound okay. At times it was almost courageous in its own self-conscious way, and one track, 'Gate To The Mind's Eye', I played over and over. It had a solo with some feedback squeaking on it before it hit the right, perfect note of distorted sonic purity, that uptight air-conditioner noise that The Who used to such great effect way back when. The jet sound was, I decided, the sound the '60s artists tried to copy – just like Bing Crosby tried to sound like the big boomy propeller planes of the '40s – and Pete Townshend used to coast on it. Pete himself would physically coast too, King Mod incarnate, blocked out of his brain on speed, arms held out wide like a plane flying at thirty thousand feet – he'd done it. He'd done it all. 'Everlasting expression of something that need no longer be expressed.' Chorus, chorus, ad-lib and fade . . .

All Aboard For Fun Time

The phone's shrieking brought me back into a world of bleary hot sunlight – was it never gonna cool down? Dawning consciousness brought the knowledge that my head was throbbing like an open wound. As I reached for the phone it suddenly hit me that my stomach too was walking a tightrope – the tightrope between nausea and cramps. I licked my dry lips but that didn't help, since my mouth felt like some small furry animal had crawled into it, vomited and died. Why was the phone so damn loud? I had its volume turned down low and there were even two strategically-placed cushions completely covering it on the floor. Yet it still sounded like a police siren being blasted through a 50,000-watt PA. And all 50,000 watts were wired up within my aching head.

'Do you remember ze old country?' said a familiar voice, using a familiar catch-phrase. An in-joke I wasn't quite ready for.

'Huh?'

'God, you sound rough.'

'God, I am rough . . . Who is this?'

'Nick. I'm returning your call.'

'Oh, right . . .'

It was the pop columnist, Nick. Or one of them. I'd called him about getting work – I thought. I couldn't quite remember. It had all been a long, long time ago. Yesterday at least.

'What did you want, Pete, when you called me? Or is this a bad time to ask?'

'Nicky, this is a bad time for anything except a large hair-of-the-dog.'

'Well, get yourself a double brandy then.'

'And I'm skint.'

'Don't worry about it, there's a lig on. At the North Atlantic bar.'

'Well, put us on the door if you can. Mind you, what time is it? I'm s'posed to be going to some rap gig tonight.'

'Relax. It's at one o'clock, this afternoon.'

'Great. What's the time now?'

'Twelve . . . Look, I gotta dash, I'll be outside at one and I'll get you in, allrighty?'

Allrighty. Nick is, I should have explained, something of a legend in the ligger stakes. Some record companies don't like him that much – his reviews tend to be critical – and some staff journos are lairy of him too. But he has a certain honesty that's worth its weight in gold. Or Tequila. He'll settle for either.

Enthusiasm was Nick's trade-mark when he started out. In fact, he was so enthusiastic that some might have called it aggression. A few years later, after cracking several ribs with Oliver Reed and getting forcibly ejected from various other parties, Nick got engaged to a girl. He used his position, something at a music rag, to get a record company to fly him and the girl to a tropical island where he was supposed to cover a video shoot. The label also, legend has it, stumped up for two weeks' holiday in a luxury hotel. Nick had a great time, naturally – covering the shoot took up one short afternoon. The label, of course, expected something substantial in return. Like a few magazine covers. Which, ahem, they didn't quite get. So they rang up the editor to complain and, what with the back-issues scam Nick was running through the ad department, well . . . exit Nick. Nick's version is that he ran into the video shoot when he was already out on holiday. And he did win the industrial tribunal case that followed it, so take your pick. He also denies another record company story, namely that one day he rang around all the majors, claiming his house had been burnt down. This domestic disaster had destroyed his entire music collection so, he's alleged to have asked, could he please have the company's entire back catalogue of rock, soul, rap and jazz?

I met Nick – all twinkling eyes and leather jacket – at some MTV party a year or two ago. He was talking to the men who'd signed Menswear – at their second rehearsal or something equally crazy – for a 'mere' hundred grand. Nick later talked me into liberating two bottles of Tequila from the bar as it closed, and we ended up in the offices of Tony Techno records, under the Westway. As receptionists fussed and pluggers plugged, Nick put his shades on and quietly passed out, oblivious to all the jive-talk bullshit being directed at him . . .

It was twelve o'clock and I only had an hour to get to the West End. And it was gonna take me about four days just to stand up. I could see that the radio's power light was still on. I turned the volume up. Some mandolin stuff. And then a voice. It was Radio Helena, Athens – as in Athens, Greece – on short-wave. Too much. When the hell had I tuned into that? And why? I snapped it off as I dragged myself into top gear, shaving as I dressed. The only really good thing, I decided, about a frantic, hung-over lifestyle was that it took your mind off the aching boredom of being single.

At two minutes past one I was strolling towards the North Atlantic Bar, Grill & Niterie and, of course, Nick wasn't outside. Typical. I could, I thought, probably have used my NUJ press card to get in, but it was an unnecessary complication when I could barely speak. Luckily, as I reached the entrance, the bouncer was busy steering some junkie beggar away from the front door. The obligatory blonde with clipboard and fuck-me boots was too absorbed in all this to even notice me as I slipped past her into a corridor already moist with heat.

I was so happy I was almost skipping down the plush stairs, taking them two at a time, all cares forgotten. My coke hangover was wearing off and I was feeling much better. I'd got away with it! Free food, free drink, free music, an afternoon's pleasantries . . . what a life! Who could possibly ask for more, and how long could anyone get away with it? For a few years yet, I hoped. I stepped into the functions room and spied Eye.

'Hiya, babe, what are you up to?' she said with a kiss as her eyes snaked a look around the room.

'This and that, Eye,' I murmured, grabbing a couple of champagnes off a passing waiter. 'The usual. So what's this afternoon in aid of?'

'Don't play the hardened ligger with me, young man,' she smiled a crooked smile. 'You know full well why we're here.'

'No, I don't. I've had no info at all, which probably means it's one of your efforts.' I jabbed a teasing finger towards her diamanté-studded belly button.

'No,' she said, with a hint of a sulk. 'It's *not* one of mine, and you know it.'

'Yeah, but who—'

Before I could protest any more she was swept away by a couple of juniors from *Encore*. One of the juniors was a girl who looked about fourteen but who must have been at least three years older. Her super-tight red T-shirt had the word 'FUCKER!' emblazoned on its front. Subtle, huh? The gap the girls forced in the crowd revealed Carston, the rock author who'd started *Groove* and a dozen other magazines, though he'd since been booted upstairs. He raised a glass in silent salute as I wandered over.

'Didn't know you were a fan,' he said by way of greeting.

'Fan of who? Who's on?'

'Hang on . . .'

A big radio producer, who considered that he'd already

booked Carston for an argument, returned with a couple of glasses. That producer would probably be considered brave by some superstitious hacks: some won't drink with Carston at all, since he was allegedly drinking with Hendrix, Joplin and Morrison on the various nights before each of them died. When the producer's need to take in some air briefly silenced him I asked Carston again what we were actually there for. He chinked his glass against mine.

'I know what you're here for, Pete. And it's not the solid refreshment, is it, lad?'

Everyone seemed to think I was degenerating into a total party animal. An apprentice alcoholic. A dipso. Maybe I was on that slippery slope. Or had been. Now I seemed to be working a combination. Less liquid and more powder. Not up or down but . . . well, sideways . . . or diagonal . . . Was that progress?

'But tell me,' I re-started my pointless quest, 'who is actually performing here?'

It was too late though, the producer had already gulped down the minimum amount of oxygen required for another few seconds' chat and he launched into it. Again.

'But thinking about it, it can't have been Rita Hayworth you were talking about, because she didn't marry what's-his-face, she married Orson Welles . . .'

'Oh, she bloody married everyone,' Carston replied with just the right amount of amused irritation. But the producer had yet another angle on that angle so I took refuge at the bar. Some *Groove* hack who was playing the bar-fly thought he'd heard about some review work going at *Raw Soul* magazine. If I needed the work. I said I'd check it out. This conversation took place, I should admit, after we'd shared a line of coke in the toilets. My coke . . .

I turned around and, next to me, as I poured two cham-pagnes into a single half-pint glass, was Rendall. I looked twice to check it was Rendall since I was really amazed to see him again; someone I'd not even glimpsed since the Eighties. I met Rendall years ago, on one of a thousand endless hypnotic soul nights when you could make a friend for life in a few frenzied hours. Frenchies in Camberley, the Lacey Lady in Ilford, Dingwalls, the Wag, the Mud and Shoom in town, the beach – and everywhere else – in Hastings, Brighton, Bournemouth. Runnin' away. Big fun. Humanoid stakker. S'Express. Nights of neon and flashing road signs and frantic strobe lights. 'Nights In White Sulphate' as the Moody Blues never quite got round to saying. *And the beat goes on.* Driving us down the A3, driving us down the coast, driving us round and round the orbital. Here we go again! Listening to pedestrian crossings as they bleeped out their warnings to empty dawn streets while you tried to find your own rust-bucket Beetle. It was your town at that time of night – at that time of morning – with all the straights asleep and the place deserted like it was now. One big adventure playground for all the hip town teens. There were even some all-nighters back then that I'd managed to get through entirely without chemical stimulus. Twenty-four hours or more and still kicking just on music. I bet that doesn't happen any more. Not in the E'd-up, coked-out UK . . .

But my main train of thought was about Rendall and the cigarettes, cars, records, rave tickets and guest-list places we'd shared. It was all a few years ago now, though Rendall still looked like a spring chicken, still had that freckled soul-boy charm that made him look years younger than he was. Last time I'd seen him he'd just shifted from A & R to promotions at one of the bigger labels. It turned out that he was now running some PR company that specialised in 'streamlining' radio stations. Creatively speaking.

'So you're responsible for the state of the air-waves, are you?' I asked as we pumped each other's hand.

'Yeah, yeah, it's all my fault, OneFM in the Housey House, maaan,' he said mockingly.

'So how are you . . . and how's all that?' I asked as I wondered what happened to his job at the major label.

'I'm good, very good, and that stuff's all going well. So what are you doing here, then?'

'I'm still misrepresenting the fourth estate. *Groove*, *The Mix*, you know . . . the usual suspects.'

'Oh, that's all right. It's a living, isn't it?'

'Yeah,' I grunted.

'I was thinking of dabbling in that lark myself, actually, Pete, on the quiet. From a publishing point of view, of course.'

'Oh yeah?'

'Yeah, we're just assembling backers at the moment. Gimme your phone and fax and all that and I'll give you a shout.'

'Yeah, do that,' I said as I scribbled some numbers down and wondered if I should tell him that my second-hand fax had given up the ghost long ago. 'Be an excuse to go out again as well, eh? Now you're a radio star.'

'Of sorts . . . Yeah, be nice to go out. Thing is, I don't do too much socialising any more, mate, to be honest with you. 'Cept when I'm working, of course.'

'Oh, right. So who's here then?'

'Everybody they invited, I think,' he said before turning to me with a friendly, ironic grin and adding, 'and quite a few they didn't . . .'

'I thought I'd turn up anyway and class the place up,' I blustered with a smile. He grinned back, he didn't give a shit about all that.

'So tell me, I've asked everyone else in the room, who is actually performing this—'

But my question was drowned out by applause as some female musicians appeared to answer it. Rendall disappeared with a wave as girls in lace-up boots, skirt suits and ties took the stage. Very formal in a pervy kind of way. A now familiar face appeared, Joanna something – you know her, the classical rock chick, the black one – and tuned up her steel guitar while her sidekicks fiddled with their fiddles. One of them held an electric see-through violin, the other wrestled with a damn-big-thing-on-strings the name of which I couldn't recall. I turned around to look but Rendall was completely out of sight. Was he busy or was he avoiding me? Both, probably. I concentrated on the stage. I might, I decided, end up reviewing this. For someone. If I was lucky.

An A & R man came on-stage, tapped the microphone then started speaking as Nick elbowed himself into position next to me.

'This industry spent one hundred and seventy million pounds developing new talent last year, and that was in the UK alone—'

'Liar!' Nick hissed in my ear. 'Let's see a break-down of those figures . . .'

'—and,' boomed the A & R, 'even our MD, though he isn't quite as young as he used to be—'

'He was never fucking young,' Nick moaned. 'He was born at the age of sixty . . .'

'—still goes out to small clubs and pubs. Because he still enjoys looking for new music, because he's still searching for dynamic new talent—'

'Still searching for little boys, more like,' Nick wise-cracked. 'Though I must say that he wasn't gay when I slept with him.'

'You didn't sleep with him, you just had an affair.'

The A & R was now hardly able to contain his excitement. Another gig, another mortgage payment . . . his voice rose like a newly-born baby discovering its lungs.

'—but all that hard, hard work becomes worth-while—'

'What hard work? The old fool just said he enjoyed doing it.'

'—becomes truly, truly *worth-while* when someone of the calibre of Jo here gets discovered. With her *and* all her band here, this is probably the greatest gathering of musical talent these walls have ever seen—'

'Except when the cleaners were here this morning . . .'

'—well, people, I won't go on and on—'

'You are, you are . . .'

'So here she is! And she's gonna *do it to ya in your ear-drums!* Do it, kid!'

Do it to ya in your ear-drums! You'd have to have a stomach of stone not to puke. Nick was saying something else to me but the rest of his words were cut off by the blast of the first few bars of music. Joanna and her gals were actually quite listenable, in a bland wash-all-over-you way. But her face disappeared from view when the very flushed, and very tall, A & R stood right in front of me, worn out by his triumphal speech. I did, though, get a chance to study his dandruff-flecked Red or Dead bomber . . . and his Rolex, whenever he deigned to scratch the back of his head. It was a good Rolex, too. An original. The type that kids would cut your hand off for if you were ever foolish enough to stop at red lights in New Cross. Which probably made his head-scratching deliberate. A record company lig like this was one of the last safe places to flaunt it. All ten grand's worth of it. And if you've bought a CD or tape in the last decade then welcome to the club, sucker, 'cos you helped pay for it too. Being a major label A & R, a so-called talent scout, has to be the ultimate yuppie job. Giving out the best chat-up lines at parties – 'Hey, babe, wanna be a star?' – and wearing designer clothes, resting in the Bahamas, eating seared tuna at Mezzo . . . and getting paid ninety grand a year to stand at the bar saying 'nice little band, all they need are some more gigs to make them really tight . . .' Getting paid even though they didn't actually like music, and most of the few acts they did sign would flop miserably, at great expense. Any one of the trendies hanging out in Chinatown's Dive Bar, or down at the George on Wardour, any one of them could do a better job. In fact, you could sack all A & R men – and women – tomorrow and just release demo tapes at random and it wouldn't make things worse musically. Things might even get a little better. At least we'd have a level killing field.

I suppose my main objection to most A & R personnel also happens to be the same as my main grudge against some of the modern music writers. So many had no feel for it, no passion. They'd never saved every penny they had to buy some record. They'd never rocked. They'd never even danced. Not even alone, in the privacy of their own teenage bedroom. So determined to be hip that they never actually were. Even when they had little 'credibility meetings' as one of the music week-lies did, gatherings earnestly designed to quantify what cannot be quantified. Being on, or near, the cutting edge of anything always, I felt, involved some risk. Or should. Whether you were risking looking crazy or risking falling for the wrong person or championing the wrong kind of band or whatever. Risk. Buying a subscription to half a dozen magazines and buying everything they recommended didn't really cut it. You had to risk something, no matter how trivial. And these people were not risk-takers. They were, in fact, the very opposite, the sort who'd had three pension schemes sorted out before they'd even left infant school. They'd never believed that music was their world or that it could change anything. They'd never wanted it to. It had never been that important to most of them. It wasn't a way of life. Music was just a hipper way of getting money and girls – or boys. And drugs, of course. Never forget mother's little helper. If the City whizz-kids had continued to attract big headlines, and if their firms were still hiring, most of today's A & R folk would now be sniffing their coke in the Square Mile, playing the finance casino where it's easy to make millions – if you can but get past the doorman. A task that got tougher and tougher with each passing year – *I'm sorry, sir, but I can't seem to find your name anywhere on the list* . . .

I know one particularly obnoxious character called Zak, who fitted perfectly into all this. He was a writer, allegedly, not an A & R, though he'd probably end up being both. He gave 'good meeting' and had subsequently been given huge advances for his half-dozen books. The latter were all about various bands he didn't particularly like and which he'd never actually seen live. I wouldn't have minded that so much if it hadn't been for his arrogance. He was always saying, 'Read this, Pete, you just might learn something.' I always did and never had, if you know what I mean. When a publishing director once surprised everyone by resigning in support of Zak, some wag had commented, 'That's right, the Captain always goes down with his shit.'

My idyllic view of the A & R's back was soon disturbed by something just out of vision. I turned slightly. Shit. It was Jerry. He was standing outside the room. He was alone and shuffling his feet awkwardly in the big downstairs foyer. When he caught my eye his tentative wave turned into a more frantic gesture. Gesturing for me to go over – *C'mon! C'mon!* – and I thought I could guess why. Maybe I could have skipped out the back, through the kitchens, like they do in movies. But, in reality, this being London, all the fire escapes would have been locked shut. Nailed shut, probably. Ah well, I knew I'd get found out in the end. Nemesis. Him or someone else had to find me. And it is about time. What had I got to lose anyway? *Your knee-caps*, said my gut instinct. *You've annoyed Jerry's big boss Vee – or you're about to.* A song ended and in the near-silence that followed I could hear Nick denigrating some dead photographer that everyone else was crying over – another coke'n'smack victim – when they weren't reminiscing about the memorial the week before.

'Why wasn't I invited to the funeral?' some other ligger pouted sulkily.

'I never liked the bastard,' said Nick, as I wondered if Jerry would be saying that about me soon. Was he, in fact, already saying it? I knocked back someone else's drink and walked away from Nick and Joanna and everyone else. Time to really face the music. Glancing back I could see that the A & R had now gone off to one side, away from 'his' music. Typical. A second glance revealed that he'd started to chat up one of the *Encore* juniors. The girl with the FUCKER! T-shirt. Even more typical.

'What's happening, Pete?' Jerry demanded. 'Vee wants to know where his advance copy is.'

'Vee's advance copy of what?' I dead-panned, playing for time as ever.

'The advance copy of your *Groove* piece on his band? The Nomads, remember?' he explained, as if to an idiot. 'The band on his label, don't you remember?'

'Oh yeah, right . . .'

'And the floor-fillings chart thing, a photocopy of that. He can use it in the ads for the record.'

'Jerry, I'll have to cross that bridge after I've burned it, son.'

'Huh?'

'Relax. I'll deal with it. I *will* deal with it.'

'When?'

'Soon, son, soon . . . Here, Jerry, we are mates, aren't we?'

'Yeah, a-course we are.'

And as he said that a wave of affection swept over me. I really did like him, I dunno why.

'You'd do us a favour if you could, wouldn't you?'

'Yeah . . . no problem. If I can help – I will.' He was looking down. He obviously hadn't been on the white line trail yet today. He wasn't a bad lad, Jerry, but he wasn't completely altruistic. Maybe some coke would help, encourage him to shield me when the time came. And, I felt, I could do with some more myself.

'That's good, Jerry, that's good . . . Want some tink?'

'Geezer, I thought you'd never ask – would you care to step into my office?' he grinned as he steered me toward the gents' toilet, his spiel continuing seamlessly. 'I took some to them Scallies last night, y'know? I known 'em years, man, fuckin' years, got 'em started I did. Did you know that? Did I ever tell you that?'

'No, when was that then?' I asked, genuinely amazed that he'd never told me any of this before. Everyone has their little secrets, I figured.

'Yeah, it was a year and a half ago. They was nowhere, remember?'

'Yeah, I remember.'

'It was all Britpop then, The Scallies couldn't get arrested. No front pages, no nothing. And then I said to 'em, well, I said to their management team, like, "You gotta charlie everyone up, y'know? Give some bugle to the boys on the weeklies, or you're going down the tubes, y'know?" And they agreed with us. And fuck me! Did they go for it or what? They splashed out, man, took over a hundred grams off me, nearly five grand's worth and just gave it away . . .'

'Gave it away to who?' I said, but I already knew the answer to that.

'Journos, all the boys and girls at the inkies were invited to a big gig down on the river, and everyone who got backstage got given two or three grams of good solid charlie. And who gets backstage at gigs? Friends, groupies . . . and hacks. All the journos were there. Someone from *Groove* must have been there, too—'

'Yeah, I heard about it,' I said, and it was true, I did dimly recall some major party that I'd missed for some reason. Jerry watched me unfold the paper twist of coke as he pushed the cubicle door shut behind him. The need on his face was so obvious it was almost disturbing – at least, I thought, I was never that desperate – and it reminded me about some experiment with rats and coke I'd seen once on TV. Rather than waste time eating, the rats actually gave up food and cocained themselves to death. Literally. All natural instinct over-ridden. It can be that addictive.

Despite his hungry expression, Jerry still managed to look all slick, streamlined and stylish. Real man-about-townie – even in the dim yellow light of the toilet. He should've been a model really, that or some kind of rock star. He had the presence for it, the front. The sheer bloody nerve that you need for that kind of stuff.

'Two weeks later,' Jerry was still saying as my mind clicked back into the present tense, 'it pays off – The Scallies get their first big piece in the weeklies, a fortnight later they're on all the covers. Then Radio 1 start playing the third single and that's it! Top! Launched on a sea of coke, million-selling an' all that . . .'

'Did you really shift a hundred grams to 'em?' I said as I chopped out two big fat lines.

'Yeah . . . well, me and Vee did.'

'Yeah, that's what I thought,' I said as kindly as I could.

'Is this Vee's stuff here?' said Jerry, turning investigator in reaction to my mild put-down.

'Yeah.'

'Have you cut it?' he asked with just a hint of accusation, worried in case I had diluted the joy of the joy powder.

'No,' I answered as he greedily sniffed up one of the lines.

'Nah, you're right,' Jerry nodded as he rubbed his nose, 'this is uncut. The full monty. I can always tell. That's the spirit, my son, never tinker with the tink. Not if you're taking it yourself. Yeah, that's the stuff all right. Pukka, pukka . . .'

'Do you still get on with The Scallies?' I asked, as an idea began to form behind my bloodshot eyes.

'Oh yeah. I'm well down wiv 'em. Tell you what, I'll get you an interview if you want, an exclusive or something.'

'Cheers, Jerry.'

'Yeah, yeah, yeah.'

'No, I mean it, that would be really good.'

'Yeah, yeah, yeah, put me on the door, put me on the tour . . .'

6

Honey, I Don't Want To Do What You Want Me To Do

The rap fusion gig was spread before me like an audio-visual feast; a sensory overload for those suffering under the liquid cosh. The self-inflicted liquid cosh. I'd had too much fire-water and my stomach was feeling pretty loose. Even when I drank a pint of kiddie's chocolate milk it didn't help much. I must be in a bad way, I thought, if I can't take one of those on board. This had forced me to sink a few Camparis. A double Campari can stop all that nonsense, but you had to be prepared for some funny looks from the bar staff.

I was sitting at the back of the balcony, the Astoria's distinctive round table lights pointing the way to the stars on the stage – a tidal sea of pregnant orange stars. In the mosh pit several dozen metres below 'the kids' were going ape as the heavy-duty beat pulverised the peeling black paintwork. I began to think how the growth of bass really *was* the growth of modern music. Rock, R & B, dance – whatever you want to call it. The bass guitar sound is bigger and bigger now – and has grown in volume and compression ever since the early Fifties – because bass is the sound that completes the circle, that cements the marriage between Afro rhythms and European melodies. Because the bass is part drum and part rhythm guitar. Lots of musicians like playing bass for that very reason; it is *the* sound of modern music for them, even if they're not bassists.

I'd done another line of charlie on the way there to keep me buzzing after the afternoon lig. And why not? What had I got to lose? I hadn't brought that much with me and this gig wasn't, sadly, like one indie event I'd once attended where I could see two distinct piles of envelopes, one bulkier than the other, the bulkier ones containing back-stage passes to the after-show party and a twist of coke. This I discovered by reading an A & R name upside-down on one of the fat envelopes and then claiming it was mine. What could the real A & R have done? Call the police and demand the return of his drugs?

Still, I *had* done some coke earlier. And I did have a bit on me. And the afternoon's white powders were combining nicely with the white wine. The mix safely added distance to everything. Zap, pow! Now that was okay. I had fine-tuned the picture. It looked good. It was just like real life.

Caledonia, the deflowered flower of Scotland beside me, was already bored. She'd thought it would be some sort of exclusive back-stage party-type thing where her video credentials would mean something, would get her introduced to top TV people, but to me it was all kind of interesting anyway – watching myself and watching her as we watched the rappers. I've heard a lot of rap, and it's had its moments, but, for me, they were mostly in the past. The main rapper was draped in last year's gold chains but he did at least have a bit of stage presence, a bit of character. His biog said he used to 'pump gas'. Weird.

What was also fun for me was watching the expression of mild surprise on the rapper's face. As his gaze went out to the audience – not seeing anything of course, just a blur beyond the footlights – you could see a special look that seemed to say: 'What bizarre miracle of the modern world brought me here? What thing brought me – a thirtysomething black mechanic who never graduated – to London, England to get paid thousands for swearing in rhyme? I mean, has the world gone freaking crazy?'

There was a ten-minute break so we went up to the top bar. After a few seconds of merciful silence the disco re-started. I braced myself for a blast of techno but, instead, James Brown came through the speakers, getting on up, then Flash doing 'White Lines' – the vocal backing soaring over me as Flash irresistibly stuttered out his warning on the beat. The DJ ended each record with a dead-stop – *squelch!* – on the beat as vogue dictated. Neat. Then came something new from Sven Van Hees – slow and hypnotic – and then we were Soul City walkin' with Archie Bell and The Drells – *tighten up!* – and getting heavy with Heady D – and then it suddenly struck me that I still loved this shit, still loved music like the air I breathed. Soul, dance, rock, R & B. Music. The best of it, any of it, all of it. Music being the stuff someone once called the heart of a heartless world. All those OTT feelings swept over me. I did still love it, God knows why . . .

7

Keep On Steppin', Brother Man

The music high, a buzz that once would have kept me twitching all night, lasted only until Caledonia stuck her bony elbow in my ribs.

'I hate this shit, Pete, I fucking hate it.'

She was jerking her head in the direction of the speakers. She really hated it. It figured. She liked death metal, Manic Manson and shite like that. Another head-banger after coke – now she'd split with her Dalston dealer boyfriend she was on the scrounge full-time . . . and then another DJ was on, playing yer techno, and the musical dream was over.

I nodded hello to Nick as he arrived – I didn't think he was gonna make it there that night – and then various label people came over and lied about the rapper's influence and I lied about what I was going to write about said rap artiste. No food had been laid on by the label, which didn't matter to me as I couldn't keep anything down anyway, but it was bound to irk others. The label's glamour couple soon got bored talking to me and switched their beams on to Nick.

'Nick, baby, so nice to see you, so glad you made it.'

'Nick, what do you think of the first half?' they asked eagerly. Nick looked around, sighed and then answered.

'Are you fuckers gonna feed us or what?'

I'd loved to have heard what came next but my 'date' kept looking around, distracted, tugging at my sleeve like a demented five-year-old. Caledonia had just been someone to walk in with anyway. The wrong someone. The feeling was probably mutual, being realistic about it. So I left Nick to it, moving away from the bar to humour Madam a bit and, as I did so, I noticed a Goth girl who kept looking over at us. Well, she was Goth-ish. She had a pretty snub nose with a tiny ring in it, a leather skirt that ended a foot above the knee and spike heel boots which ended a couple of inches above the ankle. The boots had real metal spikes – or were they studs? – placed in them, which made me think they must be Westwood originals. She looked, despite the come-and-get-it element, very neat. Her neatness was rare. Rarer still, for a Goth, was the way she had managed to keep her slim face clear of crap white foundation. Spider from *Raw Soul* mag was there and he noticed me noticing the semi-Goth.

'Sweet, ain't she? That one over there?'

Spider had said it to try and embarrass me. Bastard.

'Is she?' I bluffed back. 'I haven't really noticed her face, I was looking more at those boots. They're amazing. Westwood, aren't they?'

'Yeah,' he said. 'They're real fuck-me boots, ain't they?'

'Fuck *off!*' Caledonia butted in, her feminist hackles rising abruptly with her voice, 'you two are just so fuckin' sexist!'

'I dunno what you mean, darlin',' he said, winding her up further.

'You know exactly what I mean. Can't you talk about anything more *meaningful*? Eh? Or are those girl's boots "it", the limit of your fuckin' conversation?'

'Shall we ask her?' Spider said. 'Ask her where she got 'em?'

'Whatcha mean ask her?' Caledonia sighed. 'Do you actually *know* her?'

'Yep,' said Spider as he turned to Caledonia, 'sure I do. She used to temp for our ad department. Satisfied?'

'Very rarely,' said Caledonia, determined not to cheer up even when Spider brought the Goth over. Especially when Spider brought the Goth over.

'They're Westwood boots,' she said. 'Cost me a fortune. Look okay though, don't they?'

'Yeah,' I nodded. 'Classic stuff.'

Spider went off to ring his pregnant girlfriend – *I'm going to be late again, baby* – and the small talk of our awkward little triangle got smaller and smaller, at one point it was barely visible, and I was relieved when Caledonia finally went off to the bar. This left me alone with Ms Goth but Spider came back just seconds later. He angrily re-lived the phone chat for us. Chat isn't really the right word. Frank exchange, more like.

'So I finally get through and I explain that I've *got* to be here,' raged Spider, 'so I am gonna be a bit late and she says, "Well, I dunno if there's anywhere for you to sleep tonight then, I might have to lock up early."'

'I think, if you call back,' I offered, 'you should try and hit the right conciliatory note—'

'I'm gonna tell her that if she locks that fucking door, I'll fucking kick it right in!'

'Yep,' I sighed. 'That's the right conciliatory note . . .'

The Goth flashed me an amused grin at this – a tiny curve in one corner of her mouth and there was a touch of cruelty in there too. It was still a lovely mouth for all that. Sexual too. She was up for it, to put it in *Loaded* language. She was up for something.

'Sometimes she is so far up herself,' Spider ranted, 'she's coming out the other side.'

'So what are you gonna do?'

'I'm gonna get completely off my nut!' he said, draining his glass in one before adding, 'before getting back as late as humanly possible . . . Later, if I look like I'm gonna throw up – don't worry, I probably am.'

'You haven't actually introduced your friend,' I finally butted in as I realised I didn't have a name to hang my hang-ups on. This was happening more and more. Names not being passed on, as if a name was some kind of secret they wanted to keep all to themselves.

The Goth smiled at this. Sally was her name, and she had a heart-shaped mole under her bottom lip. She offered a hand for me to shake, as coy as any nice new convent girl meeting a pal of Papa. Touchingly formal, considering what she was wearing. And then Caledonia, returning from wherever, grabbed my shoulder and breathed some gin-flavoured words into my ear. It wasn't what I wanted to hear. I suppose I'd known what Madam was after when she agreed to come along tonight. That was the down-side of holding stuff – yes, people did seek you out but the suspicion remained that the gear was the main reason they did.

'I hear you're holding, Pete, make with the stuff, huh?' she hissed as her fingertips brushed my neck.

'I thought you had some gear,' I mumbled back.

'I've only got a tiny bit o' that pink champagne shit,' she said, shrugging. She was talking about the rose-coloured speed that dealers targeted at girls. Even speed-makers were into niche marketing now. I felt in my pocket, there were two paper twists, one had nearly a gram, the other had barely a line – and some of that was dust. I slipped the latter to Madam and she glanced towards the girls' toilet.

'Back in a minute, Pete,' she said, smiling for the first time that evening.

'Missing you already,' I said. She run-walked away. *Hooked*, I thought. *Desperate is not the word.* I actually knew maybe a dozen like her. Always female, usually from some deprived, depraved city that was hundreds of miles away. Media intellectuals who'd got loads of qualifications and a fair bit of talent too but, because they'd 'deserted' the home fires they seemed to feel some big guilt. Especially about some old boyfriend they'd left behind. And so these girls would then try and get over this by getting even more wasted than the rest of us. They'd take anything. In vast quantities. Coke, E, acid. Even H, even crack. Crazy shit. Worse than crazy. Downright fucking stupid, in fact. Some of them wrote well enough but, at the rate they were going, they were all destined for some white tile place. Either a clean-out clinic or a mortuary slab.

Spider told us that there was another party on, to launch some new indie label. Of course, like most indies nowadays, it was really just a front for a major label.

'Do you wanna go?' I asked Sally the Goth straight out.

'Yeah, why not?'

'Okay, let's go.'

'Yeah,' chipped in Spider, 'what have we got to lose? I'm all rapped out anyway.'

'What about what's-her-name?' asked Sally.

'Caledonia?' said Spider, grinning. 'Don't worry about her, she'll be chopping out the Sani-lav by now.'

I thought about waiting for Caledonia but then dismissed the idea. Sod it, she'd stalked out and left me alone at the bar enough times – usually over some completely imagined slight. And I'd usually be left with a large bar bill, just to rub salt in the open wound . . .

As we headed toward the exit, Spider looked at Sally, leading the way, before winking back at me. It was an ambiguous wink. It either said 'You're a lucky man' or 'You've got a live one there, matey!'. Or both.

'That's it!' ranted some record label flunky by the exit, 'Take! Take! Take! Go on! Leave before the second half has even fucking started!'

'Huh?' The flunky had had a few drinks, but the amazing thing was the venom in his voice. And the fact that someone from the label was now ranting at us. This was a real rarity. A label man accusing a hack of being shallow. A label attacking the hand that bleeds – before it's even been bled . . . And I resented that *take-take-take* bit too; a bit of a pot–kettle face-off.

'Yes, I'm talking about *you* lot,' Mr Record Company went on, unstoppable now, 'journos like you who breeze in late, leave early and drink all the drinks! Your attitude is just plain criminal—'

'We're criminals? Have you seen the price of your CDs?'

'You've never paid for one in your life anyway! You just take the piss, don't you? Take the piss! It's just take-take-take with your sort. Isn't it? You lot never give anything back, do you? Do you?'

Behind him, a hack from *NME* was vomiting majestically over a corner table. Something was certainly being given back tonight . . .

Shocking stuff, I thought. *Leaving under a cloud. Counting them all down and bringing 'em all up again. Must we fling this filth at our pop kids?*

8

Show Me The Way

Time, I thought, for another. And another. And another. And a line. And another – shared. And then another drink . . . brandy'll settle your stomach . . . I don't know how we got to the indie party or how long it lasted. I just remember Spider being on the brink of tears about something. Maybe it was his girl? No, it wasn't that, he'd been forgiven after two more phone calls. But he did keep mumbling something, some great news he'd just found out. Something of great urgency too. And something I didn't understand, not the way he bawled it at me in the middle of the dance floor . . . and then things got *really* blurred . . .

When the mists cleared again I was in bed with Sally. We were getting it on and we were at – I glanced around – my place. She'd done all the right things – keeping her heels on, keeping her leather skirt on but inching it up, and she made all the right faces. All in order to drive me on, to drive me crazy, so I'd keep on doing what I was doing, to really drive me crazy. And she *did* drive me crazy. When you're making love to a girl you're really into then that's it, that's as good as it gets – so if she gives you the old go-code then, at some point, you're gonna go for it, attached or not. And, at some point, you're gonna lose all control.

She pouted, bit her lip, gasped, fluttered her eye-lashes, arched her smooth neck, lived a little, died a little. The Hollywood way. Not necessarily fake or insincere but, in bed, she did express herself the Hollywood way. And I wondered if it had been different getting it on with females before the late Sixties, before nearly all Western girls had seen hundreds of other women making love in endless movies and videos. Which must have had some sort of influence, if only subconsciously. This is how it happens; this is how you act. This is the way to *do it*. A hot hybrid of Goldie Hawn, Mary Millington, Linda Lovelace and Sharon Stone – and all the actresses that lot have ever influenced. Maybe, nowadays, most young men were making it with the same woman, artistically speaking. Which didn't make it any less fun . . .

Despite the coke still chugging around my system things had started pretty damn well. She had the kind of collar-bones that belong on a statue, and her shoulders moved very nicely, very slightly up, at each forward movement. As I took all this on board two thoughts occurred.

Thought number one was how coke, like speed, can get in the way on these occasions. Both guys and, more often, girls can get hot on speedy things. But, and it's a big but, the more speed you shoot – or the more snoot you sniff – the less likely it is that the male sex drive will make it out of the garage. It's quite simple. Sex is natural but powders are not, and, thinking about it, I'd had some real 'mares on chemicals. Though that was long ago, back in the days of teenage stupidity. I once foolishly borrowed some uppers from some housewife's pill box – uppers that were, I found out, really downers. They completely blanked me out, taking me, after two long lost days, to stare doomily into the Thames on the South Bank – unshaven, unwashed and trembling. To add insult to injury I was getting some slurred suicide counselling from some foul-smelling tramp. When you're getting advice from some dribbling alcoholic then you really are in trouble. Every time I yawned – and this went on for weeks afterwards – a kind of evil cerebral electricity crackled between my ears. It was a vile feeling, a ragged power surge that went right between my temples, right across my jaw and brain. Really nasty. None of which shone much light on my coke–sex difficulty, should it arise. Freud once wrote about cocaine making him sexually potent, but that just goes to show you what a Viennese fruit-cake he really was.

By that time, though, the dope me and Sally had smoked earlier combined with the wine to cancel out the charlie and thus activities continued. And the continuing activities brought me to thought number two. Was it safe sex I was involved in – as recommended by Her Majesty's Government – or was it unsafe? *You can't*, I thought, *be too careful in this day and Aids*. But I saw the discarded Durex wrapper and everything was all right – it was definitely safe. It was kind of reassuring to know that I was still thinking even when I wasn't thinking. Leaving me to get on and enjoy things. And then she was gasping again, her sharp fingernails creasing up the dog-eared pillow, white at the knuckle, and I couldn't think about anything except her and her body. Her body and my desperate need for it. And how good it felt to be on her, in her, around her. As I kept pushing, a slow smile spread across her face and then turned into a fleeting sneer before she gasped again and then I knew I wouldn't be able to slow things down. Sound, sorted, safe. Relax. And then it was all over and I was so damned grateful I actually wanted to thank her as I nuzzled my face into her neck, soft-biting the smooth skin above her collar-bone. I decided not to. *She'd probably sneer*, I decided. *This is, after all, the modern world* . . .

As Sally lay there afterwards, I suddenly thought – just for a second – that there was something very, very disturbing about her. Something disturbing about the thought of actually laying my head down next to her big eyes. Maybe it was the Moroccan black we'd smoked; sometimes dealers would add a touch of diesel oil to make the weight, texture and colour right. It didn't normally do anything – except maybe give you a minor headache later – but it was said to add a touch of paranoia sometimes.

But her eyes *did* look bleak afterwards. Bleak as hell. It wasn't my imagination. If the eyes are the windows to the soul, then hers had had the shutters nailed closed years ago. A grim thought. I really hadn't noticed that before, when I was looking for a kiss and she was looking for Mr Goodbar. And so what? Honey, this wasn't no romance. She liked me, a little. And she looked good. End of story.

9

The Pay-Off

The morning was rough so I opted to get up in the afternoon instead – that was the one joy of freelancing, you did have a bit more freedom than the nine-to-fivers. Sally had to get back to college but she'd left a note which had her phone number on it. I thought I probably would call her. In a day or two . . .

I went through my pockets – the toot twists were gone, of course. I'd actually sold a tiny amount of coke – well, swapped it for a half-empty champagne bottle and a tenner, which was something I'd never done before. Not with coke, anyway, and not with strangers. I made a mental note not to deal again – if you could call it dealing. I still had a little coke in the wardrobe drawer that I kept my T-shirts in. I thought about taking a line to buck me up, but it was too early – and besides, that way lay madness. Later, later . . .

There was a second note on the floor. It was so badly scrawled it took me half an hour to translate it all and then I wished I hadn't. It read: 'Pete, you deaf bastard, don't you understand? *Raw Soul* is closing down! And *Groove* is being taken over by *EM*. We are both dead, mate! DEAD!'

It had come from the Spider, the *Raw Soul* man, and raw was how it left me. But was it true? Three phone calls and a glance at the *Evening Standard* confirmed the worst. No more *Raw Soul*, and no more Pete contributions to *Groove*. The latter was now part of the *Express Music* empire and they'd fill it with their hand-picked hacks and hackettes. As for freelancers, only their own little favourites would get a foot in the door now. The end of an era. And an error. My error – for relying too much on one source of cash. Never put all your expenses in one basket – a big mistake which had now come home to roost. It was all a power trip, really. Being a freelancer means always having to say you're sorry – and I'd stopped apologising.

I could have called *Encore* – no, skip it, someone at the party had said they were closing next week anyway. *How long can I get away with it?* I'd asked myself at the North Atlantic lig. Not that long, as it had turned out. That was the real freedom that everyone now had – they were free to feel insecure all the time. Great. Now the two months' rent I owed seemed like a real problem, not just some temporary irritation.

I was up against the lot. There were fewer mavericks than ever now, and that was the battered bracket I'd sidelined myself into. The battered cul-de-sac. Nowadays there's also less staff on magazines, films, TV, anything. Less chance to get your feet under the table. And those that did had got their qualifications at the same universities and attended the same schools before that. They'd probably started networking in kindergarten. Which might explain why most mags have the same guys on the cover every month. It's not just down to the PR gurus, it's because most people these days tend to work and live with people from exactly the same background, earning the same kind of money. More of the same. All of which left me depressed and more nowhere than ever . . .

The afternoon got more and more disconnected. I rang around various record companies, trying to stock up before the word got out. I tried a few other editors too. I did have a big story at the back of my mind, something that might be worth thousands if it worked out. But it was a big if and I didn't want to go off half-cocked, so, on the phone, I went for the straightforward hustle.

'Of course I'm still okay at *Groove*, but I want to branch out,' I said, being frugal with the facts. 'I like what you guys at *Bloated!* have been doing recently—'

'Really? You haven't called of late.'

'Well . . . nor have you.'

'Pete, I'm an editor, I don't call anyone – people call me.'

Smug bastard. There were even a few fellow hacks I had to call but they were all having meetings, on their way out, on the other line . . . I tried my 'In' people – they were all out. The yes-men all said maybe. And the word 'maybe' is English for 'no'. Calls went out in dozens and came back in singles. I should have expected it, really. Absence makes the heart forgetful; you're out of sight when you're out of your mind – and so my get up and go got up and went.

I did another line of cream that night and tried to balance it with the last of my grass as I wondered what the hell to do if the big story didn't pan out. What to do with the rest of my life. Not yet thirty and all washed-up. It was all very well having walked the walk and talked the talk and lived the life and all that, but living the life didn't count for too much any more. If I'd gone to college then at least I'd have been lined up for some cosy twenty-grand pay-off, complete with full pension rights. That at least would have kept me alive for a year or two. *If* I'd gone to college.

But then again, in the nasty Nineties, they aren't taking on too many staff anyhow. I'd been a bookie's assistant once, for a few weeks. I should've stuck with it, maybe. Maybe I'd have been running William Hill Turf Accountants before my twenty-fifth birthday. *It was all a mistake, honest, guv* . . . I got into music journalism via the night-club evenings I'd been running back in the days of Acid House, in '88. I discovered a lot of semi-legal drinking dens when I was doing clubs. I'd also learned a lot with clubs, though – like how the off-duty cops would go down, in little gangs, to one of the ballrooms in Leicester Square. Every Saturday night. There one of them would pick on some kid who was out with his girlfriend. The off-duty cop would then insult this girl, push and shove her until her boyfriend would finally lose his rag and take a swing at him – at which point the other cops would leap in, flashing their warrant cards at the bouncers and proceed to beat the hell out of this unfortunate kid. Then they'd drag him down the cop-shop, blood pouring from his broken nose or black eye, and he'd be charged with affray and get a hundred-quid fine. And the cops who'd hammered him would get a day off work because they'd been brave enough to make a valiant off-duty arrest. They get paid two or three grand a month for doing that. *And don't forget, mind how you go, kids* . . .

I'd originally got into night-club promoting, as opposed to anything else, because I was sick of sweating blood on building sites. I'd done a year and a half of that, eighteen months that felt like a century. I wasn't going back to building, or to starving in some garret on the coast. I'd actually done that, done the artist bit when I thought I was a photographer. I'd been kicked off the dole. Made a small fortune – a very small fortune – and lost it. I'd gone bankrupt, even gone without food for two or three days, more times than I care to remember. Me and various pals often gate-crashed parties early to get at the food and drink. Mr Integrity, I thought, though Mr Dumb comes closer to it. I wasn't in the Sudan, I didn't *have* to starve. I could have grovelled my way into a McJob but what would have been the fun in that? I have had some money in my time and you soon get used to it, but you never get used to being without – even if you were born without. There's no such thing as *you don't miss what you've never had* any more. Not in the West, not anywhere, not with all those TV ads and posters showing you in great lingering detail exactly what you're missing. So if anyone tells you about the nobility of poverty and all that shite then laugh out loud, because in most cases that stuff just doesn't apply. Poverty corrupts and absolute poverty corrupts absolutely. Ask any skint junkie and, between hustling you for fifty pence, he'll tell you about the care-free fun of it all.

I knew what I had to do though, and I did it. Between putting out the feelers on the story of the year, I spent the next few days trying to talk up small amounts of writing work and borrowing from those who'd borrowed from me before.

That was daytime. The nights were spent frantically necking with Sally. Yes, we'd almost become a couple. I wasn't a single loser any more; now I was a loser in a relationship. Me and Sally were an item, as much as anyone could be an item with Sally. Considering she was an item all by herself. The third time we got it on, for instance – well, just after the third time, actually – she held my face in her hands and smiled.

'I like you,' she'd said, 'and I don't like many people . . . not many at all.'

'We're not worthy,' I deadpanned, but she didn't react so I just kissed her forehead and ruffled her hair. And then she jumped up and got dressed.

'Where you going?'

'Gotta get back to the dorm – and study.'

'Are you out of your skull? It's two in the morning.'

'Doesn't matter. See you later.'

'But—'

I'd started to protest but she'd already blown me a kiss and fled. Crazy . . . After a couple of weeks of this I was supposed to meet her parents. I kept asking why. She kept saying it'd be fun – 'And don't worry, it's just a visit, doesn't mean anything. They won't try and marry me off over the sherry . . .'

I finally agreed to go the following weekend. Maybe it would be fun – Daddy was a life-long Tory who'd just had his new car nicked. I thought I might rag him about that – *Ha! ha! You voted for it, mate, now enjoy it.* He and Mumsy lived somewhere down in Sussex. Meeting them was, I felt, one of those life experiences I could well live without.

The phone rang the day after we arranged the meet-her-parents session. It was a news editor telling me to interview some rap combo. A rap group who just so happened to be on Vee's label. I no longer wanted to avoid Vee, not especially; I mean, it wasn't my fault the Nomads review had gone missing. It had been an act of God, technically speaking, and, besides, Jerry had told me he'd squared it: 'He's bin fired, Vee baby, what can he do?' This he did in exchange for another gram of my charlie. Not that he was being mean – he'd just run out. A little toot does go a long way – at the right time – but I still wasn't sure I wanted to see Vee, just in case he did bear some grudge after all. But I had no choice, really.

'Speak to that Vee guy himself,' said the news ed, 'there's a big cross-over between music and video now. Find out the whys and wherefores.'

'The whys?'

'And wherefores.'

'But why?'

'Just do it.'

Just do it. I couldn't argue, freelancers can't be choosers. Refuse too often and you won't get asked again, ever. And, as I turned it over in my mind, I saw that interviewing Vee might just fit in with my plans anyway . . .

Vee's offices were exclusive, expansive and expensive. You had to get past *three* sets of receptionists and guards. The other highlights were two big video editing suites, one small studio and a private bar. Pop videos and EPKs were knocked off in the small studio – EPK meaning Electronic Press Kit – and I just can't recall the rest of the place. It was all a blur of fierce little halogen lights, earnest young staff working all hours, empty pizza boxes and cola bottles greasy with finger-prints. The record label seemed to be a mere toy, a diversion compared with the video side. The latter was too big to be a front. If it was his. Maybe everything was hired. Maybe there was a whole dormitory of sleeping partners.

Vee was even friendlier than before though, and insisted on

treating me like a long-lost pal. I did the interview with his label's new wonder group – two rappers, one of whom could play guitar – and then Vee insisted on buying me a drink or two. He didn't tell me how he got his money but he did reveal how his video biz had taken off so quickly. Seems he used some of his ill-gotten gains, and he didn't have *that* much to start with, to buy one broadcast VCR and one VCR with hi-fi sound. Oh yeah, and Vee had something else you or I wouldn't have had, an undeclared shareholder. This guy had got friendly with Vee through the coke and he just happened to work for a big record company, WEAMI, so he made sure that Vee got all the video duplication work. It was all pretty pedestrian at first – copying someone else's pop videos on to stereo videotapes for hacks who'd watch them in mono, if they watched them at all. But WEAMI paid him thirty quid a time anyway. And that was thirty times fifteen or twenty copies. Up to six hundred quid a time. And it was happening two or three times a week in the Eighties when a lot of A & Rs thought the only way to break a new act was on MTV.

A few years ago Vee had bought a warehouse near Caledonian Road. He wasn't even VAT-registered but by then he could afford to pay cash. And he did. Nearly two hundred grand. All in one go, in fifty-pound notes crammed into a bulging suitcase. After that it was all over bar the shouting – or in Vee's case, the sniffing – because a fortune was definitely going to be made. Or that's how he made it sound anyway. But, I figured, he couldn't be doing that well video-wise or why would he still be dealing coke?

10

You Run The Numbers, We Rig The Jury

Vee had a big red Audi in the pub car-park. It was new, naturally. He fielded calls on his mobile phone as we drove back to his house. Every one of the few things he said on the phone sounded like some minimal foreign language. 'Yuh, no . . . no way . . . huh? . . . uh huh . . . yeah.' It could, I supposed, just be the way he talked on the phone.

His place had five bedrooms and was somewhat spacious. It was worth a quarter of a million of anyone's money, maybe more. He had some huge loudspeakers in the L-shaped lounge and a pair of shotguns on the back wall between them. They were intricately inlaid with gold, so I assumed they were deactivated antiques. But a longer stare quickly revealed that they were not antiques; although they were pretty damn flash, they weren't toys. They did undoubtedly work and they did get used, I could see that. There was dull grease trying to shine near the trigger mechanism. They got used. If only occasionally. If only on some private shooting range. They didn't inspire any feeling of well-being in me . . .

Vee introduced me to Anna, his girl. She had a faint

American accent although she was from further south – Latin America. That was the closest she got to naming her home-land – Latin America.

She was either a very experienced 22-year-old or a freak-ishly young thirtysomething, it was hard to tell exactly which. She wasn't particularly narcissistic but she played with her hair so much you couldn't help admiring it as much as she did. More than she did, in fact. She was, in the words of the poet, elegant. More than attractive. You looked when she moved. You listened when she talked. You wanted to be close to her, to touch her . . .

Vee also had me exchange formalities with the house-keeper, a fat, happy, middle-aged Spaniard who had a couple of small kids dozing in her arms. They were her children, the house-keeper's, by some long-departed boyfriend. Vee and Anna let them live in, which was all very generous, though I couldn't help wondering what the Spaniard would do if armed cops should ever come sledge-hammering their way in through the windows on account of the toot. Maybe Vee didn't worry about that. Maybe he didn't keep any there. Maybe he paid off. 'The Met,' he later told me with a cynical grin, 'are the best police force that money can buy and, believe me, they can be bought.' Vee was all right. Vee had cover.

We all talked about getting wasted. Caning it. Getting full-on, spaced-out, out of it. The addictive perils of music, journalism and the entertainment media in general. I waited about half an hour before casually slipping in one of the important questions I'd been saving up.

'Did you really get a hundred grams to The Scallies?'

'Them? Hmm . . . yeah, I did. Well, I did through Jezza. It was his deal really . . . that's how they broke through, innit?'

'He still supplying 'em?'

'Ask him. Yeah, he probably is, on and off – they still owe him dosher, y'know? Number one and they still won't pay on time.'

That confirmed one of the planks of my big story. Just one.

Vee would never swear to The Scallies' connection in court, but that might not matter. I did have a confirmation, of sorts. It was a start.

When Vee went out of the room I could no longer resist asking Anna, as casually as possible, what she actually did.

'Whatever I want,' she shrugged, smiling with mock innocence as she added, 'doesn't that sound terrible?'

'Yes and no,' was all I could come up with as Vee breezed back from the curved cocktail bar. Anna did have a rich-bitch air but, at the same time, she was really sussed – she'd done a mock yawn when Vee had talked about his next car. Big boys' toys and designer labels didn't impress her. In fact, most things didn't impress her. I was damn sure I didn't, which was a big pity, for me at least.

'I bet you think I'm on the charlie all the time,' Vee said, ignoring my shaking head. 'But I'm not. I only do it socially, 'bout once or twice a month these days. Sometimes, not even that.'

'Never try your own supply,' Anna quoted.

'Never try and enter your own fucking movie,' Vee added with a touch of gloom. 'And that's one thing you can fuckin' quote me on!'

By midnight the house-keeper and the kids were in bed and Vee suddenly stood up and smiled.

'It's late. Let's do it, eh?'

'Yeah, sure,' I said, before asking, 'Do what, Vee?'

'What?' Vee quietly laughed back at me as he pulled a fake book-set from the wall. He opened out the book-set and pulled out a huge bag of coke – thirty grams at least – and spilled out a couple of grams. He took a razor and swiftly chopped the charlie into six fat lines.

'Have a line, go on . . .'

'Nah.' I tried to resist, as if I had a reason to be up early in the morning.

'Nah, go on, Pete . . .'

'Maybe half a line . . . maybe later . . .'

Anna encouraged me. I think I vaguely amused both of

them. A poor man of words in a flash palace like this. I've never actually been poor, but I *was* a man of words, which meant something. If you're a writer, other people can be you. You can make them see things from your point of view completely. It may only be for a nano-second but they *are* you. That's why dictators hate writers, the good ones anyhow, since the big boss man is forced – as he reads – to share someone else's critical point of view, someone else's conscience, someone else's enthusiasms. Vee knew all that, instinctively; he even, vaguely, respected it.

He sniffed a line in a second. One second. Superfast. The doorbell rang, once then twice again. Vee tensed the first time then, as the bell went again, he relaxed. Friends. The friends were Ally, an A & R man that I'd seen before somewhere, and two girls – Styla, a dark-haired model that half the country would recognise, and her equally attractive sister Silvia. She reminded me a little of Anna. Sultry-looking, as they say in airport books. These two were a little uptight and I ended up speaking to Anna more and more. She later told me that she'd once been a bit of a debutante where she was from. She'd run away from all the luxuries to run weapons to the Sandinistas and a few other uprisings of recent times. It didn't sound as if she could easily move back there – not if she wanted to live. She was real left-wing, real militant. A cocaine communist. I'd once been an amphetamine anarchist myself, a few years ago. All that stuff about the world, the world that never listened. The world that never stayed the same and never changed. The world that, instead, changed us. Us, like water over stone, like ghosts, nameless lives leaving no trace.

But they were strange together, Anna and Vee. Strange because they were so different yet always in . . . in what? Not in love. Maybe in league with each other? Because here was affection, fondness even, but nothing more. Not from her, anyway. Curious. Curious because she seemed too intense, too real, to put up with that kind of distance, that kind of emotional fraud. The kind that makes up most long-term relationships. Habit. Fear. Boredom. Emotional black-mail . . .

I could see her attraction for Vee – the long hair, the eyes, the long limbs, a Latin Disney babe come to life – and maybe I could glimpse what he *might* mean to her, but there was something missing, and something extra as well. Vee and Anna were, in short, a little mysterious to me. At first they seemed to confirm my pet theory, i.e. that women didn't need men but they *did* want them, whereas men really *needed* women and therefore desperately pretended that they didn't. But that theory didn't fit them. Maybe money kept Anna there, but that seemed too mundane.

Vee talked about how Reagan really helped get the cocaine ball rolling back in 1981 by using his mandate – '*Give them liberal wet-backs hell, Ronnie!*' – to push the wholesale coffee price down two cents a kilo. This meant that thousands of Latin hill farmers were suddenly facing bankruptcy, and soon most of them were forced to start laying coca crops for the big boys. Within a year, the US was flooded with cheap coke and people were dying daily in gun battles in Miami and LA. Well worth the two cents, huh? Then to make matters worse, the CIA themselves started shifting coke into the States so they could use the profits to fund the Contra terrorists.

'Most of their coke ended up as crack, ending up killing people in the black ghetto,' Anna interjected. 'Did you know the KKK have meetings at the CIA's main offices? They've got so many Klan members in the CIA they're actually allowed to hold meetings there.'

As I shook my head at all this – not in disbelief, it was more than likely true – I couldn't help noticing how long Anna's warm eyes tended to linger on me. Me? *Could I have the slightest chance with this one*, I mused, knowing, as I did, it was dangerous to even think about thinking about it.

I asked Vee if he knew anything about how his stuff was produced. Ally and Vee then talked about jungle clearances, about the way petrol is used to turn the coca paste into powder. About his supplier. About the crazy things friends had done on coke. About how the once-mighty Casablanca records – a million-selling outfit – had allegedly been brought low by coke. About how Major Lance, a soul singer of serious distinction, had been brought low and jailed for it. About how Vee himself hardly touched it now (and they all said that as they snorted more and more). About the England footballer who had supplied some of his team-mates with it – no wonder he was never dropped and no wonder he never scored. About how you cut the stuff to re-sell it – toothpaste powder, baby powder or laxatives. Seven or eight lines got sniffed. The *modus operandi* quickly became clear – stuff came in, sometimes from an embassy or some such untouchable source, and twenty or thirty grams each were instantly dished out to a dozen trusted middlemen who then passed them on to their own, smaller street dealers. Then there were the fringe people – dealers-cum-users, designers, City types, hairdressers, video cameramen, nightclub promoters, bike couriers, mini-cab drivers, session musicians who couldn't cut it any more, so they chopped it out instead.

These were people who were s'posed to get around a bit, get around and meet people, that was part of their various jobs. That way no one would have too much on them at any one time. All *in* and all *out* very quickly. And all connected by mobile phone. Deliveries to your house, deals on wheels. But why did Vee have so much coke stashed here? Surely it was dangerous, even for him. More coke was poured out, chopped out, lined up, inhaled.

I wandered around the lounge. Time for a more detailed inspection. Everything was designer *designer* to the *n*th degree. The hi-fi's six-foot loudspeakers were made from some polished wood. It was the colour of pine but had too many dark lines. It looked more like walnut, like a Jag's dashboard, but more luxurious, more glossy. They were, a plaque indicated, 'electro-static Jebbsens'. I'd seen that brand of speaker once before, at auction. Going for fifteen grand a pair. Second-hand. What the hell did they cost new? Twenty thousand? Twenty-five? If you could afford to hire these things, you could afford to buy them.

Vee's money was big money. Seriously big. The video studios had shown me that, with FX machines which cost more than a car. And the state of his place confirmed it. Pounds sterling. Six figures. Maybe more. Which presented another mystery about Vee and Anna. Why still deal in coke if you're that rich? It couldn't be necessary now. Why risk even the slightest chance you might get busted? The others present didn't really count in any of this. They were users or six-gram dealers. Small-time. It soon became obvious Ally made much more money this way than he did from his tiny label, which had not actually charted since God knows when – and how much cash do you actually get anyway when a record hits No. 98 and then drops out? Especially when you've paid two grand a week to buy it in there in the first place. So five grams of coke would be taken here, two grams given away there. And those that received it were just a bit more receptive in their dealings with Ally. It all added up for him. And all tax-free, of course. I began to remember where I'd seen Ally before – it was at a big publishing house, going into a lift with someone. Maybe that meeting was about music. Or maybe it was another deal. I'd heard about that publishing house. They'd discovered who their own in-house dealer was and were about to fire him when he threatened to make his little black book public. Most of the creatives, half the board and the chairman's daughter were registered in his book. Registered as accepting packages. He even had a few recorded-delivery receipts; bike chits that had been signed for at the offices and at the homes. Delivered to the door. And guess what? The in-house dealer wasn't fired. He was still there the last I heard. He probably knew Vee. Or did Ally prevent such a meeting? Maybe a meeting like that would have meant him losing his percentage – see how hard you have to work when you're an A & R?

As Vee talked it became obvious how much toot could give you a head start in the music biz. It could win you friends, allies, influence and contracts. And that was just for starters . . .

The charlie on Vee's table was finally all used up and people moaned discreetly. Anna was doing something out in the kitchen as Silvia suddenly subjected me to a lascivious charm blitz, hanging on my every word as her finger stroked my arm. And then she realised that I didn't have any coke – for some reason it wasn't done to ask our host for any more – and she suddenly recalled that she had to be home by two-thirty to let her boyfriend into their Highgate hideaway. Ally and Styla said they'd give her a lift, and they all rose together.

Just before Anna disappeared up to bed she emerged from the kitchen long enough to chat some more. And all the time she was looking at me with her eyes – those dark brown eyes of hers that managed to be so intense and yet so light at one and the same time. And then, at one point during our chat, a car alarm went off outside and I tracked those same eyes of hers flicking from Vee to the window and then back to Vee again. They exchanged glances and there was a moment between them. A look. A moment. A look that spoke volumes. There was an entire story in there somewhere, in that look, but I couldn't understand a single line of it and felt like a failure because I just couldn't suss it all out. Little Miss Mystery, our Anna. Before she went up she kissed Vee goodnight and pecked me on the cheek. At the bottom of the stairs she stopped and remembered her bracelet on the side. I threw it to her and, from beneath her curled tresses, she gave me a harmless wink. It made me ache for her, made me hope that, somehow, it wasn't harmless. That, somehow, I did have a cat in hell's chance of getting to know her better . . .

By five-thirty in the morning Vee and I had told each other our life stories, with lots of highlights and quite a few low points. There was only one real low point for me: that night with Beth Aden. I left that out, but was still thinking about it when Vee suddenly snapped, 'You still owe me, Pete, you still fuckin' owe me something.'

He remembered. And he still bore a grudge. It threw me

completely. Even if he was joking, it was no joke. Vee suddenly smiled. He *was* joking, but I wasn't laughing.

We went out through the open door of his French windows, out into the small walled-in garden as my nerves slowly stopped screaming. The garden had the kind of wet dewy haze you only get when you're on an over-hung lawn near sunrise in summer. I was smiling but I noticed my fists were clenched – index knuckle forward – like Vee's. A clenched fist was, I decided, the Nineties equivalent of the Sixties peace sign. Seriously wired. *The Summer of Love this ain't*, I thought. But then Vee, flushed with coke and Chardonnay, suddenly decided to declare undying friendship for me anyway.

'You're all right, you are, Pete. Safe. A diamond geezer,' he said. All I could see in his eyes was an alarming lack of pupils. He looked like an alien, like the girls in the club. Like something frightening.

'So are you, Vee, you're safe too,' I said without thinking. Because safe was the one thing Vee wasn't.

'You ever need anything, call me. I swear I'll get it.'

We can help you, we can help you, I thought. *Yeah, yeah, yeah*. Vee had probably sworn friendship a hundred times before with God knows how many different people. He'd probably meant it each time too. At the time. Were they customers? Or friends? Was I there as a friend or a customer? The dividing line seemed to get blurred quickly with Vee. Not that he'd ring or anything; I knew dealers better than that. They're not all the same but they never will call anyone because they never have to – someone's always calling them.

I mumbled my excuses and stumbled off into the dawn. I walked for an hour to get some fresh air and then jumped in a cab. It cost me my very last tenner. There was a cheque clearing, wasn't there? No, there probably wasn't. I would have to nip down and sell some records I hadn't even had a chance to play. I'd go to Steve's Sounds, they did a fair price on stuff, once you knew them – or maybe even re-visit Chas. When my nose had stopped aching. My nose and my eyes and my jaw. And my back. Too much standing up. Too much pacing around. Too much of that snow white. The sun was up and bleaching everything out. I'd arrived here on some sort of mission, but I was no longer sure exactly what it was. All the details were disappearing fast. Goodnight Vee, goodnight Vienna.

11

All This Time I'm Wasting - Whose Is It Anyway?

I walked through Berwick Street market as it died, kicking the scuffed cabbage leaves as I strolled along. A day had passed but the night hadn't yet started.

'Whatta lotta Ocelot *I* got!' yelled a white-haired street trader as he frantically waved some fake leopard-skin around. I went down to Shaftesbury to score some Chinese tiger balm. I figured that if I rubbed enough into my temples it might make me feel better.

As I passed a take-away I could see a wall-eyed hooker inside, smashing up the vinegar bottles. It complemented the scene, ten yards on, of some drunk with a baked potato trying to hit a bemused tourist. Turning the corner into Dean Street was nearly as bad. Leaning against some ripped Bowie posters – with Mr Jones finally looking like the Weimar artist he always wanted to be – were a gang of loafing yobs.

'Want some fucking charlie, mate? Eh? Want some?'

I shook my head. I wouldn't have bought Pepsi off them, let alone charlie. If it was charlie it was probably cut with some dodgy speed. Or rat poison. My refusal to buy got a mouthful of abuse. I didn't mind that so much but the thug nearest me was holding a double-stan. A double-stan consists of two Stanley knives held together by a small slab of plasticine – the whole evil point being to leave a bigger scar on your unsuspecting victim. Pleasant, huh? Looking at the yob's blank expression I figured that someone, somewhere, was going to have an unpleasant meeting with Ollie's friend Stanley . . .

And then there were the gangs of Essex boys – uptown to have a drink and giggle at the freaks, the same freaks who'd put London back on the map – who were getting way too rowdy. I almost thought about tipping off a copper and then I suddenly realised I hadn't seen one for more than an hour. No, nearly two hours. Not a cop, not a cop bike. Not even a van. Not in the whole West End. And this is at *night*. It was like they couldn't be bothered any more. Some of them were pissed off by the Crown Prosecution cost-cutters and some were just bone idle. You want security? Hire it privately. Behind me the mob were spitting at some tourist. As the poet said, 'I love the Third World, that's why I live in London . . .'

Then, thank God, I found myself back on Compton Street. Since about 1991 Compton Street had developed into a shaven-headed poseur's paradise, with more cafés per metre than anywhere else on earth. Despite the presence of the occasional, equally shorn, woman, the Compton poseur's life did not seem to be one enlivened by female intrusion. The shops there had more chains and leather than you could shake a whip at. As Eric at Boy once put it, 'We get more heavy breathing in here than most sex shops. One guy was trying on some rubber stuff just so he could expose himself. And he was, ahem, in a state of serious arousal.'

'You should write to your MP about it,' I'd told him. 'I think it *was* my MP,' he'd replied gloomily.

After I'd said a quick hello to Margherita at the Carlisle I hit out for the Cambridge, where I was supposed to meet Jeff. I stopped briefly at a late-night newsagent so I could flick through a copy of the *Chronicle*. I'd filed three small stories but they'd only used one. Shit. It still wasn't going to bring me down, though. I might yet, I thought, have a big surprise for the big boys at the *Chronicle* – Maurie More and all. Things were going well. Potentially.

The IRA had once fire-bombed the top bar at the Cambridge, which I thought was over-doing it a bit but, then again, they do always charge a lot for their drinks up there. Which was a drag as Jeff wasn't there on time – he never was – and so I had to lash out the few quid I'd brought with me for the cab, on drink. I'd expected to wine and dine at the lig that Jeff was taking me to. It was also where I expected to see Eye.

The Finnish put ice in their cider, which I always thought kinda novel. This gives you a chance to order a glass of ice with your cider, which makes it last a lot longer as well as implying some kind of pseudo jet-set sophistication – 'This is how we do it in Helsinki, dwarling.' The permanently full glass also gives out the impression that you're still solvent. I had actually discovered that I liked my cider cut that way. I was well into my third when Jeff finally showed.

The lig we were going to was at a newish place called the Hyper Viper Venue. There were six bouncers on the door and one was wearing a flak jacket. I'd seen that in Hamburg, where Turkish gangs with guns often attacked local bouncers, but I'd never seen it in sleepy London town.

'Has someone taken a pot-shot at you?' I asked the bouncer in the flak jacket.

'Yeah, two shots, last week.'

'Shit! Where'd it happen? Here?'

'Yep.'

'Shit.'

'It was a thirty-eight.'

'Shit. That's progress, huh?'

'That's progress, Peter.'

A couple of people milled around aimlessly as a name DJ pumped out MOR House at pain-threshold volume. The DJ was one of the House Mafia, and he'd left his invoice lying around the DJ's box – 'For Services Rendered, 3 hrs; £2,000.' Two grand! For clearing the dance-floor! He must have seen them coming. His set was so lacklustre that only three girls were dancing – I found out later that they were being paid – and Jeff looked ready to leave within minutes.

'I might go soon,' said Jeff, 'I can't stand these places any more.'

'And what about me?' I kidded. 'I'll get lost in here on my own.'

'Eye will look after you, she'll be down soon. So you didn't bring Sally?'

'No.'

'But you're still seeing her?'

'Oh yeah, she's studying again, you know these students . . . She asked me if I was serious the other day. Serious about her, she meant.'

'And what did you say?'

'I asked her if she was serious.'

'And?'

'And she said that she'd asked me first . . . so I said I was serious if she was.'

'And what did she say to that?'

'Nothing.'

'Do you get along with her?'

'Yeah, between times. It's okay. She's okay.'

Jeff left after a few moments as I wondered if maybe the WAIFs were also getting paid to drape themselves around the place. You know what a WAIF is, one of those Why Am I Famous? people – an It Girl or He-Hunk or whatever. Maybe they'd been hired in too. The paparazzi outside had looked fake as well – I hadn't recognised one of 'em – and where was that TV crew from? WTV? XTV? Never heard of 'em. Maybe even they were being paid to be here, posing with empty cameras. I always thought that one day I was going to be in some club where everyone present was being paid to be there. Fake paparazzi, fake TV crews, fake hacks, fake dancers, fake trendys, fake bar-flies . . . so maybe that was it. A fake club. The virtual reality dive.

Reality virtually broke down, however, when something

electrical got disconnected and the sound went off. The three paid dancers went on moving silently for a few seconds – maybe they thought it was a special mix or maybe they didn't get paid if they stopped moving – and then they slowly shuffled to a standstill. The House supremo took off early and the following act, a couple of funky DJs in berets, came on. They had white shirts and braces and looked like something out of *A Clockwork Orange*. They spliffed up almost immediately, but got the sound working again. By the time I went to congratulate them on their set they were smiling blankly. What they were smoking must have been skunk or something since they were completely out of it.

'Nice stuff,' I said and they smiled quietly, encouraging me to go on. 'Those berets you're wearing look well *Clockwork Orange.*'

'Crash yer dermott, kid,' said one as he attempted *Orange*-speak with a sick weak smile. A few seconds after I'd arrived and had taken a few tokes, the venue manager appeared. The DJs hid the smouldering joint under the console and lit up a herbal ciggy as the manager came closer.

'What's that smell?' asked the manager, and one of the jocks silently raised the herbal fag packet. The manager nodded, seemingly unaware of how wasted they really were.

'So, boys, you finally got the sound sorted then?'

'Sound,' said one.

'Sorted,' added the other.

The manager raised a thumb and they copied him in dumb-show. Reassured, the big boss man then went back to the bar. After I'd finished the boys' joint I offered them a drink.

'Wanna beer?'

They were beyond speech now. Lost in music, lost in smoke, the lost boys in love with sound . . . but they did, finally, succeed in raising one thumb between them. At the bar I got a dig in the ribs.

'So from bar-fly to bar-parasite in three easy moves, ladies and gentlemen, I give you Big "Charro" Pete, the last cowboy in the Wild West End . . .'

I turned around to see Terence, the unshaven MD for Pounds-Sterling Discs, a man who'd ironically made a fortune out of black music. I say *ironically* because our Terence, who'd been a very well-educated young man, had also been a racist teenager who encouraged others to attack Asian pensioners or black school kids or whoever.

All of this was somehow made more complicated by the fact that one of Terence's new promo men was a black racist – he'd forbidden his daughters to ever date whites, a bigotry which at least he was honest about. This dire duo had survived a recent scandal wherein CDs were being pressed up and sold off without paperwork, which meant their label got all the dosh while the artists knew – and got – nothing. It had been hushed up, of course. Written off as an accounting error. Token fines all round. I disliked the pair of them – especially Terence.

'I'm only kidding, kid,' he said in his fake East End accent, 'Whatcha want? Anything you like for a penny. No, seriously, Pete, whatcha want?'

'Five beers.'

'No, seriously.'

'Five beers, seriously.'

'*Five?*'

'I need some for the DJs,' I said.

'No skin off my nose, they're all free,' smirked Terence as he shouted at the barmaid, 'Hello! Over here, pur-lease! Six beers, and can you—'

'Havana beer? The big ones?'

'Yeah, whatever.'

The barmaid was cute and had an Afro. She approached Terry with a bill. Her name badge read 'Spliff', which I thought was quite funny, if unlikely, but Terry wasn't laughing.

'That'll be twenty pounds, please.'

'You what?'

'The Cuban beers are four pound for the big bottle—'

'This is supposed to be a party, lovey, a fucking party, the drinks are on the house, they're freebies. Do you know the word "freebies"?'

'Yes, I know what freebies are, mister, and all the freebies have run out. That'll be twenty pounds, pur-lease . . .'

It was, I figured, an occupational hazard. Which was actually Terence's problem. Miss Spliff opened the bottles as if to cut off all means of escape. She had one of those bubbly faces that deserves to be permanently on the cover of every teen mag. Determined not to lose face – although he did have a few to spare – Terence slapped a twenty-pound note on the bar.

'Thank you so *fucking much*!' he snapped at her before shoving the bottles in my direction and stalking off. His sulk didn't annoy me. It didn't even irritate me – nothing could touch me that night. I was on a near-natural high and I was going to be higher still. Thirty thousand feet to be exact. Eye was coming down to give me two air tickets to Holland, a flight that was leaving the next morning, taking me to old Amsterdam. I was going to drag Sally along but she had an exam or something stupid, and her main concern was that I got back in time to make it over to her mum and dad's. I would, I reckoned, need a good lig to prepare for all that. The trip had actually come out of the blue, at the last minute, as these things sometimes do. Feature stories like this had got me to New York twice, although I'd refused a return match three times since – thus missing Aretha Franklin, M People and someone unforgettable I've since forgotten. Now that I was barred from the DPC building, and instant access to a glossy mag, I wondered how many more big ligs I'd go on – maybe tonight would be the last. I knew I was on a few blacklists – too many signed petitions, too many strikes – so it seemed unlikely – unless my ace in the hole came off.

Spliff the barmaid asked if all the drinks really were for the DJs, and when I nodded a reply she gave me a tray and a smile.

'You're very kind,' I mumbled and she smiled again, this time with lips slightly parted. Her eyes and mouth made a triangle of real interest and I couldn't help noticing that her pink tongue was always teasing her front teeth. Maybe there was something happening here. I didn't wanna do the dirty on

Sally but, hell, she hadn't come with me, had she? As I turned back toward the DJs, I could see a would-be model give them some flyer. Maybe there was something happening somewhere else. Later. Wasn't there always?

It was the gentle rocking which brought me back to full consciousness. After some two hours of incredibly uncomfortable sleep I decided that I should have drunk more. I hadn't even been that drunk, not really. If I'd drunk more I'd have slept more. A little dope helped you sleep, but too much dope, on a warm night, made you think too much. And I'd had too much dope.

I was in a car, a red Honda which belonged to Spliff. That explained why I was so cramped and uncomfortable. We hadn't found the all-night Essex rave we were looking for, and were so doped up we'd had to park somewhere and rest. I'd had my exhausted eyes shut when we parked. That was my excuse, anyhow. She'd had her eyes open, though, and she was the one who was driving.

We were in a quiet B-road lay-by, or so she'd assured me as she'd snapped the engine off just after five.

'No funny stuff, huh?' she'd warned. ''Cos I'm dead tired. Okay? You're staying over there. And I'm staying here. Well, we are tonight anyway, got that, boy? Got it?'

I'd been too tired to do more than nod. *Sure, babe, whatever you want. The athletics can wait.*

And then it was early morning. I blinked as I looked around me. The gentle rocking of the car was being provided by huge lorries. Every thirty seconds the car was being rocked slightly by the sheer turbulence they created as they swept past. She'd actually parked the Honda on the hard shoulder of some motorway. The motorway was flanked by scrub. Could have been anywhere. The start of the country? The end of the country? The end of the East End? M11? M25? I had no idea. I *did* know it wasn't that busy – the slow stream of lorries passing the Honda were the only vehicles in sight – and that being on the hard shoulder was still the worst possible place to be. The car was just waiting to be hit by some dozing lorry-driver. Some eighteen-wheeler would have made mush of that not-so-hot hatchback.

So where was Miss Spliff? Not in sight, not anywhere. I looked at the ignition – the keys were still there, slowly swinging. She must be nearby, I figured. But so what? I was still a sitting duck. I painfully stretched my shoulders back into shape, then crawled out of the car to stretch my legs. The stream of lorries kept coming. One would disappear around the curve in the road, and just as its dull roar faded away, another one would rumble into view. I kept well back from the road as I waited for her to return. Return from where? Had she walked down to some motorway café? Gone to the toilet? For a walk? A wash? A manicure? I looked at my watch; it was nine forty-five. I had an hour and fifteen minutes to get to Heathrow. Wherever that might be from here. *Oh for cryin' out loud, where was she*? I counted another dozen passing lorries then finally gave up on her and started hitching.

Hitch-hiking normally involves walking along as you wave your thumb. If you don't walk then almost nobody stops – unless you're an especially fit girl. You have to be walking, glancing back hopefully, your thumb luring them in. In other words, you have to show *willing*. To show your prospective host that you *are* walking and indeed working and generally trying in life, i.e. you're not some anti-social dole queue cowboy who laughs at honest tax-dodgers. And even then only one in a hundred drivers will ever stop. Or one in thirty lorry-drivers. Those boys were all over-worked these days, often dangerously, and some needed hikers to keep them awake. Some wouldn't give lifts as it wasn't company policy. Some wouldn't simply because they were complete bastards. Not that you can blame the non-stopping motorist that much: there are a lot of crazies out there. And I knew about crazy at that moment because I was going crazy, insane with frustration. How was I going to make it to Heathrow in time?

What had that stupid girl been playing at? Where had she gone and why? And why for so long? My fury drove me on and on and soon the car was way back behind me, around the curve and unseen. After about forty lorries had passed me, one finally trundled to a halt.

'What the bloody hell are you doing out here?' asked the tired driver, his leather face looking mildly amused at my predicament.

'Looking for a lift.'

'Bollocks!' he said with a superior smile. What can you say to that? I shrugged and attempted a grin in reply.

'Whereja wanna go then, lad?'

'London.'

'I can get you as far as Stratford. Past Leytonstone. Will that do you?'

'Yeah, great, cheers,' I said as I clambered in. 'How come no one else is stopping these days?'

'We're not s'posed to. Company policy. You get rigs being hijacked these days, didn't you know?'

I shook my aching head as I clicked the filthy seat-belt on – never trust a tired lorry-driver – and the lorry crawled away. I say crawled because he didn't get much beyond 35mph.

'You're not worried about speeding, are you?' I asked.

'No, I've just got the whole maximum load on. Well, more than the maximum, to tell you the truth . . . and this is not a new rig, see?'

'Oh, right.'

I felt the flight tickets in my jacket and sighed. He sensed my impatience and tried to cheer me up.

'I saw something funny this morning. Not two minutes ago, would you believe.'

'What was that then?' I asked, trying to fake interest. He had a dusty CB radio and mike under the dashboard but the thing had a few wires askew and was obviously broken. That had been a relief. I didn't think I could have stood all that nonsense at that time of day. Not after a night like that.

'I'm driving along about a mile back,' he went on, 'and as I take one of those slow curves past the bridges, guess what I see?'

'No idea.'

'This girl—'

'A girl? No kidding?'

'Yeah, there was this black tart coming out of the bushes—'

'Black?' I said as my heart sank.

'Yeah, black and she's pulling her shorts and knickers up. Like she's just been caught short, right? Pretty little thing she was – and as she goes to her car, she sees me coming along – you know, I'm not going that fast – and I can see her seeing me and I can just tell that she's so embarrassed 'cos she's ducking down behind the car and putting her head down an' that as if she's lookin' in the car for summat . . .'

'Did she get in her car?'

'Yeah, she did – look, that's it now!'

He pointed a pork-pie finger at the red Honda as it shot past us. Shit. Why hadn't I waited another five minutes? I had lost all my patience since I'd started hitting the charlie in a big way.

Ms Spliff was hitting seventy-five as her car passed the lorry in front. With a sigh I finally twigged that I wasn't going to make it to the airport in time. Not at all, in fact. Now I couldn't even see her speeding car any more. Uptight. Out of sight. Goodbye Amsterdam. I groaned inwardly.

But then, sitting in the warm lorry, away from the dawn chill, it slowly dawned on me just how exhausted I was. So *what* if I missed it? I was too worn out anyway. I would, I decided, get someone to tape it for me. Then I'd see the photographer's contact sheets afterwards. Reconstruct it all in my own mind. Yeah, I'd ring him there. On location. I'd ring the hotel from home. Yeah, it would be easy. In fact, I thought, some of my finest reviews were written about events I'd missed entirely.

There was, if you considered it, a certain bravery about covering something you'd completely missed. Never mind the quality, feel the vibe. You had to be there, maaan. Or not, as the case may be . . . and, as an added bonus, I thought I might actually get some real eight-hour sleep later. It would be yer actual deep REM sleep – neighbours permitting. I was just stuck in this truck for half an hour or so, that was all. It wasn't so bad. No great tragedy.

'Do you ever play word puzzles, lad?' the lorry-driver asked, puncturing my rising optimism. He was getting his second wind now.

'Er . . . no.'

'Well, maybe it's time you *learned*, eh laddie? 'Cos I really love 'em . . . Open that book there. That one. If you don't mind.'

'Oh, right.' I was too weakened, too dog-tired to argue.

'So you don't mind then?'

A word-puzzles fanatic . . . at dawn . . . all I needed.

'No . . . I don't mind,' I said, thinking, yes, let's get it over with.

'Get on with it then, lad. Some of these puzzles can be fantastically fascinating.'

I took it all back. That morning *was* bad, *was* sad. It was, in fact, a bloody tragedy.

12

Did He Tell You That You Were Beautiful?

I don't know if you're aware of this, but there are certain weird things that happen in your head when you're out of it. Your memory takes on board certain scenes and then instantly forgets the very same things. Things that you can then only recall when you've had a few drinks some days later. When you're sober, between times, they're gone, blank. Wiped from the memory banks. That thought, that talk, that movie clip in your head, that *whatever* has vanished into the mists of time. Yet the moment you get a few drinks down you, it can all come back to you. Sometimes days or weeks later. And one of those moments came flooding back to me as I hit the hip-flask for the fourth shot of the morning. The train was rattling through Blackfriars station. Just crossing the bridge where the Masons hang their dissidents. North to south. On the left was St Pauls, that immense monument to creation, and on the right were the Express newspaper building, IPC's King's Reach Tower and DPC's Dee-Pee House. You couldn't have had a greater contrast, really . . .

Dead ahead and already breaking some by-law by lighting up her ciggy was Sally the Goth. She had her legs crossed and they were covered for once – albeit in some sheer black fabric – though she was showing a fair amount of Wonderbra cleavage up top. It wasn't the outfit I'd have chosen to visit home in, even if I was a girl.

'Do you think we'll get away with this?' she waved her fag guiltily as she glanced around.

'You look chic, chick. Smoke yourself to death. If anyone objects . . .' I tailed off into a shrug.

'Yeah, if anyone objects . . . what?'

'Well, we'll say we're expressing free speech. Since you are a half-breed Apache—'

'Huh?'

'Well you could pass for one – an Apache princess with the God-given right to send smoke signals.'

'That's really, really stupid.'

'What the fuck do you expect at dawn? Oscar Wilde?'

'It's not dawn.'

'It is for me.'

She rolled her eyes heavenwards as she took the Soviet Army officer's flask from me and took a deep swig. The vodka was burning its way into my own gut a few moments later when the flashback occurred. My memory banks suddenly snapping back into action. *The* flashback. In my mind's blurred eye, I was back at the indie party and the lad from *Raw Soul* was rambling something to me in the toilets. But not about the magazine closure. I'd already been there, missed that. What then? What had he been talking about? I remembered his voice; once again it was loud and clear over the now-distant rumble of the party.

'I'd be careful when you try and sneak Sally through the alley,' he'd mumbled, sickly grinning like a village idiot holding back news of murder.

'Huh?'

'Don't you know? She's got more hang-ups than a dry-cleaner.'

'Yeah, yeah, yeah. Well I've known more space cadets than Captain Kirk, so don't worry about it, son.'

'Pete, you have no idea, mate, no idea. When her last

boyfriend tried to chuck her – she fuckin' stabbed him. Stabbed him but good. It was a miracle he ever recovered. She's hard-core, Cap'n, fuckin' hard-core. You'd better be ready to say "Beam me up, Scotty!"'

He'd roared with laughter at that and the laugh percolated through my brain. It had all seemed too unreal to take seriously then . . . Maybe that was why I'd buried it deep in my sub-conscious. I wished I could have spoken to Jake about it – he'd have known if it was legit or not.

I seized the hip-flask back from Sally and took a slug. The stabbing story probably wasn't true, I decided, and, even if it was, so what? I wasn't too worried. I could handle Sally. She was a bit uptight about some things, I'd discovered, mainly because she was a feminist vegetarian who took it seriously – she only wore the Westwood boots because they were heavy-duty PVC . . . But she wasn't too po-faced about the feminist bit, not most of the time – well, I mean, you can't be if you're in a micro skirt and four-inch heels.

So I decided to just watch my mouth and see how far things went. She stared hard at me as the train went through Loughborough Junction in south London. I looked outside, still considering it all. Loughborough Junction was like Fort Apache, the Bronx, totally abandoned. According to the radio, a gang of girls had kicked some pensioner senseless there the week before, and although it was still a working BR station, graffiti covered all the name signs on the platforms. Even the broken windows were spray-painted over. If you didn't know the route, you'd have no idea where you were – and it didn't look like the kind of place to get off and ask. Too dangerous. Just like our Sally? My cynical smile died. She detected something might be wrong. I was thinking with my eyes and she was nothing if not astute. Sharp as a razor. She nudged me with her foot.

'What are you thinking about, boy?' she asked in a cod country accent.

'Nothing,' I lied as people lie whenever a lover asks them that question. I turned to face her again. She was undeniably cute. Clever too, in that blinkered academic way that some student girls are. Not that she was your typical student. She wasn't your typical anything, least of all your typical knife maniac. I put my hand on her shoulder and pulled her toward me. All this danger talk was exciting in a weird way, and it was making me make-believe like we were on some trans-Europe express with her as my Bond-girl-spy diversion. From Russia with lust . . . my other hand explored Sally's half-open shirt as I put on a barrow-boy accent: 'Ya know what you're askin' for, doncha girl?'

'No, I honestly do not know what you mean, kind sir.'

I pushed my mouth on to hers and our tongues met and slivered around each other a bit, gripping and ungripping, as I unfumbled another of her shirt buttons. *Why not?* I thought. *Let's go for it.*

'Yeah, you do know what I mean, doncha?' I mumbled softly.

'I wish you were just a little bit more interested in my mind, Mr Shelldrake,' she whispered, now sounding like some New York bimbo.

'Of course I'm interested in your mind, honey,' I said deep and low, kidding that I was De Niro. 'I wanna hump your brains out—'

She sighed in mock shock and amusement.

'You are so totally, totally unreconstructed.'

'You mean unreconstructed like a building site?'

'That's where you belong, boy,' she said, sounding like herself again.

'We should go down to the toilet now,' I nodded down the empty carriage. She bit her fingernail, looked around with big eyes. Half-joking, of course, but half-aware of how effective it all was. It worked on me, anyhow. A great performance from a great performer. When she put her mind to it she was great at having fun, whatever had spooked her hadn't taken that away from her. No one could take that away from her . . . and yet I still didn't know. Could this one really be some knife maniac? Could she really be hard-core? At that moment it didn't seem likely. Why had I taken the *Raw Soul* rumour-monger seriously? I asked myself. He was drunk, he'd probably made it all up. But I knew he hadn't; not all of it. There was definitely something there, something crooked behind Sally's little mask.

Our lips were raw against each other, hearts pounding. I managed to pull my tongue away for a second.

'Let's go to the toilets – now!' I whispered to her urgently.

'Umm . . .' she glanced at me for an instant then nodded, '. . . um, yeah. Okay then.'

So I stood up and led her by the hand. She was sussed enough to know that being led, that obeying all orders was very sexy in itself, at times. Especially in a feminist Goth student. *Beat me, daddy-o, eight to the bar . . .*

13

In Every Dream Home . . .

The house in Sussex was set in picture-postcard surround-ings. Green fields, hedge-rows and fields of rye. Horses grazing in clover. It was so sweet but I was bored within min-utes and began to hark back to the hectic train journey – tearing Sally's clothes off in the closed confines of a grimy Railtrack wash-room, stroking her naked skin, making her go down on her knees . . . It all had a certain sleazy glamour. But the operative word was 'sleazy'. I felt sleazy in other ways too. Me being there, meeting the folks, presumably meant young Sally was semi-serious about us. Whereas I was not. Not really. Not because I didn't care for Sally – I did, believe me – but because . . . Because I was in love with Anna? A girl who hardly knew I existed?

We went for lots of walks and by Sunday night I realised that – between meals – we'd avoided her parents as much as was humanly possible. This was kinda weird because we were actually there to see them. But it was also kind of weird because *they* were kind of weird. I'd never known a family quite like it. Sally just didn't fit in there. She didn't fit in anywhere, come to think of it, but you'd have thought that at her own home, if anywhere, she'd seem like she was more . . . in setting. Some people don't make sense to you until you've met their parents, but not our Sally. She made even less sense now.

And there was something else wrong. It wasn't anything you could easily put your finger on, but there was something wrong. The way her mother was so far away, drinking almost as much as me at night. But no matter how much she downed, she always remained suburban, all very polite and very nearly normal – even though she must have been drunk. Never aggressive, never emotional. She wasn't even argumentative. She'd given it all up.

The way her dad acted around Sally was strange too. Too close, and yet too distant, and too jealous of me. Even for a concerned father. And although we were granted a double bed, Sally wouldn't get it on with me there, which was her first refusal with me. She just lay there, all glassy-eyed. I didn't pursue it, but it did set me thinking. I couldn't ask too much because she didn't like talking about her parents, even when we were in their house. Strange; too close and yet too distant. It was like her old man was some ex-boyfriend. Like she'd been abused or something and . . . what? Forgotten it? Been made to forget it? Maybe I was putting two and two together and coming up with five. Maybe there was some other innocent explanation. I just couldn't figure it out. Whatever it was, I was convinced it was something heavy.

Beside that, the *Raw Soul* rumour about Sally seemed, well, just plain silly. Just a stupid rumour. So I decided to bring the subject up; kill it off once and for all. Late on the Monday morning everything seemed the right time for an earnest discussion. It was blisteringly hot. We'd been out really early – like before ten – and Sally had finally come across in some open fields. I'd never got it on outside before, never in my life, to be honest. Not in broad daylight. I hadn't planned it that way, although I must admit that the disrupted sleep had been sending my hormones crazy all that morning. And she'd been wearing a T-shirt and she was flapping that around to make some breeze for herself. Sally had sat down on a slight slope above me. As she lay back and smoked and flirted, I lolled about. After a few minutes I caught a glimpse of the grass poking up around the lace-edged underwear she was wearing. For some reason, it affected me even more than it would have done normally. Hot blood pumped through my chest. It seemed exotic, erotic, exciting. Like she'd planned it, like she was asking for it. Both of us hoped we were unobserved as we frantically pushed together; me thinking of her body, both the way it was then and the way I'd seen it the morning after we'd met, with her perfect skin looking good despite the goose-bumps of the cold dawn . . . And then I wondered if it was sexier if someone *was* watching us, which probably meant that she was thinking the same, which probably meant . . . we moved faster and faster until we lost all the complications.

Back at the parents' house afterwards Sally was busy packing her rucksack – black leather and studs, *of course* – smiling her head off and everything seemed groovy. We had a couple of hours before we had to get the train and were sneaking a friendly little joint together, upstairs in her bedroom – she still had pictures of Take That on her wall – and everything seemed mellow. I figured that I'd never even get near Anna, so why not have fun with Sally and forget her? I might even fall for her one day. She'd passed the joint back to me with a dreamy smile and I thought that had to be the perfect time to softly kill a rumour. A rumour that was coming between us – in my mind, at least.

'You know, I heard this really funny thing, back in London,' I breezed.

'Oh yeah?' she said, quite perky now that we were going back to town. 'What was that then?'

'It was about you.'

'Oh yeah?' she smiled, still very cheery and completely unconcerned.

'Oh, it's just that . . . someone said that when you and your last boyfriend were—' I adopted a diplomatic tone at this point, 'were, er, were splitting up, like . . . you, er . . . stabbed him.'

Even as I was finishing the question I knew it was the wrong thing to ask. I knew it implied I was thinking of finishing with her at some point, maybe soon. It also implied distrust and there was something else, something worse. Without realising it, I had put myself on the spot. If Sally did say 'yes' then she was, in all probability, some kind of sociopath. And I would therefore be at something of a disadvantage in any future dealings with her. Maybe she'd been in some institution – or maybe she should have been. *Release the psychotics!* was fun when it was just a piece of punk graffiti on a Mount Pleasant squat, but now it was official government policy and every week some poor sod was burying some slaughtered relative. Who knew who'd be next? Would it be you who'd be killed at random? Or maybe me, who had just asked the unaskable. Who had just handed Sally a loaded weapon, emotionally speaking. What would she do with it? Sally took it and, without batting an eyelid, aimed and fired it. *Bang! Bang! You're fucking dead, man.*

'Yeah. I stabbed him,' she said, all matter-of-fact. 'And in the end he was okay . . . So what?'

Despite the heat, I shivered. So what? So *what*? She was so relaxed about it, bored even. What kind of attitude was that? The worst kind. It was my own fault, I'd asked for the worst and I'd got the worst. The very worst: the truth. How could she be so cruel as to tell me the truth? Nothing stung more than truth when you weren't expecting it. And now what was I to do? The girl *was* probably psychotic. I'd suspected it and now I knew it – and *she* knew I knew. Or she knew I suspected. I tried to do a firm-but-friendly stare and I failed. There was a silent pause that lasted five seconds and several lifetimes. I had to end the silence or explode. When all else fails, try the truth. She had. Why couldn't I?

'I had something similar happen to me, once . . . once upon a time, well, once upon a drug deal, really . . . Well, it wasn't that similar, but, y'know . . . similar . . . I was in Bournemouth with this trendy, Beth Aden, and I, er, killed her, kind of. Except that she isn't really dead.'

Sally looked at me blankly.

'Shall I go on?' I asked feebly. She didn't say anything. I looked at her closely and then she shifted her thousand-yard stare on to my face. She even managed a faint smile as she nodded her reply.

'Okay, well Beth asks for some speed, some blues, you know? And I give her two. Then I took some myself in the toilet. Came back. She asked for another. I gave her another. The Leicester contingent was there, the same lads who always got pissed Sunday night and sang "You'll Never Walk Alone" at the tops of their voices. And they want some so I give this Leicester lad half a dozen blues – I had fifty or sixty half-hidden in the lining of my jacket. That way, I figured, the cops would never find them. The night goes on, lots of energy, anything's still possible and suddenly this brickie comes back and asks if my blues are all right. I said they were, they were as good as possible, I thought. Reliable source and all that. But then this brickie tells me that some of his mates are really ill, there must be too much strychnine in the blues. And I say, no, that the blues are all right, the blues are pukka, forget it, and then Beth, who's taken five by now, suddenly falls against me, eyes rolling white. And I'm thinking, *"Oh my God. I've killed her! I've killed her!"* Tap her face, tap it again, slap her – thinking, the blues have killed her – no, I've killed her. I thought things couldn't get any worse and then this side door bursts open. It was a raid, cops coming in through the fire exits, coming down the stairs. And I have enough blues to get classed as a serious dealer – three years minimum. The house lights come up and there's so much sweat there's a mist in the air and the DJ, he leaves the amp on but turns the record deck off so the music just slides to a halt. Sounded really weird. My heartbeat must have hit a hundred an' fifty, completely out of control. And I'm throwing mineral water in Beth's face. Her facial muscles don't even twitch – nothing. All around me kids are frantically dropping drugs on to the floor and kicking them away and some of 'em are still getting busted, a few scuffles break out, the cops hit a couple of people. Three guys come out of the bog in handcuffs. And I'm thinking, *Three years, minimum.* And I couldn't casually get the blues out and chuck 'em away – it would've meant digging in my jacket for half an hour and then shredding the lining. And I thought the decent thing to do would be to call an ambulance for Beth. But if I did, I might draw attention to myself – just why had she passed out? Why was she so ill? And they'd keep me there till some student cracked and pointed a finger at me. He had the blues, he sold the blues. Maybe they could do me for manslaughter, if someone had really died, like.

'And then this big police sergeant elbows his way through and asks what's wrong with Beth. Instead of telling the truth I saved myself. Lied blatantly. Said she was a mild asthmatic and she just needed some fresh air and no she hadn't taken any drugs, I know that 'cos I've been with her all night, officer. I've seen her do this before, officer, she'll be fine outside, in the fresh air, like. And this copper stares at me for a minute then shouts "Gangway!" and helps me carry Beth out the front steps and all the cops who wanna stop and search us, well, he just brushes 'em aside. So he helps me prop her up against a wall and he goes back in while I run to the nearest phone box. And, just as I'm calling the ambulance, wondering if the delay has killed her, knowing that I can't risk waiting around for the doctor to arrive, there's this tap on the phone box window and it's her. She's okay, smiling her head off, it wasn't the blues at all . . . but I knew I'd done it, you know, chosen to avoid the law rather than get 'em to call an ambulance. I coulda killed her, you know? Could have been a fatal delay . . . *if* . . . Funny thing is, I never told her all that, she never knew it – and a few weeks later she chucked me 'cos she said I was a bit too soft . . . Can you believe that?'

Sally said nothing to all this so I went on, lamely.

'Well, there it is, my own brush with whatever you wanna call it . . .'

'Shall we go downstairs now?' she said as I realised that she hadn't heard a word. I couldn't believe it – my one heartfelt confession and no one had heard it. How typical, how very fucking typical . . .

'We ought to have some tea before we go,' she smiled, all sweetness and light again.

14

Beat Me, Whip Me, Bite Me

I had to meet Rendall in the Portobello Road. I phoned him a few days after we'd met again at Joanna's lig and we'd arranged a meet. He was starting something which just might get me some donkey work, hammering out single reviews and such-like. Some Internet thing. But donkey work wasn't all I was going there for. As a former A & R man, young Rendall would also be able to give me some more inside dirt on the music biz – something that might help with the Scallies exposé.

Although I'd said I would see Sally, I'd postponed it with a phone call. I still wasn't sure whether to blow hot or cold with that one. Despite myself, I did still fancy her a lot, though we weren't in love, that much I did know. Although she was highly inflammable, a certain spark was still missing, and I couldn't help being crass and wondering if she'd stab me if I left her. Or would she leave me first? That would make things easier – when the time came – or maybe we'd just drift apart. But then again, I didn't buy that 'drift apart' thing – I knew she wouldn't ditch me until she had someone else lined up. She was quite realistic, for a possible psycho. Everyone has to be realistic nowadays. If, say, Anna left Vee – when hell froze over – it would be for me . . . or someone like me. And that was Realism Lesson Number One: when a lover leaves you there is *always* someone else. Always. Even if it's temporary. So forget the 'I need my space' spiel, forget the 'I've been abroad and I'm in culture shock' shit, forget the 'It's only for two months' mantra, forget all that. Quite simply, there is always someone else. And if that someone else doesn't work out, or the idea of them doesn't, then the party in question – your own sweet practical lover – might just wander back to you. But don't bank on it. And don't forget – there had been someone else. There always is, always was, always will be.

The meeting with Rendall was at the Market Tavern, which was crammed with raggas and arty types, all with bundles of cash the Inland Revenue knew nothing about. Once, and it wasn't that long ago, a pub was a pub was a pub. White faces, flocked wallpaper, bitter beer from the barrel. Looking around the Tavern – a dread here, two Chinese girls there, a French bike courier in the corner, Indian beer behind the bar – made me see how much had changed in the ten or so years I'd been frequenting pubs. Now every other city pub was like a bar in the tropics. Exotic.

The framed photos at the Tavern are the sort you'd only have seen in sex shops once upon a time – some guy getting a blow-job off a kneeling Latin, a naked blonde lying on top of a pensioner . . . As I studied them I could see a white Trustafarian lifting up his three-year-old kiddie to show him the photos – very educational. I knew one publisher who kept naked pictures of his kid, and various other people, all over the lounge. I could imagine what his tiny mind was thinking: *We don't want Josh to be sexually repressed.* What a dip-stick.

Rendall's firm were doing well, he said, and had turned over half a million plus in the last twelve months. When I asked him if he'd lined things up for Christmas already, he laughed.

'Did that months ago, mate. At the moment we're being booked out for the millennium, 1999. Four years in advance!'

Of course, the party of the century, the party of the last ten centuries . . . With a bit of effort, and after three more pints, I eventually dragged him back to the point of our meeting, which was, primarily, to find out more about Rendall's stints in A & R and record company promotion. He had been at a major label for over four years and, with a bit of prompting, he'd hopefully spill the beans on what went on, what really got results. Or, should I say, on what *usually* gets results – nothing's ever got a cast-iron guarantee. Except that it will all be very expensive, that's one thing you *could* be sure of.

Most of the ingredients I'd heard before, but Rendall baked the cake for me and then added some whipped cream on top. Which just about made it *the way it really was* . . . There were a few lessons to be learned, some of which you'd know, most of which were obvious, when you really thought about it.

'All post-Eighties signings, as far as the majors are concerned, are based on fashion,' he said between sips. 'All of them. Fashion-based. Music does not come into it in the UK. Or rather, it comes in despite the music industry, not because of it—'

'Mind if I use this?' I asked as I plonked a Pro Walkman on the shiny wooden table.

'Go ahead.'

'So how would you go about things? If you were the manager of an unknown band?'

'Well, for a start, unless the band are life-long pals, get a watertight contract on 'em. Every other group ditches their first manager and it doesn't matter what you've done for 'em – clothes, songs, gigs, record deals, whatever. If someone offers them a few pence more they'll blow you out. Never drive or you'll end up a roadie, and never learn too much about studios or you'll end up engineering for nothing . . . Anyway, once you've got a contract, never waste time sending *any* tapes to a record company. Someone there might just rip off your ideas.'

'And in court the majors will always win.'

'Yeah, ask George Michael. And the fact is that no major has ever signed a band from a cassette tape. Not in living memory. Talking to publishers is just about okay, but never, ever chase labels – they have shelves of unplayed tapes and none of them know a tune anyway. And even if they did, how would they promote it without a gimmick? What's the band's angle?'

'You have to have some kind of buzz about you?'

'For sure. You've got to gather up as many gimmicks as you can think of, arrange a few off-the-wall gigs – never call them showcases – and you'll be halfway there. If you're a dance act, think in club terms. Your own club night or something. Whatever. Then get some photos and make sure they're hot. Would you look at them twice? Would teenage girls, or boys, use them as pin-ups? Would they cause mayhem at the Midem music-fest? Would they make *you* pause?'

'And then you're halfway there?'

'Not even ten per cent of the way, Pete, not even ten per cent. You have to get a publicist on board – the biggest firms are so well-connected they can virtually guarantee a page in *EM* or *Groove* or wherever you want – if the PR firm take you on. And you know what PR really stands for, don't you?'

'Pretty ropey?'

'No, it's pretty *and* ropey, 'cos it's all about getting pretty things to chat up ropey-looking journos. The big tease, you can look but don't touch, and everyone's everyone's friend until they get promoted. As well you know.'

'For sure. What about gigs?'

'It's all connected. The gig venues are controlled by booking agents, but where the PR mob go the booking agents will follow. Independent thought isn't their strong hand. Almost *any* publicist is better than none. Almost. But you'd have to ask around.'

'What do publicists charge?' I asked. It's always good to put cash amounts in a story, it's what makes editors go hot under the collar. As stimulating to them as porn, maybe more so.

'They'll charge you anything from zero to a grand a week. And a percentage on top, of course.'

'So what happens next?'

'Well, if you really wanna get on with it then the band or their manager or publicist have to get busy . . .' he raised his eyebrow archly as he rubbed the end of his nose. His gesture said 'coke' – his gesture actually screamed coke – but, unfortunately for me, it wasn't a gesture my little Sony could record.

'I take it you mean cocaine, m'lud,' I said, trying to make a joke of the fact I needed him to spell it out.

'Possibly,' Rendall smiled back, 'possibly . . . Anyway, once your act has got some press, then the record companies should eventually follow.'

'And then you've got to . . .'

'Then you've gotta play hard to get. Record labels need to be wound up – and, God, can they be wound up. Remember that the label never wants you until they're sure you don't want them at all.'

'Just like a girl?'

'Exactly – and as for song publishers, never, *ever* send them more than two or three songs on a tape. If they wanna hear more they gotta pay for the studio time, see? Get the best production you can for your demos, as ninety-nine per cent of publishers can never actually "hear" songs. They listen more to the fucking production than *anything else*. A classic put down on cassette will get less interest than a well-produced dirge.'

That was probably true enough. Several times in the past, mischievous journos had sent old demo tapes, by big hit acts, to the very publishers who'd eventually signed them. Without fail, every single publisher unwittingly rejected their own star signings – the same trick has been used on various labels too, and they all fell for it.

'A good engineer is a must for your demos,' Rendall was saying, 'and I'm assuming here that your act can't afford Nellee Hooper or Trevor Horn. The engineer with the joint in his mouth is usually the one to avoid.'

'Yeah,' I said, 'but by the time you've finished your session with him you probably won't mind if you don't get a deal.'

'That's true,' smiled Rendall, 'but any engineer who plays you his own material should also be scrubbed off the short-list – if you're worse than him he'll rub it in and if you're better he'll sulk and tell you that whatever you want can't be done: "Nah, can't do it, geezer, the mushroom valves will fry if we add more reverb to the snare."'

'Anything else about demos?'

'Never mix demos, or anything else come to think of it, on Yamaha NS tens. *Never*.'

'They're speakers, right?'

'Correct. And nearly every studio has 'em.'

'Yeah, they're little ones, aren't they? I've noticed them in places, they make things sound good.'

'That's why they're a piece of shit, in my humble opinion. They've got no objectivity. Every mix sounds sweet on them, even when it's not. If you do get offered studio time by the publishers then take it, of course, and afterwards, if their offer is no good, which it won't be, take the finished work else-where. Which means hanging on to your master-tapes – both multi-tracks and DATs. Buy your own if you have to.'

'What would they set you back?'

'Labels always claim they cost five or six hundred pounds a time, but they're really about a hundred and thirty quid, all in. And if the tape's yours, it usually ends up as your recording.'

That figured, I thought. *Possession, as the dealer once said, is nine-tenths of the law.*

'The last scam is the hardest one of all,' Rendall was saying. 'Getting a nice tight recording contract. If you're lucky enough to get offered a record deal, then make sure you go for the biggest possible advance – if all goes wrong at least you'll have enough left to do a runner. Don't worry if a deal with a small company ties you up for several singles and an album – as far as the majors are concerned there are no deals with indie labels. There's nothing that can't be broken in court or bought off with ready cash.'

'So a big advance is the best?'

'Nearly always. A nice large percentage isn't bad either, say forty or fifty per cent, as an alternative to a mega-advance but . . .' He shrugged.

'But what?'

'Well, you don't know if you're gonna sell, do you? And, more importantly, the label will work much harder for you if they've already advanced some serious dosher – they've got to try and earn it back. Gotta try and make your band big, right?'

'Right.'

'And you should get a lawyer to write into the contract stuff like release times – they put it out within sixty days et cetera – and you should specify that you want press parties, artwork costs, flyers, radio pluggers, PAs, independent publicity, EPKs, promo videos and a vast amount of money set aside for street posters and tour support. All non-returnable, of course, though the label will want to make 'em recoupable off royalties, which is fair enough.'

'Tour support is when you pay a few grand to get on some tour with a bigger band, right?'

'Yeah, you need big money for that, and street posters. Big because it's usually cash. And the overspend on these items can be siphoned off.'

'Siphoned off for what?'

Rendall finished his drink then leaned forward and switched the Walkman off. As its red recording light faded away he leaned back in his chair and smiled.

'Someone should,' he said, 'be siphoning it off for two main reasons. Firstly to bribe the press – mainly the music and the style press. Three grams of charlie for a good single review, six grams to make it one of the discs of the week. A dozen to make it *the* release of the week. And four grams wrapped in two air tickets to New York, or Tokyo, to get you a nice shiny page in *Visage*.'

'Charlie plus free flights, huh?'

'That's not just free flights to see some gig, that's air tickets when and where you want them – a holiday, basically, with hotels and hired cars thrown in. That's probably the best deal going, since features are more important than reviews alone, though every little bit helps, of course. You need features and giving bands coke to "innocently" share with journos obviously helps a little on that front too.'

'Anyone who gets backstage gets some, huh? Especially the journos?'

'That's about the size of it.'

'Sounds like some of it's cocaine music, eh?'

'Some? It's *all* cocaine music, now. Well, nearly all . . .'

'With the help of certain people?'

'Yeah, I mean, it's hard to overestimate the power of the music weeklies, especially on yer indie Britpop scene – I've been in the offices of smaller labels when demos of some new band have come in, demos that the label has actually paid for. But, even if everyone loves the sound, before they even think about signing the band they get some hacks from the inkies to listen to it. If they don't like the band then that's it, the label won't sign 'em . . . once you've got some press on your side, assuming you do, then your second goal is getting radio play, obviously.'

'Do pluggers still put packets of charlie inside the record sleeves?'

'No, not much,' he said, almost ruefully, 'not any more. Those days are over in the UK, mostly. I remember though, years ago, some jock screaming, "There's *nothing in this record bag! Nothing!*" and this naïve young plugger was looking totally bewildered. You could see his mind ticking over, him thinking, "*No, the record's definitely in there. Look, there it is, can't you see it?*"'

We both laughed before Rendall picked up the thread again.

'Nowadays dinners at expensive restaurants get you lots more mileage. Or go for a day at the races – food and drink provided – and then place all the bets for your radio producer.'

'It has to be the producer?' I asked.

'Oh yeah. It has to be the producer 'cos they control the

playlist. And if said producer backs the wrong horse, so what? He'll still win because the pluggers will bet on every horse there is for him. If anyone ever asks about all the excess dosh sloshing around, well, the producer can honestly say he's won it at the gee-gees – an honest stroke of luck. He supports zero tolerance. Who's to know any different? Other pluggers opt to take 'em for a night at the casino – with the chips supplied *gratis*, of course. And nearly all such social occasions call for a short call from our mate charlie.'

I had suspected most of this stuff for a long time, but it was still weird to hear it all spelt out – from the horse's mouth, as it were. It also made my piece on The Scallies more and more important. Potentially. They were just the tip of the iceberg.

'But what if the press and the radio play isn't enough? What if the record gets to ninety-nine and starts to die on you?'

'Then your label buys you a higher chart position. Top seventy-five, at least, or the top fifty if you can afford it.'

'Yeah, but how?'

'With a few kids and some cash. There's nearly two thousand chart return shops but they usually use half that number on any given week. These shops are not exactly secret – the staff all use those computerised magic wand things to log the time and name of every sale . . . they even fiddle the barcodes now, but chart-hyping is an expensive lark.'

'I'll bet,' I said, signalling for the barman to set us up for another round. Another few hundred more words . . .

'Hyping costs at least three grand a week all in, and you can't just do it for a fortnight. If a disc zips in to the charts and then drops straight out, then questions get asked.'

'Isn't there a ten-grand reward offered for any info that'll convict chart-hypers?'

'Yep, and no one's ever claimed it.' *Not yet they haven't*, I thought. *Not yet.*

'Corruption, corruption, everywhere. And most of it linked to tink . . . it's all a bit naughty, innit?' I said as I passed another pint to Rendall.

'Cheers. Oh yeah, it's naughty all right, boy, naughty as

fuck . . . but it's even worse in the States. Did you know Gene Vincent had to carry a loaded Colt .45 after gigs, just to make sure he got paid something? And that was forty fuckin' years ago.'

'Ruthless stuff.'

'You want ruthless? Well, one pretty-boy group once had their valuable bachelor image threatened by the lead singer's new girlfriend. When he wouldn't dump her the American label began to arrange an "accident" for the girl – to kill her off. Their manager only managed to talk them out of it at the last minute.'

'I heard that it was a five-piece, name of The J—'

'Could have been,' interrupted Rendall teasingly, 'goes on all the time over there . . . Their record companies usually give a promo company a minimum of a quarter of a million dollars to promote a record. Sometimes it's half a mill, sometimes three-quarters, sometimes even more. This money is, officially, "promotional tour support", to enable artists to visit fifty or sixty radio stations to push the record. The reality is that the singer will visit maybe ten DJs with the key promo people following behind. Then the promo guys go on to visit all the other stations and everywhere they visit, they'll be dishing out sex 'n' drugs 'n' rock'n'roll.'

'Chicks, cash and coke.'

'Of course. Every other British band who does tour support Stateside gets a farewell present of half an ounce of charlie. It's always placed in the dressing-room after the last gig.'

'Do you remember that Scallies gig on the river-boat? The one that launched 'em?'

'Who could forget?' He roared with laughter. 'They thought I was a fuckin' journo, I got given a gram of gear just because I was wearing an old *Express Music* T-shirt.'

'Naked bribery.'

'I thought it was very honest . . . in a dishonest kind of way.'

'But it started 'em off.'

'Oh yeah. No one was really writing about them before, and that's a fact.'

'Yeah?'

'Oh yeah, you could check back issues of the mags and I'm sure you'd be able to track it all down to that date – well, track most of it down to that date. That was the beginning.'

'Really?' I said, though I'd already photocopied all the back issues in question. They revealed how the tiny trickle of stories before the gig had become a mighty flood afterwards. It was evidence, cold hard evidence. But I didn't tell Renny-boy that.

'Oh yeah, it's much harder for most others. Kids should be aware that it's really fucking difficult . . . record companies, publishers . . . most of 'em know very little.'

'Decca turned down The Beatles.'

'They *all* rejected The Beatles – the only reason EMI went for them, in the end, was to humour Brian Epstein 'cos he had the biggest record shops on Merseyside. That's why EMI gave the boys George Martin as their producer, he hadn't produced much rock'n'roll stuff before, he'd mainly done comedy for Peter Sellers. It was probably an insult to the Fab Four that they didn't even notice because they didn't know a fuckin' thing at that time. All the labels rejected 'em just like they all rejected The Who, The Doors, The Sex Pistols – you name it . . . Rhythm King could have signed Jazzy Jeff for $5,000 but they turned him down – can you imagine how many units he's shifted since?'

'How many?'

'Over twenty million.'

I whistled softly as Rendall continued his diatribe.

'They had Schoolly D too, but they let his contract run out and that little slip musta cost 'em half a mill. And look at Al Stewart's *Year of the Cat* album: all Al wanted was five grand, six and a half tops – most labels said no and another zillion-seller had got away . . . the simple fact is, ninety-nine times out of a hundred, the labels just don't have a fuckin' clue. I was once, I'm not too ashamed to say, an A & R and I *know*. It's fuckin' pot luck out there.'

'When it isn't bribery.'

'Yeah, when it isn't bribery,' he repeated dully. We drank some more, and when the music biz chat died down Rendall and I entered the land of more personal reminiscences – and I began to see the big problem with meeting him. Seeing someone from those days really brought back memories. And, when you're a bit stressed anyway, the good times get forgotten. You tend to dwell on the bad. And I had enough problems as it was – what with young Sally and dreaming about Anna and earning a living *and* nailing down my big Scallies scoop. *Let's talk fast cash business*, I thought. *Current business – cut to the chase. Chop 'em out.*

'So what about this Net mag then, Rendall, do you need me or not?'

'Oh yeah, sure – you're in, end of story.' *That was easy,* I thought. *Way too easy.*

'Yeah?' I said questioningly.

'Oh yeah. Music correspondent, first-class. And you get to keep all the empties.'

'What's the catch?' There's always a catch.

'Er . . . we're not starting for a few months yet.'

'Uh-huh. And?'

'And we haven't got that much money behind us so we're not paying out that much money at first, not to the writers.'

Great. This looked like a real Nineties affair – bound to end at the official receivers.

'Ah well,' I said cheerfully, 'never mind, we'll do it when we do it.'

'Yeah, that's the spirit,' he said as he stretched and checked his watch. 'Be positive.'

'Yeah,' I said as I continued to humour him.

'I've gotta run, lad, or the kids will suffer, which means madam will make sure I suffer too. Good to see you, Pete.'

'And you. I'll give you a shout soon. And thanks for your time an' all that.'

'No problem, mate,' Rendall said as he stood. 'I'm just sorry I had to say some of it off the record.' He tapped the inactive Walkman again before strolling out.

I waited a few seconds, until I was sure he wasn't returning, and then I looked at the second Walkman, the Mini-Disc that was hidden in my jacket, the Mini-Disc that was still record-ing through its tiny microphone. I checked it – 'sorry I had to say some of it off the record' – and it had captured every single word.

I hadn't wanted to set Rendall up and, with luck, I wouldn't have to use his name in the actual feature. But his quotes, used in a story proposal, would help get my feet under the door at the *Chronicle*. And that would help get me a photographer, a lawyer and the easy cash that I needed to finish the piece properly . . . Anyway, I decided, I was only, in Rendall's own phrase, being 'honest in a dishonest way'. Sometimes you just had to lie if you really wanted to tell the truth.

15

Up On The 29th Floor

Although I was, officially, *persona non grata* at DPC's Dee Pee house, the girls on reception still had a soft spot for me and they'd turn a blind eye if I ever nipped back to pick up my *Groove* hate mail. After seeing Rendall I went there to make a few free calls abroad – a New York magazine still owed me $400 from way back. I also knew that the director's meeting room was still being kept unlocked, which gave me the chance to liberate some drink. A bottle of brandy for me and maybe a bottle of vodka for Maurie More, the *Chronicle* ed, since what was on my Mini-Disc had pushed my Scallies idea a few miles further forward.

Both receptionists, Conluda and Fontella, looked like models, but I couldn't tell if both of them knew it yet. The pair of them had been sweet once but their milk of human kindness had curdled a little in the West End. Just like mine had, I supposed. They both now had bleached blonde hair, although Conluda's was in an Afro. They'd given up smoking recently but, I could see, they'd both re-started – it was difficult to give up anything any more, there was just too much stress. As I walked in, they were wearing those chic little headphones-with-mike things that airline pilots wear and, between chatting, they seamlessly fielded calls in stereo.

'Oh no, it's that awful Peter person,' said Fontella, but she lifted her hand when I went to reply, 'DPC, working for music – can I help you? . . . Yeah, I'll put you through . . . So, how's our favourite hustler?'

'Still hustling,' I answered.

'You would be. DPC, working for music – can I help you?'

'Can you help me, Con?' I said, switching my attention to Conluda.

'How so?' she answered, teasing.

'I wanna get on the guest-list, miss.'

'Difficult today – there's a big security clampdown. We're awaiting a superstar.'

'Don't con me, Con.'

'I'm not, it's Bee Jay himself— DPC, working for music . . .'

'Is that a fact, Fon? Bee Jay's coming here?'

'Yep, live and in full effect for a big interview – for Pete's sake, Pete, would we lie to you?'

'Is seven up? But why would he come here? Why not do the interview at the Ritz or at—'

'I don't know, but that's why we can't let you in.' But even as Fontella spoke she was scribbling out a temporary pass. She then passed it on to Conluda who counter-signed it.

'You're now George Giles, lift maintenance engineer, third-class.'

'It figures,' I said. 'I owe you one, gang.'

'You owe us everything,' said Con.

'So when can I take you to dinner?'

'When you can afford The Ivy,' Fontella said with a professional smile.

'How about the Ivy Motel, Hounslow? Wonderful room service.'

'Here! What kind of a girl do you think we are?'

'The expensive kind.'

'Damned right—'

'All property is theft, girls,' I said as I moved toward the Securicor men guarding the lift.

'All property is best, you mean.'

'That's cynical, Con—'

'DPC, working for music . . .'

The boardroom on the 29th was unlocked, as I knew it would be, and I couldn't help smiling as I walked past the huge mahogany table toward the drinks cabinet. On my way I kept half an eye on London – the west wall of the board-room was a huge slab of glass overlooking the city. As I reached the end of the room a voice suddenly sounded.

'Hey, do you remember ze old country?'

I spun around as Nick rose from under the table, clutching the papers he'd obviously just picked up. I smiled and contin-ued the routine.

'Ja ja – who could ever forget?'

'What vos it like again?'

'I do not remember . . .'

We grinned like idiots at each other.

'You're on the DPC shit-list, Pete, how did you get in?'

'Love laughs at locksmiths . . . How you been?'

'Fine – that old turd Bee Jay insisted on them using me for the interview. Said he respected my writing.'

'Really?'

'Yeah, the real reason is I rolled him a few joints once, way back. He might have forgotten his roots and all his old mates, but drugs? Never!'

'Typical. I hope you give the old Tory a hard time.'

'I'll sound him out – the drinks cabinet is locked, by the way. And there's nothing in the fridge except ice.'

'A press card can get you in anywhere,' I said as I flourished the NUJ freelancer's card that had cost me two pair of Levi's and a round of drinks. 'You should know that.'

'What you gonna do?' scoffed Nick. 'Show it to the men on the door?'

'No,' I said patiently as I slotted the thin edge of the ID card into the gap between the cabinet lock and the door. A second of twisting later and it clicked open. I pocketed the brandy then discovered that there was no vodka. I picked up a bottle of whisky instead, but it had already been opened.

''Ere, Nick, fancy some Scotch?'

'On the rocks,' he said as he yanked the fridge door open. I poured the drinks.

'Cheers.'

'Up yours – and well done, you coulda been a contender.'

'I coulda been a bar-tender.'

'So how's tricks?'

'Tricky. Got an ace up me sleeve, I think, but I haven't got last month's rent – well, not yet . . .'

He smiled sadly at this news and walked to the window and looked out over London.

'The battle's over, lad,' he said without smiling. 'The only thing to do is surrender gracefully.'

'Huh?' I'd never seen him acting semi-serious before.

'Freelancing, I mean. It's over – you should forget it. It's hard enough for me, but yourself . . . well, you're in an awkward spot. You're not a teenage whizz-kid any more and you're not some fortysomething the board can trust with any responsibility.'

'Are you trying to cheer me up?'

'I'm not trying to bring you down, lad, you're good and all that, but since when did being good mean anything?'

'True.'

'You're hardly thirty so—'

'I'm not thirty yet!'

'Exactly, so you can start again, in something else, another industry . . . either that or—'

'Or?'

'Or start at the bottom – again. Here or somewhere similar. Get into the office early every day, kiss a few arses when you're fighting for life inside . . . that's what it's all about.'

'I thought I'd bypassed all that.'

'No one bypasses all that. The most you can do is get well paid for it.'

'Want another one?' I asked.

'Yeah . . . don't put so much acid in this time.' I poured and we drank.

'Well, drink up, old boy,' Nick finally said. 'I'm gonna need this room soon. Me and Bee Jay, master of rawk.'

'Maybe I could hang around, lurk in the background and steal a few quotes.'

'No way – talking to Bee Jay in daylight is like dealing with the President of the United States. There'll be police guards here and all sorts. DPC are sending up someone to keep an eye on me before we even start it.'

'That's paranoia.'

'Yeah, the crazy bastards think we're gonna steal their drink or something.'

'How ridiculous.'

'Cheers.'

'Yeah, cheers.'

16

A Good Clean High

My idea of a good night out didn't normally embrace being at some Jungle event. Jungle is, I suppose, the first truly modern 'music' in that it's mostly generated by computer and vari-speeded up until it's so fast it's impossible to play live. No percussionist can play that fast for more than a minute or two. It is basically unnatural, faster than the human heartbeat and therefore best listened to on cheap speed or crack. Not that it was all bad – some was even pretty good in a relentless kind of way – but it wasn't my cup of tea.

And yet here I was. Getting blasted by 120 decibels of stuttering, maniacally fast drum-and-bass rhythms while young raggas tried to start fights by walking into people. I wasn't the only white there; there was a couple of other guys, one doing the bar, as well as six or seven girls. But while most of the people there were fairly friendly, the gangs weren't. Ugly little knots of threes and fours would occasionally flair up into a scuffle-fight or disappear at high speed into some back-room – and somehow I didn't think they were playing tag. At midnight a record I'd never heard before came on – King Killer? Gay-smasher? Goldie? – and the crowd went berserk. A dozen girls pulled huge hair-spray cans from their bags – you know, the maxi-mega cans that are the size of fire extinguishers – and pointed them skyward. Then, as they started spraying their Harmony upwards, they'd shove a burning fag lighter in front of the vapour jet. This turned each can into a mini flame-thrower, putting out a yard of fire. It was like a Mad Max version of the Hollywood Bowl candle tribute. At that moment it was all very entertaining and innocent, but I could see trouble coming. One day, soon, some bright spark was going to use these in the middle of a cat fight and the victim's face was going to need even more plastic than Michael Jackson's.

As the fave record started to fade into the next, a guy pulled a snub-nosed handgun – I'm not making this up – and pointed it at the roof before blasting away four times. Funnily enough, the gun-shots didn't sound too loud with all the noise around them, but it concerned a few people all the same. I grabbed a few sensational shouted quotes – for a magazine story that would probably never run – and ran. Was it Hitler or David Bowie who said the strength of a nation lies in its youth?

The big house (small 'h') party I moved on to was, in a way, even more disturbing than the drum-and-bass gig. At the beginning, at least. Here there were lots of little kids – three and four years old – running around while people spliffed up and chopped them out. Complete abandon. Mind you, even our host Dee-Dee, a white dread who fancied himself a singer, balked when he caught a couple of drummers chopping out lines of coke next to his baby's crib. *A Nimby*, I thought cynically. *A not-in-my-back-yardie.*

'I knew it would be a drummer, they're the worst,' Dee-Dee said, semi-seriously. 'What do you call a guy who hangs out with musicians? A drummer.'

'Oh yeah?' said one of the drummers, still smirking.

'Yeah,' went on Dee-Dee. 'And what question do you ask a man with zero IQ? Answer: what drum-sticks do you use? And how'd you know when there's a drummer at the door? Because the knocking keeps getting faster.'

'You know it's a singer at the door,' retaliated the nearest drummer, 'because he never knows when to fuckin' come in.'

Later on the musos stopped jawing and, as I hit the skunk for a return match, they started jamming. It was awesome to behold, three guitars, a bass, bongos, congas, a trumpet and a biscuit tin all being played in perfect unison – which meant they were a tiny bit out timing-wise, but that was all part of the fun. Perfection isn't perfect, it struck me as they played; technical perfection just sounded like a drum-machine and a sequencer. Real perfection was imperfect. Those guys were all slightly out – it was all part of their tightrope act – yet they swung. How far out can you be and yet still sound in? How far out can you be and still swing?

One of the guitarists got bored keeping the groove and started mucking around – 'No Fun' became the middle eight of 'Anarchy In The UK' became 'Let's Spend The Night Together' became 'Here Comes The Night' and then became 'Sugar Sugar', before slipping effortlessly into 'The S'Express Theme' and 'Ride On Time'. And then it got *really* strange. 'Hotel California' became a *Zorba the Greek*-type taverna dirge, starting slow and getting faster and faster until it ended up as a stupidly fast cabaret version. You had to laugh. But they were good people. Even the drummers were all right really – one of them could even play a listenable solo – they just lacked the necessary drug etiquette for that particular gathering. It was because they were young, barely out of their teens, and they'd only recently stopped being beer-boys.

In the kitchen I realised that one of the musos who'd been playing was Barry.

'Barry, how stoned are you?'

'Well out of it . . . the in-crowd are always well out of it. How long have you been here then?'

'How long's a piece of dope?'

'Yeah, right.'

'Got any gear, Baz? Charlie, I mean.'

'Nah, I don't touch it, not any more.'

'No? How'd you get by then?' I asked, because, at the time, I was genuinely puzzled. 'I mean, where'd you find the time and energy to do everything?'

'Pete . . . I find the time because I don't waste it asking questions like that. You're gonna go snow-blind if you're not careful.'

'Yeah? You used to do it a little bit, as I recall. Are you always this consistent?'

'Sometimes. But you take it all too far. For sure.'

'It's easy for you to mock, Barry, old boy . . . at least you've made some great tracks, written some great songs. If you died tomorrow, you'll have done more than most, you'll have done something.'

'Oh yeah, what? What have I done? Recorded other people's stuff? Sold a few thousand singles in Spain? A household name in three towns near France. Big fuckin' deal. *You* probably get more done. In your own mad way.'

Typical. Was it Hitler or David Bowie who said the grass was always greener in someone else's joint?

'But you created those things, Baz, and they're good, and abroad you—'

'And here,' he jumped in, 'I can't even catch a fucking cold. Can I?'

'Rome wasn't wrecked in a day, Bazza . . . I take it from that rant that you'd still like to score some kind of hit here?'

'Score some kind of hit? I'd be fuckin' grateful just to hear myself on Capital. Or OneFM. Or Virgin. Just *once*. Just once . . .'

Yeah, yeah, yeah. He'd said it all before. Just once. Just one clear chance. That's all he wanted. That's all most musicians wanted – that's all any of us wanted, come to think of it.

'What are you sighing about now?'

'The crap that is my life.'

'Barry,' I deadpanned with polite malice, 'I wouldn't actually call it a life. Not . . . as such.'

'No, you're probably right.'

And that, funnily enough, cheered him up. He was doing

okay really – flash car, devoted girlfriend, some work lined up – and he was smiling as he talked. It was all enough except when it wasn't enough. He told me about some charity mix work he'd been doing and how the producer involved had asked for him especially, because he was so good. And I thought, *No, mate, you're good but they actually asked because they knew you'd do it for free. Haven't you sussed that yet?* But I didn't say anything to him. Why bring him down?

'There's some suit in the downstairs bog, snorting *smack*,' moaned a passing drummer.

'That's not smack,' said Dee-Dee, trying to rescue his party's damaged reputation, 'that's one of them new speedballs. It's like a Banana Split.'

'A lot of that City mob are doing it now, you know? Got it from Wall Street. Snorting or smoking H or Splits. You get a lot of Hoorays too, they use it to get their wives off crack. Cheaper than whatever, innit? Cheaper than dope now . . . Lasts longer.'

So crack had reached Belgravia, huh? How tragic. The rich are not like us – they have more money. Must be funny doing a drug heavily and knowing you can always, always, always afford more of it. And more of it. And more of it. And with crack there was no limit, technically. You could keep going until you ran out of money and went insane. The choice was yours – although you probably had no choice at all once you'd started. The drummer mentioned some stockbroker who'd flipped because his year-old baby Lucinda could say the crack-dealer's name before she could say 'Dadda'. And then hubby forced Lucinda's mother, poor darling, to switch to sniffing smack. Just on weekends. And not in front of the nanny. And the funny thing is that you see these people every-day, all looking respectable in suits or twin-sets, running record companies or estate agencies or boutiques or selling stocks and shares . . . and sometimes killing themselves on smack because it was all too easy to overdo, too easy. Two or three fat lines of coke won't finish most folk but beginners – usually cokeheads – doing that with heroin are going to be in serious trouble – like those kids who take E for the first time, at the start of an evening, and who, when they start to feel weird a few moments later, drink so many pints of water they dilute the blood in the brain and go into a coma. No one had told them that you only need to drink water if you've dehydrated yourself by dancing for hours . . .

Most people took drugs because they had nothing to do, no money to do it with and *time was running out.* The rich do it because they have everything to do, all the money to do it with and because they have all the time in the world. At least they think they've got all the time in the world, but they haven't. The one who dies with the most toys still dies, doesn't he?

'Doing smack? They must be fuckin' mad,' I said.

'That's the height of bad manners as well, you know, OD-ing in someone else's toilet.'

It was another sick muso joke from Barry. We started giggling again. Too much drink, too little food. And then everything made you smile . . . but, despite the mellowness of those in the kitchen, I was still looking for a buzz, I still wanted some cream. The full Monty. I just wanted a bit of it, I think. What made it worse was when people talked about it. Dee-Dee had talked about meeting some old funketeer when the latter was doing more cream than Unigate.

'He had this big brace around his neck. Seems he'd been up all night – buzzing on coke – and he ended up hiding in some tree so he could hunt deer. And, after fourteen hours, the guy starts to flag and he closes his eyes for a second. When he opens them there's this deer two foot away. And the deer looks up at him, opens its mouth and does this enormous burp – *blah!* – right in his face. So he fires his gun in surprise, misses the deer, of course, and gets knocked right out of the tree by the gun's recoil. And he does his neck in.'

'Was he doing any pain-killers?'

'That's what *I* asked, and he says, "Yeah, mah *usual* pain-killers." And he pulls out the biggest bag of coke I have ever seen. I mean, it must have been *four ounces!* Must have been!

And, right there in this plush boardroom, surrounded by suits sipping Perrier, he snorts his way through most of two grams in fifteen minutes. Madness.'

Yeah, madness, and still no one had offered me any. Upstairs, however, someone was wielding a bong. So we went up as a reggae oldies CD began to sound out on the third floor. After a couple of hits of the bong everything musical sounded much clearer. The guitar solo in Ken Boothe's 'Everything I Own' seemed almost painfully brilliant after the second hit, brilliant and supple. Dave and Ansel Collins' 'Monkey Spanner' had a chunky, rubbery bass that – with a cheesy, swerving Hammond organ over the top – sounded spectacular, the perfect driving swelling sound of the Hammond lifting the entire song. Song wasn't really the word. The term 'talkover' was closer. A kind of talk, shout and sing ad-lib style they had perfected in Jamaica around the end of the Sixties. Long before American rap had been recorded. Marvin Gaye once said that he thought he knew all about hip music, thought he knew it all until he heard 'Double Barrel', a record that, he admitted, blew his mind with its echoed, shouted intro and its ice-cool piano riff. Both KLF and the self-styled Fastest Rapper In The World had taken samples from it, and it was easy to see why. And as for Marvin 'Sexual Healing' Gaye, he apparently went on playing 'Double Barrel', having it blow his mind musically until his transvestite father grabbed a handgun and blew Marvin's mind physically. Blew it out for good. I suppose anyone who, like Gaye, had said that coke was a good clean high – anyone, in fact, who had a hotel suite with a priest in one room and a coke-dealer in the next – was definitely riding for a fall. What's going on? Coke, that's what's going on. All the time. No wonder he beat up his dad a few times. And no wonder the old man finally took revenge the hard way, all the way.

There was a disc change, as Dee-Dee dropped the hookah pipe and passed out and Longsy D's 'This Is Ska' came blaring out followed by Prince Buster's All Stars doing 'Ryging (Was

Here But He Just Disappear)', a song about the real-life gunman who was the subject of Jimmy Cliff's film *The Harder They Come*. Mr Ryging wasn't, all told, that much of a hero. In fact he doesn't even qualify as an anti-hero, as his biggest shoot-out consisted of him running out of a hotel waving his gun which he·then fired at some cops – he missed the latter completely and killed two pensioners instead. Not exactly Robin Hood, is it?

But it was the sheer nifty nature of the All Stars track – complete with a killer clarinet solo, would you believe – that made me consider why reggae had changed from the slower blue-beat rhythms. And then the real reason hit me. It hit me as I looked at a room full of musos and their friends, nearly all of them off their faces – just like I was. The older blue-beat rhythm was, quite simply, the rhythm of the herb. The rhythm of the easily-grown grass that was then the fashionable drug in JA. And its rhythms only got faster in the mid-Sixties when the drug speed started to wash over Kingston from Britain and the US. Speed – like the sound systems' rivalry – had to be a big influence on Ska just as London beat groups like The Who, Kinks, Pretty Things and Small Faces were themselves getting faster with their own over-driven, choppy guitars slamming out three-chord wonders like 'Come See Me' and 'You Really Got Me'. And then the psychedelic thing happened when acid and coke came in – the first Summer of Love – and now, reggae was ragga was Jungle was drum-and-bass which was getting insanely fast because it was the sound of crack rocks. Rocks that would truly screw you up. For years. Big-up, big-time. And usually for ever, or until you freaked out and got locked up somewhere. Two or three hits, some reckoned, and you were gone. Hooked. Which is appropriate as it was, is, the choice of hookers, junkies, headbangers and other folk best avoided after dark. Which was why it had so affected everyone in the ghetto. Everyone, even those that didn't take it, had to be influenced by the aggression, by the sheer amount of crime and violence crack had unleashed all around them.

Modern music, its rhythms and mannerisms, did, undoubt-edly, reflect the drug of the time – 1969: Summer of Love, acid; 1988: acid house, E. Get on one, matey! We really thought we'd had Summers of Love – but it was all just a chemical imbalance in the brain. Artificially induced. And maybe that is too cynical in itself because some people who thought it was real weren't on it then and aren't on it now. And some of that emotion was real, chemically inspired or not. Some of it was real. Some of it always is.

Which made me think. Most musicians took some kind of drug, or at least drank heavily, because of fear. The fear that was implicit for them in modern music. Fear which musicians hadn't faced before the last half of this century. Before the Forties you just learned your craft and then learned a song. After that, the decline of the Tin Pan Alley song-writer and the rise of the solo artist left modern musos with a fear of having to create – *Just create, just get out there and do something totally new, just launch into the complete unknown and can you please do it brilliantly?* – which was doubled by the need also to improvise. At the heart of modern music – R & B and jazz and every one of their noisy bastard children – is the need to create and improvise. Which, while it must be fun, must also be like taking a parachute jump into the unknown. Especially when it's in front of a few thousand strangers.

Which is probably why nearly every musician worth his salt wants, at some point, his sulphate. Or his hash or weed or coke or beer or Scotch or whatever. The one-in-a-million modern muso who has no fear of improvising – people like Bird, Hendrix and Morrison – also had, sadly, no fear of anything, and thus usually wound up dead, having over-done the drugs they didn't ever need to use. Musicianship is like any other art, the real skill lies in learning the rules and then knowing when, and by how much, you should break them.

That's why musicians hate it when you unplug the radio halfway through a classic song. Or even when it's halfway through some fairly average dirge. That song had a beginning, a middle and an end. Something that can be learned, under-stood and clung to in a world of composition and impro and change. Something definite and whole. And *you* just snapped it off. Dead. Cutting off a musician's own song halfway through is like murdering one of their kids. So can you imagine what it was like when, face-to-face, some A & R character talked all the way through your new track, talked over your new-born child? And they did, frequently, I'd seen it a hundred times . . .

I staggered downstairs, slipping from side to side like a sailor in a storm. Barry followed. The guitars and stuff had been put away and a discussion was raging about British music, the gist of it being that rock was what the locals were good at. Most British dance stuff hadn't sold much in the USA. Or so Barry said, before going on to explain that Brit-dance just wasn't that good, all in all. Not abroad, anyway, which is where it really counts – Germany, the USA and Japan.

Only Britrock, and/or pop, worked abroad. U2, Simply Red, Dire Straits . . . and, of course, The Scallies. Barry had, it transpired, been engineering for a big guitar band that day. Or so he said.

'This guitarist walks into the studio and pulls out a three-grand Les Paul, a big beautiful polished antique of a guitar. A real rarity. And he says "This is over twenty-five years old." So I said, "What's the matter? Couldn't you afford a new one then?"'

'Walking your tightrope again, eh?'

'And when he set up for his solo he was really taking his time so I said, "Look, we know you're always crap, so just relax." And then he stared at me for a whole minute before he saw the funny side and burst out laughing . . .'

'Are producers still wiping the time-code off tracks?'

'Oh yeah, some of them. More than ever, actually. It's a cut-throat business.'

Time-codes are a signals track on a multi-track master. These signal tracks help keep all the computers and MIDI sequencers in time, all synched together. So when the original producer wipes it, he makes it difficult for anyone to remix. Which just might force the label to get the original producer back in, as he knows where everything is, to assist with any remixes.

'Hi, Bunny baby, we called you back 'cos we really think you've got the right vibe to help out on the remix of the track. We really think it'd work better with you being there, artistically speaking . . .'

Yeah, yeah, yeah.

17

The Whiskey-A-Go-Go

At the far end of Gerrard Street in Chinatown, on the west side of Wardour, is a pokey little bookie's. Under it is the basement that used to be the Flamingo Club. The likes of Jimmy James, Georgie Fame and Chris 'Buzz with the Fuzz' Farlowe brought uptown air-base R & B to the masses here, and a couple of seminal live albums were even laid down on that site, all in glorious mono. Now it's a derelict storeroom, but upstairs, the Flamingo's contemporary, the Whiskey-A-Go-Go, or Wag as it's now known, still go-go's on.

The Beatles, Stones, The Who, James Brown *et al* stumbled up those very same stairs and got damaging lungfuls of the very same smoky air that we mere mortals can inhale now. In those days, floods of movie stars, models and bespoke photographers were also in attendance and, on some nights, there are still one or two to be seen today. I was there early, eleven thirty – looking for Jerry or one of his mates – but it was already crowded. Northerner Ralph the K was at the controls, giving us the original mix of the Human League's 'Don't You Want Me, Baby?' and every chorus was provoking a big singalong by the assembled throng of go-getters and foreign trendies as the 1980s revival moved up a notch. There was no one I knew on the first level so I went upstairs, but the Scots barman who knew Jerry wasn't much help either.

'Haven't seen him, Pete. He's probably over at the Ministry or the Happy House. Or some party. You know Jerry, finding him is a full-time job by itself. You could try speaking to his ansafone.'

Yeah, that was true, I should have phoned Jerry earlier. I usually did, on nights like these. But he was always out with the ansafone switched off. And I needed some coke, frankly; I hadn't had any for nearly two days, and fighting the good fight was getting me down, that's why I was seeking out Jezza. I had to get a buzz.

'Yeah, you're probably right . . . You haven't seen his mate Rush, have you?'

'No, he's just flown to New York.'

'Rushin' around again, huh?'

'Yeah, he probably flew over several miles higher than the plane.'

'Yeah, I'll bet . . .'

'Last week I said to him, what you doing these days? And he says "Everything" . . . Jezza said you were goin' to do some exclusive chat with The Scallies.'

'No, they didn't wanna do it.'

And they hadn't – The Scallies had blown me out, Jerry had finally admitted. This, funnily enough, was a relief, in a way. If they had met me and we'd got on . . . well, I could never have attempted the Scallies corruption story. But now the gloves were off, there was to be no turning back . . .

I just knew, though, that everything would be easier if I had just a little charlie, just a little . . . I went down to the dance-floor below, where another blast from the past was pounding out.

In the queue outside I saw Desdemona, the Asian girl 'designer' from Bournemouth who Jerry and I had briefly spoken to at the Happy House three weeks and several light years before. She was buying something illegal from a mobile-phone user. I thought it was an E, or two.

'Twenty nicker, darling, and *that* is a bargain, take it or leave it,' said the hustler.

'Okay, where are they?' she snapped back. She had to be uptown most of the time now – if the dark rings under her eyes were any guide – if she wasn't already living here.

'I'm not carrying, but I've got 'em just around the corner,' hustled the hustler, 'jus' gimme the money and I'll be back in five.'

'Okay,' she smiled and then got a twenty-pound note out and, just as the street dealer had her pegged for a sucker, she ripped it into two before giving him one half.

'I'll give you the other half when you come back, okay?'

Desdemona wasn't so naïve any more. In fact, she'd become quite a sweet-and-sour young thing. The dealer nodded with resignation and wandered off as I thought, *She's learning, she's definitely learning.*

Hanway Street once had the Transat House record shop where all the Sixties mods came to get import soul and then, ten years later, it became Contempo Records as it brought all the boogie stuff in for all the punky funkees. Now it's Vinyl Solution, and is oldies only but that, I guessed, was progress. Hanway also has the Java Club (Members Only). Its location is actually more Fitzrovia than Soho, but the Java is a good blend of both. It opens at some point in the afternoon or evening – depending on how the staff feel – but is always busy by eleven. The main room, the only room, is about the size of the Wag's toilet, but since the place is always full of drunken writers, artists and art students – plus poets, trendies, clubbers and various other flotsam 'n' jetsam of the jet age – a good time is usually had by all. I first went there with Martin, a hard-drinking sea-faring painter. I had envied Martin once – in some ways I still did – for having travelled the world in the late Seventies and early Eighties when there were still many places that were genuinely different. One trip ended with him being shot at in New Orleans, another ended with him shacked up in some Nicaraguan mud hut with a thirteen-year-old girl – he was only seventeen himself at the time – and another voyage ended with him being searched by armed guards at Singapore airport. The Singaporean cops were looking for the tiny bit of dope they'd been tipped off over – stuff that would have got him twenty years in the Disney dormitory that is Singapore – dope he had clutched in the sweating hands he had obediently placed on his head. He similarly escaped getting busted in the old East Germany when the Stasi customs officers noticed, and approved of, the Karl Marx patch on his old Westwood shirt . . .

Places were much more diverse then – it was a bigger world – unlike now, when you can practically fit the whole thing into the hip pocket of your 501s. Almost everywhere is the same, every city like the last one, every city like a re-run. This was the future and it worked like MegaHertz, regularly screamed 'It's a Sony!', ate at McDonald's, drank Coca-Cola, wore Levi's, watched *Baywatch*, got drunk on Heineken and got arrested by cops all wearing matching baseball caps and all driving Ford Sierras. London, Paris, New York, Moscow, Peking . . . everywhere. Except the odd few areas like Soho that had, so far, mostly escaped character-cleansing, and which still had some decent pubs and clubs, tucked away somewhere. Places like the Java.

Martin had most definitely not been a member of the Java when he first ventured near the place. After a particularly colourful discussion about art, he had proceeded to verbally abuse some American tourist who'd somehow offended him – 'And what does "totally gnarly" actually mean, you daft cow? No, no, Mrs, don't take umbrage' – before wrenching various paintings off the wall. The owner, East – East of Java, see? – promptly threw him out.

'Are you gonna ban him?' asked the barman.

'Oh no,' said East, 'make him a full member.'

Which is part of the charm of the place. That night East had had the odd drink and everyone else in the place was six sheets to the wind and about to hoist the seventh. I was about to give up and go to the Carlisle Arms – someone once told me that Handel had performed in the Carlisle; a few years ago now, of course – when who should come strolling up the stairs but Maurie More, the editor of the *Chronicle*.

Being a London paper meant that the *Chronicle* had an influence way beyond its million readers across the city and Home Counties – not that there was anything wrong with a mere million readers, for, as I had to admit, whenever an item of mine appeared in there I actually would cut it out the same day. 'You sad southern bastard,' I admonished myself, using Maurie's unmistakable Yorkshire accent.

Maurie had a serious-faced young woman on his arm. She was attractive, in her own way, and her black velvet jacket oozed dark nights, but she was no good-time girl – discreet dinner parties over the Aga was as wild as she ever got. Which was no crime, I suppose.

'Hiya, Maurie, how goes it?'

'Oh God. Save me from starving freelancers.'

'That's not very sociable, Mo. I nearly nicked some Polish vodka for you the other day.'

'Nearly doesn't cut it, lad, especially when I'm tired and emotional.'

'Who's your friend?'

'This is Susanna, one of our new arts columnists – Sue, this is Pete, an alleged writer I sometimes have to tip.'

'Pleased to meet you, Susanna. That's one helluva jacket you're wearing,' I schmoozed.

'Thanks, I really like it myself. It only cost me ninety pounds,' she said in a South African accent, 'that's quite a good price, isn't it?'

'Oh yeah, it's well worth—'

'Pete, we were just thinking of having a quiet drink or two . . .'

'Same here, I'm only gonna get one and then go, why don't you join me?'

'*Why don't you join me?*' – now that was pretty good. Spoken as if I was doing them a nice polite friendly favour, as if I was the Java's real host.

'All right, lad, we'll join you for *one*,' Maurie emphasised.

'So how's Hitler?' I asked, referring to Sir Ralph, the *Chronicle*'s Maltese owner, a man who'd once been a neo-fascist, allegedly – hence the nickname.

'Hitler's fine.'

'What do you wanna drink then?' I offered in the silence that followed, and then wished I hadn't – I only had a fiver on me. I really did have a cheque clearing the next day, but that was no good in the Java. I was skint, which was why I had to see Jerry for coke. Not to re-sell it on a vast scale, I wasn't that crazy, but just because no one else would give me credit.

'No, no,' said Susanna, coming to the rescue, 'please, let me. What is it?'

'Vodka and it, cheers.'

'Make that two,' said Maurie, 'large ones – and get a receipt, you shouldn't end up out of pocket.'

Susanna went to the bar as Maurie looked around.

'She seems nice enough, Maurie,' I said, using his more respectful moniker now that we were going to have at least one drink together, 'but I thought that Hitler didn't like Yarpies.'

'Her surname's Goldman,' he answered, 'and you know Hitler, he loves Jews.'

'Crazy . . . Maurie, I might have a scoop for you.'

'You *might* have a scoop for me?'

'Correction, I *have* a scoop for you. Sex 'n' drugs 'n' rock-'n'roll. The gen on the drug generation . . . and their heroes. Exposed. A cover story.'

'I'll believe it when I see it.'

'I need help on it,' I said, and I did. I did need a bit of cover. Everyone needs cover.

'I bet you do,' snapped Maurie.

'I'm serious, Maurie.'

'Since when?'

'This morning – it's a real feature, a cover, for sure. Just read my proposal, I've already got some good quotes in it. It'll only take you ten minutes to—'

'My office, ten o'clock, tomorrow morning. Fair enough?'
'Yeah, sure . . .'
'Good, then drink up now and fuck off – I think I'm in with a chance here.'

18

Cocaine Christmas

That was the first time I'd been to the offices of the *Chronicle* – slogan 'Truth is our profession!' – despite having sold them a dozen small stories over the preceding months. All that had been done via faxes and the Internet, for it had become possible to work without seeing another human being at all, such were the wonders of technology. Being there was undoubtedly a bit of a thrill, though. This was like being in a TV studio or something. This was like the national press. This was big-time . . . kind of.

I had to speak to two different secretaries – and get frisked by two sets of silent security guards – before I was allowed through into one of the plush carpeted lifts. It was heavily air-conditioned, that building, for which I was genuinely grateful – it had still been blistering out on the streets, blistering at ten in the morning. God knows what midday would be like.

The lift smoothly whooshed up to the twenty-third floor as I checked my outfit in the mirror – baggy dark blue mohair suit and wine-coloured polo shirt. My Persol shades were tugging down the undone shirt collar. Cool as fuck. Well . . . I looked okay.

In the open-plan office that led to Maurie More's bolt-hole were two Union Jack posters with 'NO TO THE EU!' emblazoned on them. On the opposite wall was a small gilt-framed photo of Sir Ralph, the beloved owner of the *Chronicle* and the *Sunday Chronicle*. The picture had been snapped at some tycoons' dinner and, within view, was Rupert Murdoch. You could also glimpse a half-profile of Conrad Black, who owned the *Daily Telegraph*. I found it quite funny, actually, seeing all those papers taking a strong line against the European Union and its foreign attempt to 'dominate' Britain – especially since the owners of the papers were hardly true Brits themselves: Sir Ralph was Maltese while Black was Canadian and Murdoch an Australian-American. These were the brave fellows who were so actively defending the right to be *really* British . . .

Twenty minutes later I was watching Maurie as he fielded two phone calls at once. His chair was swivelling endlessly back and forth, facing this way and then that way – facing any way, in fact, except towards me. His prop-forward-gone-to-seed frame was slumped in repose and I wondered if I'd come on the right day. But it was ten o'clock – well, half past – and it was the next morning.

And then, after he'd put one call on the speaker-phone, he proceeded to pick up my proposal and idly flick his way through it. I waited impatiently, still feeling confident. This was going to make my name, this was going to make me thousands and thousands of pounds – it had to. Not that money was everything; I also felt like I was standing up for all those musicians who didn't have a high-powered coke-fuelled management team behind them, standing up for every poor sod whose demos had been slagged off unplayed, standing up for every band who'd had a front cover cheated away from them. And, I suddenly realised, I was standing up for myself as well. *We expose the music biz shysters* . . . Yes, this was most definitely it. I was certain of it. As certain as I've ever been of anything. If this wasn't a cover story then nothing was.

And then, at last, Maurie was winding up his calls.

'. . . yes, no and up yours . . . yes, my love. Bye. You still there, George? Well, fuck off and do some work then . . . yeah, the Archer story . . . yeah, bye . . .'

Maurie chucked my proposal on to his desk as he finally turned to face me. 'Interesting shit, kid, interesting shit . . . Hmm . . .'

'Well?' I finally asked.

'Well,' he sighed like he was already bored, 'you've got thirty seconds, lad. Shoot your shot. *Con-vince* me . . .'

'I don't understand, Maurie,' I blustered as I tried to think ahead, 'I've written it all down there, and if there's anything else you need to know about the—'

'What you've outlined here is a story. A good story, but a story nonetheless. Not a cover.'

'You what? Are you serious, Maurie? Are you fuckin' serious?' I completely flipped out, I was leaning over his desk and the words were just tumbling out of me: 'Drugs are the biggest thing in the lives of an entire generation! The next generation! They're the biggest thing! With no exceptions! They're *the* biggest thing in most London lives . . . as well *you* know, with some of your own fuckin' staff. And pop music is Britain's voice to the world. It has been ever since The Beatles. That's why the Fab Four's drug-taking was covered up until the Stones were busted first. That's why the Sex Pistols and Acid House had to be banned. They had to be, didn't they? Because pop music was Britain's voice – correction, because pop music *still* is Britain's voice. Rock'n'roll's the only thing left that we do really well, isn't it? And if even our pop charts are rigged, if even the best of our groups have to drug-bribe their way into print, then it's news. It *is* news. And half the music press, the people who are s'posed to promote new talent, are stifling it – unless their palms are being greased with charlie! It's all bent! That's news! It's big fuckin' news! It's a cover, for fuck's sake! It's a cover, isn't it? Eh?' My fervour had begun to fade into doubt. 'Well? Isn't it . . . Maurie . . .?'

The silence that followed was finally ended by Maurie softly whistling.

'Bugger me, lad . . . I'll buy that. You get all the dirt and write it like that and that's a cover. My word on it.'

'It is?'

'Yeah, for sure. "SCALLIES SUPERGROUP IN SEX, DRUGS AND COR-RUPTION SHOCKER!",' he said, leaning back as he spread his hands into an imaginary headline.

'Maurie, I haven't actually got much sex in the story . . .'

'Don't worry about that, lad, I know all there is to know about nookie stories, if we need some more I'll put that in meself,' he said, commandeering half the story, as editors are wont to do. 'I do hope you realise that if all this pans out all right, if it all comes out in the wash, then a good few produc-ers are gonna get the boot – as well as a good few music journos. You know that, do you?'

'Yeah, but so what? They're all gonna end up on Channel 4 anyway.'

'Yeah,' said Maurie, stifling a smirk. 'But as far as the music press is concerned you will have definitely pissed on your chips, no way back to them, no way.'

'I know, I know . . . I won't go back anyway. It's no loss.'

'So what do you need again?'

'I need a—'

'Yeah, yeah, I can fuckin' read,' he had grabbed the pro-posal and he was studying the last page again as his free hand snatched up a phone, 'Andrea, my love . . . yes, yes – as soon as the wife dies, it's all yours. Now listen, girl, I'm sending you a young man – no, no, you can keep your knickers on this time . . . *I'm only joking, my love, I'm only joking*! No, no, listen. Hell's teeth, woman, listen! He's here now, waiting . . . yes, he *is*, Andrea. He's standing here now – Pete, come and say hello—'

I began to lean over but he waved me away.

'Yes, my love, yes . . . He needs a good photographer – one who's done surveillance – some affidavits . . . oh, and give him some petty cash . . . no, make it nineteen hundred – if we give

him the whole two grand he'll do a runner . . . yeah, he'll
bugger off to Tangiers, where all the poofs go.'

I smiled the smile of the patronised but I wasn't annoyed in
the slightest. Inside I wasn't worried at all. Because at last I
knew I was making it. Making it. Big-up, big-time. The
biggest. *The wasted years haven't been wasted*, I told myself.
In fact, as I watched Maurie scribble a few notes on my proposal, I wasn't that far away from tears. For at that very
moment, I really did think that, somehow, it was all going to
work out. Somehow. All the mistakes were going to be recti-
fied – I'd re-found the lottery ticket and the waiting was
finally over. In spite of everything that had gone before, in
spite of *everything*, my life was still going to work for the best.
And now I could actually envisage affording loads of coke . . .
I didn't really want it any more. Typical.

'Don't those Scally persons . . .' Maurie spoke again as he
looked up, 'don't they go on some big tour later this month?'

'Yep, world tour, starts end of the week after next.'

'You got ten days then, fourteen max . . . You'd better get
on with it then, you sad-soft-southern-shite.'

'I'm off and running and thank you for your kind words.'

'Before you go, I do have one question,' said Maurie as he
passed me the proposal. I had tried to take the papers from
him but he'd hung on to them, involving me in an unseemly
tug-of-war.

'What is it, Maurie?' I said with a hint of exasperation.

'Lemme look at them fuckin' eyes, boy,' he leant over and
peered at me closely. 'Are you staying off them dodgy powders?'

'Yeah, of course,' I lied. Maurie abruptly let go of the papers.
I pocketed them and was about to turn away when he suddenly demanded, 'Where were you at two thirty this morning?'

'Er, at home, with me girlfriend.'

'Yeah? And did she enjoy it?'

'I dunno, she passed out.'

'Passed out! You arrogant fucker, I bet you had to fuckin'
pay her money!'

'You're talkin' about the woman I love, Maurie,' I admonished him as I began to walk out.

'Go on, fuck off out of it. And don't forget what I said, Peter, keep it clean! I don't want you getting nicked before we've even run your cover! Cocaine isn't just for Christmas, lad, cocaine is for fuckin' life! Got that? Life! You're a newspaperman now, so fuckin' act like it. Stay off them powders!'

19

Circumstances

'No, Vee, we can't,' exclaimed Anna with just a bit too much force.

'Can't what? Can't what?' he had jeered with drink in his voice.

'We can't just knock it on the head. We can't! I won't let you.'

'What?' he'd begun to grin but it was a faint, lopsided affair.

We were driving – correction, Vee was drink-driving – Anna was by Vee's side and they were arguing about toot. Arguing about keeping Vee's trade in charlie on the up-and-up. And me? I was just along for the ride. I'd gone on to a gig at the 100 Club a few hours before. Some northern soul meets Britpop affair with two bands, The Active Direction and Sub-Lager, topping the bill. Both had been good and lively, both with chain-smoking singers – *die young, stay pretty* – much better than the usual names you saw shoved under your nose everywhere. But they weren't the real reason I was there. I'd had to meet the *Chronicle* photographer to look at his first few shoots on the Scallies story. He was good, and already had pictures of one of The Scallies meeting a previously convicted 'drugs supplier' – who was not, thank God, Vee. We were getting there; I just had to bribe, cajole and beg a few more people into swearing to statements they'd already made. The cat, I felt, was virtually in the bag.

Outside, afterwards, a car had honked at me as I'd attempted to cross a rainy Oxford Street. It was Anna and Vee. And so then I accepted a lift. As the warm drizzle fell, we sped west at a rate of knots. They were going to drop me off by some taxi-rank or something. It didn't matter. All that mattered to me at that moment was puzzling out how the furious argument they were having somehow defined them. How that drug and its trade defined them. Defined them and somehow bound them together. And, I have to admit, I was pretty curious too, curious as to whether they'd offer me any. I would, of course, refuse.

'You can't stop doing shit, Vee, we can't afford to,' Anna said flatly.

'Whatcha mean we can't afford it? What the hell is there you want that you can't afford? What? You can afford everything from ninety-quid knickers to a fucking personal trainer. So tell—'

'We can't stop . . . not yet, Vee. We just can't. There's so much to be sorted out.'

'Look,' he sighed, and you felt the fight go out of him, 'I'm not, all right? I'm not going to stop just yet, okay? So just fuckin' relax, okay? I'm not . . . was just kidding, girl, that's all, just kidding . . .'

He wasn't drunk enough to argue with her. Men normally have to be drunk to seriously argue with their partners. If they're sober they'll always lose – and Vee wasn't drunk enough. And Anna was no way going to give ground on that one.

And that, of course, was it. That was the very moment when, with a little electric shock – and while I was looking at the rear-view mirror and its taxi-driver eyes – I finally knew the exact whys, whos and wherefores of their relationship. Why Vee was sad that night, why Anna was so adamant about all this. Why they were even together. *At last*, I thought, *now I know her and Vee as well as they know themselves, maybe better.* And in knowing them I killed their two mysteries with one stone. She was with Vee because, quite simply, she was an adrenaline junkie. 'What do you do?' I'd asked. 'Anything I like,' she'd said. Her home had been some upmarket Latin bolt-hole, down Mexico way. And back there she'd got bored with being a second-rate copy of an American debutante, got bored with looking pretty-pretty as she squandered lots of daddy's lovely money in various chic cocaine clubs. So she chose instead to break ranks and to break her nails – and various local laws – for *the cause.* Taking big risks with guns, giving it all away, running on empty. There was some idealism there, to be fair, and she had guts too, but what she'd eventually got hooked on – what, probably, had become an end in itself – was the excitement of it all. The sheer *buzz.* She'd had to leave her homeland and couldn't go back, not for years, not now daddy was bankrupt. Maybe not ever. All bridges burnt – like me in a way – and she liked to live like that.

Somehow she'd ended up in London. Here the most obvious excitement was the late-night bars and strobed-out dance-floors she'd originally run away from. The Ministry of Fun, which was no fun at all; not for her.

Until she came across Vee. Vee with ten grand's worth of cocaine on his bookshelf, Vee who probably carried a gold-inlaid pistol to match the gold-inlaid shotguns on his wall, Vee the video king, Vee, whose flunkies went to embassies and warehouses and airports and lonely beaches. She probably went out on some of the pick-ups too. Nothing ventured, nothing cocained. Vee wanted Anna and she, in return, wanted to share his lifestyle. The perfect mismatch, the perfect modern couple. And something told me that Vee had sussed all this out himself, long ago.

Unlike everyone else he knew, Vee was making seriously good money from his legit concerns. Thousands a week. Maybe thousands a day. Vee could have stopped pushing months or even years before. He should have done and he would have done – except that somewhere, at the back of his mind, he knew that the minute he gave all that up, he'd probably lose Anna too. They had to keep going. Onward until dawn – and beyond.

That's what that night's argument had really been about. *They had to keep it going.* Until God knows what. Until they were busted? Bankrupt? Dead? The love that could thrill could be the love that could kill . . . *So is this*, I wondered drunkenly, *why I want her more than ever?*

I went back to their place. Just to chat. And to consider my new-found knowledge. Vee had made a few phone calls and then got all wrapped up in the sports channel. I felt the joy of my big break fade a little. Sally had been busy for two days and Vee and Anna were two people I couldn't talk to – not about the Scallies coke splash – not that they were going to be involved but it was still too awkward to raise. My three-drink-blues descended on me like a shroud. *They have each other, there is no hope for you*, I said to myself over and over again.

Until the coke got chopped out. I said no twice and then said yes. It lifted me almost instantly, with poisonous ease – the powdered drug reacting against the other, alcoholic, drug. And taking me straight back to where I'd probably been before, naturally, just six hours previously – and the conversation soared and soared as Anna and I talked incessantly, each line hooking into the next like a chain-link. And suddenly, after an hour, I noticed I was looking directly at Anna, our eyes locked on to each other's heat like some surface-to-air missile seeking out its target. And, staring at each other, I had really wanted to blurt it out, that feeling that everyone must have felt at least once – the feeling that says *you're with him but you belong with me. We hit it off. We click like dice. You know it and I know it. Me and you. And I'm here now – what you've been waiting for. We can work it out together, because we should be together. Isn't it obvious? Doesn't it show like a neon sign? I know it, you know*

it and we all know it. Let's you and I just go off together . . .
Now.

If only it was that simple. The problem being that you never
did find that special person – well, almost never – until you
were already hooked up to someone, until you could relax
and be your good ol' self. *Be yourself!* I thought. *Be yourself
and free yourself!*

It was all still to play for, the whole potential relationship
lying before us as we lied through our teeth.

'Why,' she asked, 'do men put women on pedestals?'

'Because when you guys are up there it's a lot easier for us
guys to throw rocks at you, metaphorically speaking.'

'No, but do men do that because they can't take the truth?'

'Of course we can't take the truth, it's taken us centuries to
accept the lie—'

'But do you ever do that?'

'What? Put girls on pedestals to throw *rocks* at 'em?'

'Yeah.'

'Nah . . . I'm a rotten shot anyway.'

'Nah,' she mimicked me gently, 'I'm sure you must have hit
the target a few times.'

What did that mean? Was I somewhere or nowhere? *Him or
me, what's it gonna be*? Vee went off upstairs for a few
moments and I found myself lost in Anna's charms – her face,
her arms, her scent – and I just couldn't help chucking lines at
her like there was no tomorrow. And what did I know?
Maybe there was no tomorrow. Worse thing was, I actually
meant them at the time.

'This'll sound terrible, Anna, like some kinda ridiculous
line but . . . looking at you now . . . I can tell that there was
probably a point, when you were a little younger, when you
were just a bit more cute than you are now . . .'

She raised half an eyebrow – this wasn't quite the usual
praise and she wasn't sure how to play it. I ploughed on
regardless, ad-libbing furiously.

'And there *will* be a time, in the future, when you're older,
when you'll have even more dignity than you have now. But,

right at this very minute you, and your eyes and the whole of you is just, are just really, really . . . beautiful. It's the only word . . . just . . . beautiful. I don't mean that as a line, it's just . . .' I shrugged, all innocence, 'it's just . . . true. You're too much.'

'You, young Peter,' she smiled softly, 'have had just a bit too much charlie.'

'You know I haven't.'

'Yes, you have.'

Vee stumbled back into the room as I managed to tear my gaze away from her. He'd been at the gin and was ready to collapse. It was time to leave – something I found quite difficult to do. No one'll ever know just how difficult it was to leave there that night . . . to leave him with her . . .

'Bring your girlfriend next time,' Anna said by the door, after she'd pecked my cheek. I felt like she was probably telling me to back off fast, like maybe I'd already blown it, without laying a finger on her smooth honey-coloured skin . . . but a part of me thought that she just might be doing the opposite, that she was feeling guilty and that she was trying to say to Vee, 'Look, I'm really not interested in Pete, that's why I'm asking him to bring his girl along next time, do you see? Do you see?'

I wasn't normally that arrogant. I mean to seriously think someone like Anna could want me. Not in a normal situation. But neither she nor Vee knew if I had a girlfriend and so it was possible she'd raised the subject as a blind. For the signals she'd been giving out – along with the cosy little game of verbal footsie we'd played all night – had convinced me that something was going down between us.

Had Vee clocked all this? Could he have sensed it? Could he have caught the real meaning of all the double-talk we had gone through beforehand? Or had he just thought that Anna and I were going through all that grown-up-men-and-women-can-be-friends stuff? Maybe he'd thought that the light in her eyes was just a reflection of my own . . . or a reflection of the TV.

20

'X' Marks The Spot

The summer sun was finally fading in the west as the first fireworks exploded in the east. They were huge fireworks. The sort that half-deafen you. And they looked great. Great splashes of colour that streaked relentlessly out across the darkening deep blue sky, endless permutations of fire and smoke. Some of the rockets expanded violently into a dozen little fire-balls which then, in their turn, also exploded; changing direction two or three times in all. It was quite something, probably ten grand's worth on its own. Maybe even more.

I was at a party to celebrate the merger of Eye Scene plc with Fink, Fink, Fink & Jones. Both were advertising production companies, as if you couldn't tell. The place was crawling with credible directors and a few arts-council types, or so some Sloaney character had informed me at the beginning of the evening. Not that I was with her. I'd arrived with Damon, one of the aforementioned directors, who spent more on clothes in a week than most folk did in a lifetime. It was all designer designer. He did it pretty well though, I had to admit. He did look sharp. Even when, as now, he was staring gormlessly up at the sky as the technicolours wowed him. Him and me. He passed the skunk joint back to me with a dreamy half-smile.

'They're all right, aren't they?'

'Oh yeah, very adequate.'

They were spectacular, really. And then, right before our eyes, they suddenly got even better. A firework had ignited at about half the height of the others. As its fumes drifted towards us, a dozen smaller devices fired off beneath it. The smoke that this whole ensemble left behind looked like some ghostly galleon, some ancient sailing ship made out of smoke trails, as it undulated over us. Then the very last firework went nuclear and – how can I explain this? – three-dimensional as well. It really felt 3D, mainly because the wind was making the sparks drift over us as they gently floated down. So the display stopped being something flat, seen from a distance, and instead became something we were part of. We were inside the firework, it seemed. Sparks falling among us. The tiny flames always *just* going out as you reached up for them. It was like viewing, and then being part of, some huge space nebula, some long-forgotten picture of a distant galaxy. It felt important. Like you were viewing the nervous system of the brain, lit up with tiny lights that showed us every single little branch line – which, of course, echoed the space nebula firework thing. Or that's what it felt like.

'Did we really see that?' I asked.

'What? You mean that huge spectral boat and the 3D nebula?'

'Yeah, yeah. *That*. Did we really see that?'

'Nah . . .'

He'd then turned on his heel and started to trudge up the manicured lawn to the candle-lit mansion. Damon was one of many, all walking slowly, champagne glasses clutched in hand, as they bore down on the French windows. I killed the joint I was clutching and followed him, still stunned by the fireworks I'd seen.

'Do you know how much I made last year?' he said when I caught him up.

'Tell me.'

'Over a hundred and twenty grand.'

'Unlucky for some.'

'And I'm gonna double it this year. You know why I'm gonna double it?'

'Er . . . you've now got an agent?'

'Yep. I had to get a pimp, I couldn't make it on my own,' he said, tongue in cheek.

'So now?'

'So now, God willing, I'm looking at around quarter of a mill. Two hundred and fifty thousand would do me. For now.'

'And that, and ninety pence, will buy you a small coffee plantation.'

'But Pete, you do know what I'm saying, don't you?'

'I should be working in advertising.'

'Exactly. In ads and with an agent . . . you're wasted writing music stuff for kids who can't read. I mean, what's the point?'

'You're right, of course. It's like I'm speechless.'

'Well, you should say something then.'

'I thought my silence said it all.'

'Pete, you *know* I'm right.'

And maybe he was right. Maybe I should have been trying to work in advertising. But the Scallies scoop was rolling forward, though I'd kept it quiet as possible, and there didn't seem to be any rush. It was gonna happen.

'I know I'm right.'

'Yeah. I know you know.'

'You could help out on storyboards, ideas, scripts. Anything like that. Find a niche and work it – or make it your own.'

'Of course,' I said, 'you're forgetting the fact I'm not a Trustafarian living in Notting Hill Gate. And I'm certainly not a St Martin's student. And I'm over nineteen.'

'Age doesn't matter in the yoof industries. Look at Janet Whatsit, fifty if she's a day. Look at all the thirtysomethings who write and broadcast for the music biz.'

He was right, of course. All the idiot suits throughout the country's boardrooms had bought the notion – sold to them by ads and music and agencies – that you had to be less than thirty, under the big three-oh to be any good. Or even, preferably, under twenty-five. So experienced detectives and engineers and scholars and bridge-builders were bundled out the door – or put out to stud – as soon as poss. But the guys who'd sold the bosses the whole youth yuppie trip in the first place were probably all in their forties anyway. *You didn't really have to sack all your best workers, Mr Suit. Those blokes on the telly didn't really mean it. It was only a Levi's ad. They were only trying to sell some jeans. It was just an ad with some rock music. That was all.*

Damon went off to pull rank and get some more champagne as I eavesdropped on two old queens. Well, they were young queens actually – in their late twenties or very early thirties – which made them something of a rarity in the world of the Compton Tom macho-man. They were talking about Horace, a friend of theirs who seemed to be well in with various arts groups.

'Of course, it's partly because he's a big fan of Thatcher's, isn't it?'

'A gay black Tory in leg-irons.'

'Who can resist him? Even if he can't really sculpt.'

'No wonder the papers love him.'

'Did you know his grants from the arts council are worth over forty-five K this year?'

'Oh, he's not that talented, is he? It's because he used to serve on one of the council committees.'

'It's 'cos he can't say "no".'

'Course, he's made up with that disability allowance, isn't he?'

'Oh yes, he's lucky like that. Course, he'd be better off in a wheelchair, really.'

'Really?'

'Oh yes, if he was that bad he'd get on TV too – and he'd get one of those special flats in Covent Garden.'

'God yes, I see what you mean. If he was in a wheelchair, he'd have everything . . .'

How insane, I thought, *how very insane*. The two queens said their farewells.

'It's been great to see you.'

'Terrific.'

'Ciao, lover.'

'It's been wonderful.'

'It's been *real*.'

'Pete, meet Dixie,' said Damon as he shuffled me into the presence of an ageing American.

'Hi,' snapped Dixie.

'Hi,' I said, nodding.

'This is Dixie's place,' said Damon with a gesture that encompassed the room, the mansion, the world.

'Great. I love it. You could play hide-and-seek here and never lose.'

Dixie forced a smile as an aide tapped him on the shoulder and whispered something in his ear. Damon turned to me at the same moment.

'This guy here,' he jabbed a champagne flute in Dixie's direction, 'is going to be calling the shots in the new company.'

'Yeah?' I said.

'And I'll obviously be working with him a lot and maybe – just maybe – we can start squeezing you into a few things. Maybe,' he shrugged the shrug of the well-meaning.

'So,' said Dixie, returning to the conversation with a vengeance, 'what's your game, Paul?'

'Pete. I write stuff for illiterates.'

'Pete writes for the music press.'

'And the *Chronicle*,' I added with studied indifference, 'between times.'

'And do you ever think about doing anything else?'

'Sometimes . . . between times.'

The *Chronicle* was responsible, actually, for my growing sense of foreboding. The story was supposed to be in print in a few weeks' time – and I had a rough draft ready – but somehow it felt too anti-climactic. There should be flags waving or something. Why was my big surprise shaping up to be such a surprise? Maybe because I'd been ordered to keep quiet and had told virtually no one – which is also what my instincts told me to do. I'd been ripped off a hundred times through opening my big mouth too early or too often. *Keep it quiet and keep it locked*, I told myself, *just keep it locked . . .*

The skunk had had its warm glow reduced by my fourth champagne and the fact that I'd run out of charlie. Days ago. And I knew that this, being ad-land, meant that every other guy there was sniffing like a dog but not offering any around. And Damon, to make matters worse, wasn't interested in the stuff. So no one was approaching us. Except the people who counted – the boss man Dixie – and they didn't count. They'd never be seen taking stuff. Leastways, not when the juniors were around.

'Have you seen our new offices, Peter?'

'No. Where are they?'

'Greek Street – Damon, why don't you bring him down Thursday, we'll grab a drink then.'

'Fine.'

Dixie went into conference with his aide – *his* aide, like he owned him – as Damon and I had turned back to face the rest of the room. Someone waved and strolled over. He turned out to be a runner named Rolly, whose friend was chopping them out in the toilets as we spoke. Chopping out lines of charlie. Within seconds I'd made my excuses and left the main room. I scored a fat line and returned, soaring unevenly, a few minutes later. Damon had gone – 'He just had an urgent phone call. Said he'd see you Thursday' – but Rolly stuck around and he was, on reflection, pretty good company. He'd been running for six months and now knew more than most of the producers and directors who sent him on his errands. He'd be up there soon. But it would take a few years. The overnight-success industries always made you wait years.

'I mean, I had this shoot the other day,' he said, 'and they'd spent three hours trying to get this smoke gun to work. So I said, "Forgive me for butting in, but I was thinking, couldn't we use dry ice instead?" and so the producer screams, "You are not paid to think! So don't! Don't think – just think on your own time. Not mine, all right?"'

'Charming.'

'And then someone else mentions all this to the director and he loves the idea so the producer says, "Yeah, I thought you might like that." Like it was his idea.'

'That's terrible,' I said, 'but it happens all the time, y'know?'

'Yeah.'

'So is your job stable in this merger?'

'God knows. See if I'm still there on Thursday . . . Runners and receptionists and whoever, well, we're like the civil service in some dictatorship. You never know if the new regime is gonna like you. Whenever there's a merger, or someone big resigns and leaves, you're always left waiting. Just waiting. You're enjoying taking it easy but also knowing that that means you might be for the chop. I'll see what happens next.'

All of which made me think. *We'll be living in a truly civilised place – and the crime and suicide rates will be even lower than they were twenty years ago – when unknowns can get interviewed on TV and radio. Talking about their own lives and dreams and hopes. And those who can mock them, don't. Because wealth and power would be irrelevant and because everyone would be too fucking considerate. We are all equal now! The ordinary made extraordinary.* Some hope . . .

'Got any more charlie, Rolly?'

He said no, then launched into some doomy tale about a fellow runner. This other runner had done well, had become an assistant director, was on the up-and-up. Then he started doing serious amounts of coke and next thing he's dealing a bit on the

QT. Then he decides to forget the assistant-directing lark. A month later he turns up with holes in his jeans, asks to borrow a tenner. The next week he's found shot dead. Another victim of sniffing, swinging London. Another victim of the Essex dealers he owed money too. You had to know the right people. You had to be able to handle it. To handle *them*, both coke and London, or stay well away. Because this – the modern world – had become really quite dangerous. Sleepy London town wasn't sleepy any more, it rocked all night, every night, the same beat slamming out of every jeep, every club, shebeen, speakeasy and rave. 'Curfew, curfew,' sang the teenage girls, wailing like sirens, 'ya gotta go go go . . .'

21

Are You From The BBC?

That Thursday things had started well but then very rapidly went downhill. I had breezed into the Eye, Fink, Fink & Jones office at eleven, gracefully accepted a glass of chilled wine from Rolly, then joined a lounge lizard – still discreetly snarling – in a stretch limo which headed north. The lounge lizard had a tan that would have shamed mustard and he had a Rolex – fake – dangling off each chubby wrist, but he refused to say more than a few grunts so I soon gave up too. But what, I couldn't help asking myself, was going on? Why the limo? I could only assume that young Damon had set it all up for me.

The lounge lizard got out at Highgate and wordlessly waved the car on.

'Where are we going?' I asked the chauffeur after we'd been driving another ten minutes.

'Willesden.'

Huh? Willesden? After going down a B-road, the limo rolled along an endless concrete drive before pulling up beside a vast, seemingly derelict warehouse. The driver smartly leapt out and opened the door for me. For one minute I thought he was actually going to salute. *What is going on?* I thought. *What is it?*

There were several steel ramps leading up to a first-floor loading bay. Inside the place was even bigger than it looked. There was an ageing full-size diesel train – I'm not kidding – stuck on a hundred yards of track which ran through the middle of this huge industrial cathedral. The ceiling, which you could hardly see, was eight or nine storeys high. You couldn't tell exactly how high because there was nothing to compare it with. No floors. No overheads. Just a ten-yard-wide balcony – complete with overhead crane – which jutted out from one wall. I walked towards the balcony's stone steps as I studied the figures who were up there. The first people I noticed were four girls at the top of the steps. All of them were wearing those ultra-trendy black painter's smocks, wearing them as micro dresses so short you could see the tops of the stockings. Which you simply *had* to wear with them. The four girls there were all wearing the full ensemble, along with matching bra tops, which struck me as being just too sexy to be any kind of trend-setting coincidence. Maybe they'd been ordered to wear those outfits – which took the fun out of it all, in a way. Or maybe this was some kind of advertising sex orgy. Unlimited licence, like some Warhol porno film.

As I reached the top, one of the girls gave me a tiny gold train – and it was real gold, it had that weight – and pointed towards some blue-lit banqueting tables. I'd always known that Damon had style, but this was ridiculous. I looked around but couldn't see him in the throng of dark suits and checked lumberjack shirts that clustered around the far end of the tables. After drinking some white wine, I decided to inspect one of the glossy leaflets that were lying around. They informed me of the unlimited studio-office-nightclub possibilities of this site – *Willesden as the next Covent Garden* – now that Eye Eye Fink plc owned it. Willesden wouldn't be the next Covent Garden. It probably wouldn't even be the next Willesden. But so what? Someone might have had fun trying, eh? And it *was* a good idea. The place was too amazing to be left to crumble – though a part of me wanted it to be left old and rusting so I could re-discover it, as a ten-year-old kid, because it would be a good place to play . . .

I was about halfway through my second wine when I noticed two things almost simultaneously. The first was that one of the gold-train girls was wearing those big wedge shoes with transparent soles that are filled with heavy blue water. Except it wasn't water because it moved much too slowly. There must have been some kind of chemical in there that made it move like it was in slow-motion, like a wave machine. And then I saw that one of the girls looked like Anna. Well, she did look like Anna from behind. Which made me depressed and elated at the same time, re-opening my battered heart. I was depressed because I thought I'd never get near Anna, and yet elated because I knew I just might have a chance – it wasn't impossible. And what about Sally? Oh God . . .

I poured myself a vodka then schmoozed into the crowd as someone was telling his personal assistant about the gold trains – 'They're twenty-four carat, these things, must be worth a hundred pounds! Dixie's really pushing the boat out today!' – while someone else was announcing that there were no journos present: 'They're not invited, not this time, not till the big launch.' *No journos?* I thought. *Then what the hell am I doing here?* Maybe I was here about a job. Maybe Damon had set all that up. I had intended to ask him but he wasn't to be seen anywhere. I finally whispered the relevant question to a lumberjack.

'Is Damon around?'

'You're joking, aren't you? He left two days ago.'

'Left? Where's he gone then?'

'Headhunted. Burning Lens have got him.'

'Oh, right . . .'

'Were you here to see him?'

'Well,' I played for time, 'that was only part of it . . .'

'But who actually invited you then? Surely Damon would've told you he'd gone?'

I looked around. Oh God, James Dean help me. What was my *motivation* for this scene? Avoiding the ligger's ultimate nightmare. Avoiding it at all costs. That was my motivation. To avoid being beaten up, manhandled, insulted. The fear of being caught out. And at somewhere straight too. The shame of it all. And the repercussions. They'd probably call the police, try and sue me under some industrial espionage act . . .

My roving eye finally settled on the big Eye-Fink boss man, Dixie, who was busy thumping his way up the stone steps. Which gave me my exit.

'You're right. This *is* getting insane. If Damon didn't invite me then who did? . . . I'm gonna ask Dixie.'

I tore myself away and, stopping only to pocket another couple of trains – *How can you steal a freebie? You can't, right? Right!* – headed for the girls by the balcony exit. I nodded at Dixie as I skipped through the girls and on down the steps. As I struck out across the warehouse's endless floor I could feel eyes boring into me. I turned back to see the lumberjack talking to Dixie. They were both staring at my retreating figure. I glanced back again as I neared the ramp. Now they had some Group Grid security guard with them. Someone was pointing and someone else was wielding something. A walkie-talkie. I forced myself not to run as I moved down the ramps. How to get out of here fast? The drive was about three miles long and I'd be trespassing every step of the way, waiting with bated breath for the ad-zecs to set the hounds on me. I jumped into the limo, which woke the snoozing chauffeur with a start.

'Can you take me back to town?'

'Er . . . now, guv?'

'Yeah, cheers. If you can.'

'Course.'

As the limo moved off, a Group Grid storm-trooper came stomping down the ramps, throwing his arms around like an opera singer.

'Is he waving at you, guv?'

'No, that's just Jim, he always mucks around like that,' I lied as we sped away.

I was high for about ten minutes. I'd got away with it. And then I thought, *So what? Big fucking deal. A bellyful of champagne and a few give-aways. So what?* The suits I'd just left behind made more dosher in a month than I did in a year. I was no longer a kid, the big three-oh was looming up in my sights, filling the cross-hairs. I blasted away on the trigger but the years just kept on coming. Your life goes into fast-forward when you hit your twenties. Twenty-four, twenty-five, twenty-six, twenty-seven. When you're ten, a year is ten per cent of your life so far. When you're twenty-five, a year is down to just four per cent. Faster and faster. Older and older – the clubs nowadays had thousands of punters who were thirty. Or thirty-five. Or even older. And you couldn't blame them. Music, drugs, clothes, clubs – what else was there? And yes, my big story was coming together but it was all taking so long. And I didn't have long – my clock was up and running, running faster than anyone else's, and soon the time-bomb would go off.

22

Which Is The Way
That's Clear?

I had arrived at the Electric Ballroom early. Before ten-thirty. I wouldn't normally turn up there at that time, but I'd phoned Jeff and he said it was an all-ticket night and to be there early.

I was still wearing my dark blue suit and tie from the afternoon, when I'd packed Sally off to her last sculpture class. And it was a sweet suit, the pride of 1959, but I still felt a bit conspicuous. But there I was anyway, in the Ballroom, in Camden, walking through the echoing foyer and on to the deserted dance-floor as a Garage House beat smashed out of the huge speakers. That place can take two thousand kids. With just me walking around it seemed a trifle empty, though it did remind me of my days club-running. It was the time when warehouse parties and speakeasies were blurring into the first raves. The dealers were then mainly shifting speed, grass and E and they were all, as Wiganovski will tell you, well popular. Characters who were always full of back-chat, full of street wit, always ready to haggle – 'you're taking the bread outa my kids' mouths' – and always looking quite sharp. Dealers in clubs had been the loveable knaves then, they'd since graduated to being the jokers and now, with all the powders, they were well on their way to being the kings . . . Drugs are so powerful now. In dozens of estates they're all-powerful. You can see their sheer influence by just looking at how they turned Manchester's Madchester scene into a gold mine. Then other north-west towns started their own E-based raves. E-asy profits became that little bit harder to get. And then the 1990 recession kicked in and things got *really* nasty. From being dealer heaven, the dope boys were forced to fight for a smaller slice of a diminishing cake. Guns got bought and used. One night all the bouncers at the Hace were shot and wounded, all because they'd ejected a couple of dealers. Later some teenagers had died in crossfire in Moss Side. Madchester to Gunchester in a few short years: all down to the recession, and drugs.

I caught a glimpse of myself in one of the dark, nicotine-stained mirrors. The suit looked okay, a bit Steve Brown. He was doing clubs at the same time as I was. And Steve was – and to an extent still is – usually recognised by his trade-mark quiff: part Elvis, part Tony Curtis. Steve's Giant club was huge, his Pig night bought home the bacon and his Nirvana was, for a time, bigger than the rock group, but it's his warehouse nights I remember most. After one, I wandered into his bedroom to find him lying on his bed, fully clothed, dozing and literally covered in ten- and twenty-pound notes.

I shot my cuffs and kept walking, listening to Jeff belting it out. But, looking closer, it wasn't just him and me in the place. There were half a dozen girls gathered around the DJ's platform. And one was Anna. One was Anna. Every single thing seemed to fling us together.

I hurried to the DJ's box as slowly as I could and saw that one of the girls had a camera. She aimed it at me and I threw an arm over my face like I always do – I'm as ugly as the average guy and, besides, I prefer it if there's no evidence of where

I am – just in case. A second later I was next to Anna. She was wearing a Lycra item in black that only just covered her salient points. Every female clubber seemed to dress like she was in some sort of highly-charged strip-club. Not that I was complaining.

'Pete, how ya going?' she said, kissing me and squeezing my hand, confident and friendly – just like a girlfriend. There was something between us. There *was*.

'I'm going all right, Sweet Thing, what you doing here?'

'We're having some photos took. For *0171*.' It was a London mag. They did fashion and stuff.

'Who are your friends?'

'We're all in the same dance class.'

'I thought you danced pretty good anyway,' I said, as if I'd seen her dance a hundred times before. 'How come you're doing lessons?'

'You can always get better.' She looked around. 'I was hoping our trainer could make it. You'd like him.'

Jeff turned away from the 1210 decks and gave me a hand-shake before leaning in. He peered at the bags under my eyes.

'You should try taking it easy,' he said, 'all whizz and no play made Pete a dull boy.'

I shrugged. What can you say? I was still trying to think of some smart-ass reply when Anna spoke up again.

'Jeff, you've definitely gotta play some of the old stuff now Pete's here,' said Anna.

'I ain't that old,' I tried to protest, but she cut me off with a glancing grin.

'Dunno what you mean,' said Jeff, deadpan, 'I get all my records from the library. After listening to OneFM. Don't you girls follow the pops?'

'Come on, Jeff, I'm talking Mud club here, you know what I mean,' she pouted. Jeff shrugged and went back to his turntables.

'Is that a yes or a no?' she asked me.

'Don't ask me, babe,' I shrugged. Her eyes showed a hint of fire. *She likes getting her own way*, I thought, as the Jackson

Sisters' classic 'I Believe In Miracles' juddered into life. As soon as Anna's gang heard the staccato opening bars of blasting brass, they gave out a kind of collective school-girl shriek. This is what they wanted, and they descended on to the empty dance-floor *en masse*. And there they did their thing as the girl with the camera snapped away as if her life depended on it. And their collective thing was worth photographing. They all had it, especially Anna, they all knew the record note for note. Every bass slap, every snare crack, every vocal chorus, and they danced it to perfection. True modern grace, performed with the kind of skill that, if seen in ballet or proper contemporary dance, would win awards. Lots of shoulder pushing, spins and neat little disco steps. Turns and half-turns, pirouettes and pouts, hands slipping behind backs and the occasional head-toss. It was perfect – nearly. Before Anna had danced I'd still been half-thinking about Sally, but halfway through the record I found myself on the edge of the dance-floor, just to be closer. Anna shuffled over, tried to get me to dance. She was half-hearted about it – her performance was the thing – but the way she tugged at my tie and swivelled up around me and back, well, that was worth a month in the country too.

A few minutes later we were propping up the bar together. Me and Anna.

'So why haven't you called recently?'

'I dunno why,' I said. I decided it was time to change up a gear. 'How long have you been in this country? If you don't mind me asking.'

'A few years. Why?'

'You just seem to know a few records from way back, 1989, 1990, '91.'

'I'm old, Pete, haven't you noticed?'

'If you're old then I'm already dead, babe.'

'Drama queen. You're as young as the woman you feel.' She gave off a low-down dirty chuckle and looked away, her eyes gleaming sceptically. Why had she looked away? And why was she looking like that?

'I thought only men said vile sexist things like that.'

'Only men like you, Pete.' Huh?

'I don't know what you mean, Mother Superior,' I said, trying to laugh it off.

'Yes, you do. What about that eighteen-year-old you're always going around with? The punky one you never bring to anything?'

I was stunned. Sally was nineteen – actually – but how did Anna know about her? And how did someone who was maybe twenty-two or twenty-three years old manage to make eighteen sound like an age that requires a pram?

'That's all over,' I declared. 'She's just . . . a bit of a head-case, to be frank. So she has to be let down gently.'

'Is that right?' she said, with the amused arched eye-brows of one *who knows the score.* 'Gently?'

'Yeah, because I'm such a warm, wonderful human being.'

'Oh yeah?'

'Yeah. Well, that is the score. I *am* ending the situation.' I had exaggerated, but only slightly. 'It's not that important.'

'No?'

'No. Should I be saying this to a married woman like your-self?'

'I'm not actually married,' she smiled. 'Didn't you know?'

'No. Want another drink?'

'Are you trying to get me drunk?'

'Er . . . yes.'

'Oh, okay then.'

I ordered them as my imagination went into manic over-drive. She wanted a large Scotch and American, and virtually knocked it back in one.

'You should be a journalist,' I blathered, staring at her already empty glass, 'with your wrist action.'

'No, I couldn't be. I wouldn't like meeting people.'

'No?'

'No. I've met too many people,' she said with finality. 'And to be honest with you, I don't really like people. As a rule.'

'Nor do most reporters, so that doesn't rule you out.'

'No, there'd be too many problems . . . especially as there's one or two journos I fancy.'

Is this a come-on or what? Note the careful use of the plural. One or two. Ambiguous to the last. But when I was a certain age, that would have been a green light, the big go-code. And she had used the word 'fancy'. *Anything for the weekend, sir?* I edged my bar stool closer as she sucked her lemon-peel dry.

'What you up to later then?'

'I'm going home,' she said brightly, ending the party mood. 'In fact, I've gotta go in a few minutes.'

'So, Cinderella, when will I see you again?' I faked a half-yawn as I spoke – no point appearing eager, is there?

'I dunno when. Why don't you call me? . . . Vee's always out in the afternoons.'

Huh? *Vee's out in the afternoons?* What was that all about? *Here it is, come and get it, boy?* Yes and no. Her goodbye kiss slipped from my cheek and pushed into the warmth of our mouths. I felt one of my arms slip around her waist. My other hand was pushing her soft curves against my chest. As if we were making love. Our saliva mingled and she had that taste, that cocaine taste – she must have had some charlie at some point too – but my coke had been too little, too early, and the Bromide effect was thus incomplete. So I began to steam up a little at the nearness of her. Began to steam up *a lot*. Sex need overwhelmed me – I wanted her.

Certain types of hangovers make you feel more sexually charged than is healthy in a democratic society, and as our tongues touched, teased and inter-mingled I could feel my heart pump as my back started to perspire. A trace element of her Scotch trickled down my throat. We had something there. Passion, and longing and lust and maybe – just maybe – there was love in there too. But other thoughts were busy raising their ugly, unrepentant, uncircumcised heads. *We wanna be alone now.* I wanted her so much, *so very much.* Could I bundle her into a nearby hotel? Or Regents Park? Or even backstage? *No, no, no and no*, I told myself. *Don't force it.*

Anna put her hands on my arms and softly pushed as she pulled her tongue away.

'I have to go,' she breathed, her Scotch and perfume words making me weak with desire. 'So . . . call me, huh?'

And then she was gone, leaving me gagging on air.

23

Lost In The Skin Mine

There was a FAB song playing on the radio. It seemed to comment on the situation. After a chilling intro – cool 'oohs' and 'aahs' coming in from the backing vocalists – over a dramatic staccato beat, you got these words being sung by that guy who sounds like a hybrid of Bowie and George Michael:

Am I a face like all the others?
Should we just lie in silence, hypnotised?
Maybe one day I will recover . . .
Am I erased like all the others?
Travelled the world in this room a hundred times
Afraid that one day I will discover . . .

It must be from the point of view of a hooker, right? Singing from the depths of some brothel, right? Right. And wrong. Because then this electric chorus leapt out and you realise that, yes, it is from the whore's point of view but the words are also being uttered by some lonely punter as well – it's his song too.

Meanwhile I sell myself from nine to five
Meanwhile I dig myself this gold;
You got your labour of love and I got mine,
Then it's all over and I'm so cold . . .

Who's zooming who? I turned to look at Sally as she slowly dressed. That was part of the show too. *Who's zooming who?* This has to end. She'd been sitting on the bed, barely arrived, when she'd asked for some coke. No coke. Well, almost no coke. And then some of her own hash. Me feeling like a punter and her thinking like a hooker when I unzipped. All very fast action. *Solid gold easy action.* Brutal. *Keep that one on. Pull that off. Lean that way. Now.* She responded. She always did. This has to be the last time. I noticed – why hadn't I seen it before? – that Sally's T-shirt had the touching slogan 'Mind Fuck Baby' on it. Mind Fuck Baby? Damned right. This has to be the last time. I hadn't even wanted this, not tonight, when my mind was elsewhere. (With Anna.) But she was probably sleeping with Vee now so . . . so I got to make it with Sally – thus making everything worse.

But maybe I was being too hard on myself. I had tried to help Sally in the immediate past – and I would in the future – but if Anna was available . . . I hadn't felt that way about a woman since . . . God knows. But I would help Sally if I could; I just didn't know how. And I probably didn't have the time, not with the *Chronicle* stuff – I'd seen the roughs, 'SCAL-LIES SUPERGROUP IN MUSIC PRESS COCAINE SHOCKER!' and they'd looked terrific – not with Anna and everything else. I had thousands coming now – money. At last, at long fucking last.

'So . . . are you going to come to the party or not?' Sally asked me with a toss of her head. It was a decision I'd been avoiding for days, maybe weeks. It certainly felt like weeks. A party was something I'd leap at, even an art student's ball, normally. But if I went, it would just make things worse. And, besides, I had to ring Anna. 'Call me,' she'd breathed.

What else could I do?

Sally pushed me with her elbow, wanting an answer.

'No. I can't make it. Sorry.'

'You *are* joking, aren't you?'

'I mean, I can't promise anything, Sal,' I said as I opted for the subtle approach. 'But I'll try. I *will* try . . .'

I had to say that. Sing something simple. Say something compromising. Nearly all of us do because we're forced into it. None of us gets to write our own dialogue, not at this level, anyhow. We can't afford to say rude truths, not here. You only get the chance to do that later – up where you can say what you like – but only when you no longer need to say it. Only a deaf and dumb man wants to speak all the time, and that's only because he can't.

I thought how perfect this would all be – she'd meet some shoe-gazing idiot at the end-of-term party; they'd cop off. She had seemed to accept my indecision, though I figured that she half-knew the truth. It wasn't going to last: end of one problem; start of another. Another problem for me – namely, what do I do on Mondays and Wednesdays now? Anna seemed like an impossible dream now she wasn't in the same room as me. What to do? Ring her now or later . . . now or later . . . now or later . . .

24

This Dope Is Dope

You had to try and switch, if you had any sense, between charlie and dope. Or even from charlie to dope. Dope made you a part of the whole, whereas coke made you think you *were* the whole. You were it. These two attitudes aren't mutually exclusive, but most of the time, the second option seems to be the one you want. *Coke, I am it!* Whereas the first is probably the one you really need. Especially with the dope I'd just taken; this stuff was mind-blowingly strong. Drinking was great with it. Even passing water was a stunning experience. Comparable with, and as pleasurable as, some big-deal *Cosmo*-type orgasm. You could feel the liquid going through all the tubes before it then made the testicles tremble with a kind of passing subtle glow. Drinks were just as sensational. Any kind of drink. Even the weakest cold spritzer washed around your mouth like some effervescent electric ice. The nicest taste in the world ever, ever, ever. The earth moved, as they say.

'This dope is dope, you know?'

And it was nice, quietly inhaling more and more of it while watching some politician's baby-oil face shining unhealthily. He was on TV, trying to attack corruption abroad while

173

down-playing it here . . . Meanwhile the effect of the draw I'd absorbed got heavier and heavier. The TV sound got more and more distorted. Was the guy speaking in stereo – his voice double-tracked like some rock'n'roll chorus – or had Barry somehow wired his TV into an echo chamber via the hi-fi? I turned the TV sound down and tried to concentrate on Barry's conversation, but it kept getting lost too. His phrases began to spread out, like a scattered herd of buffalo galloping across some wide equatorial plain – only the last few words were visible, like the nearest few buffalo in my mind's eye. Too long inhaling the bong. Too pooped to pop. Too skunked to punk. Which still left me wondering, just why had Barry ended his sentence, '. . . and if it was anyone in the world, it was Chewy Louie'.

Why had he said that? And why did he have a quiet smile on his face? Was that look irony? Pride? Amusement? I closed my eyes and looked around at my fictional buffalo herd. They were slowing down now, some of them starting to graze, all of them happy to have escaped Buffalo Bill's one-man holocaust. I tried to work it out. But even at this slower speed, as I attempted to count these animals, these words, another couple of them shot past me. I opened my eyes. Barry was happy. And I was happy. I had taken a decision. An executive decision. Decided to knock the coke on the head. Yeah, knock it on the head one hundred per cent. Time to chill, at least for a few months. No more charlie. No more white lies, no more white lines.

Weed, dope and even skunk were natural phenomena. They just grew out of the ground. A gift from Mother Earth, if you treated it right, and that's why it was healthier. Maybe fresh coca leaves, if you chewed them like some Bolivian tin-miner, would have the same effortless purity, but I'd never had them. They only grew in South America and it wasn't legal to export them. Not since they took the cocaine out of Coca-Cola (it really was the Real Thing once, that's why it became the world's best-selling drink back when Great War officers legally received Lick Me! postage stamps that had been soaked in coke – every legal thing the toffs do gets banned when it filters down to scum like us – funny that, isn't it?). To take coca leaves out of the area illegally now wasn't viable either, unfortunately: too bulky; not worth the risk. So we only got the leaves once they'd been smashed into paste and then petrol-filtered into powder with a good few chemicals slipped through them. To make them into cocaine. But you had no choice. Correction. Yes you did, you just knocked it on the head, like I was going to tonight.

I redoubled my efforts to understand Barry's speech. He was criticising me, mildly, saying how I dressed sharp but thought sloppy. Whereas he was a perfectionist in thought and deed.

'Me and my loose anarchy,' I slurred, 'are perfect for you and your perfectionism.'

He laughed.

'We have a laugh, eh mate?' I asked.

'Yeah, but not together . . .'

I'd asked for that one. He laughed again but his heart wasn't in it. Then he gave me a cock-eyed look as the drink got into him like poison. Seconds later he was getting uptight. Just a little. Just verbally. He'd never lay a finger on me, but he pushed his luck verbally. Bouncers and doormen had abused him and thrown him out of one or two places before now because of his lip. He didn't struggle with them; physically, he was a coward, he said. He was proud of that and he announced it bravely. And that was the reason he always pushed his luck verbally. If push came to shove, his tongue would keep schtum. But push didn't come to shove usually, so he got away with walking his own particular tightrope.

Barry's mouth is moving again. What now? Now he's talking about another of his former flames. A brief two-week fling which started on rocky ground and fell apart after he met her uptight feminist mother. Except, Baz thinks, the mother wasn't really a militant feminist. She was just feeling a bit neglected . . .

'The weird thing is,' he announces with a sick grin, 'if I'd made a discreet play for the mother, if I'd secretly laid her, she'd have encouraged her daughter to see me. Even to marry me . . . that's funny, isn't it? I would have had to hump the mother in order to marry the daughter.'

'That's gross.'

'Nah . . . not really,' says Barry, thinking about it seriously for the first time, 'lots of people I know would probably have gone for it – maybe even I might have, if I'd known it at the time. If she'd spelt it out in so many words.'

'I've never got it on with someone I didn't fancy.'

'That proves what I've always thought. Underneath it all, Pete, you're shallow.'

'Yep.'

'Do you know what I'd like?'

'I dread to think, but carry on . . .'

'I'd just like, once, of an evening, to walk in here and hear myself on Radio 1.'

'OneFM.'

'Whatever. Or Virgin . . .' I'd heard this before somewhere. I think we all have. Jim Didn't Fix It for me.

'Dream on.'

'Just to know that one of my songs had finally got played coast-to-coast in my own country. So a few million of my fellow countrymen could finally hear one of my songs. Just once. Just for three minutes. My family hearing it. It's not that much to ask, is it?'

'Yes, it is.'

'Fuck off.'

'You're a talented lad, young Bazza—'

'Fuck off.'

'—and that talent, and ninety pence, will get you one small cup of coffee.'

'Fuck *off*,' he snarled half-heartedly.

'I'm only kidding, kid.'

I got back home late, still reeling. Five messages on the

ansafone. Two from Sally . . . seems she'd found a few people to go to the party with but she'd rather I made it. I'd rather I could make it too, but I couldn't, not without making my fractured life even more complicated.

25

The Dream Dump

The Dream Dump – famed for its tranny waiters – was the setting for the next naff night. I'd phoned Anna three times that afternoon and hadn't left a message on the first two occasions, just in case Vee heard it and took it the right way. But, third time lucky, we'd spoken and she said she just might swing through the West End – and drop down the Dream Dump. She couldn't promise anything but . . .

The Dump was promoting some clear rum – and some crap House album – by giving it away. The catch being that you had to suck up the rum as it was poured through some male torsos made of ice. And the rum emerged via the ice man's dick. Real witty stuff, huh? There were plenty of takers, of course, since there's now an awful lot of desperate, skint liggers around. But it was still kinda disturbing. Outside we'd all stepped over homeless kids sleeping rough in pools of lager piss, and inside, fat bankers dressed as French maids – probably the same fat bankers who'd help start the recession in the first place – were gawking and giggling as hungry liggers performed frozen blowjobs. Many of those transsexuals present had actually had the op, which I didn't object to, but some had done it on the NHS – which I did find kinda weird. There were kids dying on hospital waiting lists – and pensioners who'd fought for this country who were on NHS blacklists – and millions of pounds of public money was spent on helping people castrate themselves. I know some of 'em say they'll go all suicidal without the op but so what? That's a psychiatric matter. What if thousands of us suddenly got obsessed with Long John Silver? Would billions then be spent cutting off our right legs and removing our left eyes?

One of the overweight trannies had given some young crustie a huge acid-smack cocktail. The kid was swaying around in front of the bar and cringing, really cringing, wide-eyed with horror, every time someone came anywhere near him. God knows what he was seeing. What I was seeing was vile enough. They take the bread and we provide the circus. The cheque-book Czars ruled supreme . . . so Orwell wasn't quite right about the future, it was actually going to be a *designer* jackboot grinding into a human face, for ever. Exploitation, writ large. It was like all those East End pubs near the City that were now full of teenage boys obviously there to service the sex needs of the pin-striped money wizards – a little Bangkok right in the heart of London, and one that no TV reporter or broadsheet hack will rush to expose. But that wasn't my problem. My only real problem was the delay in the story's appearance – legal reasons, the lawyers were fussing again but Maurie swore there was nothing to worry about – all of which was driving me quietly insane. I couldn't cry on Sally's shoulder about it without making things worse when . . . when what? When Anna left Vee? Dream on.

I drank a few then used someone else's coke to pull me round – I only had a line, honestly. I figured it was just another harmless night out, another wasted evening being wasted. Some drunks from the weeklies were there, sneering – one of the idiots was throwing ice cubes around and caught me with one in the face – but I didn't retaliate, feeling strong with my little secret. My secret that was gonna blow their cosy world apart. *I'll finally tell Anna the secret tonight*, I decided. It would be a weight off my tiny mind.

Later, after I'd given up on Anna, I knocked back four doubles in minutes and wandered out. There were half a dozen kids outside the Soho So-Good drinking club. Three of those outside were girls and one was truly beautiful. She seemed to stand slightly apart from the others, like she wasn't really with them. Maybe she wasn't. As I strode towards them, the fact that, drug-wise, I was soaring sideways inside made me chance a glance at her. She returned it. I looked again. She was staring back, giving me a subtle smile, pushed herself towards me a little. I couldn't believe it, it was too good to be true, that kind of thing hadn't really happened to me since I was twenty-one. And, of course, it wasn't true.

'Hiya,' she said with direct discretion, like we had a shared secret, 'do you wanna girl?'

'Maybe, maybe,' I blathered as I realised that she was a hooker.

'Only ninety for the night.'

For ninety quid I want three-course sex with Kate Moss – and she wasn't for sale.

'Nah, I don't think so, honey.'

'You're cute, how about fifty-five?' She said it in a friendly way, which was something of a rarity, English whores normally being like our pubs – cold, expensive and unfriendly.

'Sorry, babe, but . . .' my voice trailed off as I thought *but what*?

'But what, babe?' she asked with what I took to be a professional smile. And then it hit me: the question I had to ask myself. Did I really look that desperate? Yes, I probably did. Correction, I *know* I did. Anna's non-appearance had knocked me for six. I'd been so certain that we were, or would eventually become, an item, so certain that she would turn up – but no, she hadn't.

I smiled feebly and kept walking past the hooker beauty as a depressive paranoia overwhelmed me. In the junkie gardens behind the cinema in Charing Cross Road I stopped to get some air in my lungs and enjoy the near silence. I looked up at Centre Point, that big majestic waste of space that had looked down on so many of my triumphs and failures. Sammy, the last girl I had lived with, had really wanted us to get it on there . . . It was after she'd dragged me to see Daniel Ortega, the red president of Nicaragua when they still had such a thing. He was speaking in a hall in Westminster because his country was under attack from the Contras. It was the new Spanish Civil War, but because it wasn't called 'The New Spanish Civil War', in quotes – and because it wasn't in Spain – the powers-that-be just couldn't see it. Everyone thought it was a little bit of a joke, most of the time.

But, as I found out that night, it wasn't a joke – real people were dying in big numbers. There were pictures from the Red Cross and Amnesty, kids with legs missing . . . from outside you could still hear the jeers of Tory students – 'Greaseball go home! Sandinista-IRA!' – and there were cops patrolling the aisles like Dobermans, looking for a fight, when Ortega finally got up to make his speech. And he was magnificent, electrifying, as he begged, beseeched and finally demanded that Reagan's Contras stopped slaughtering his people. The Working Week jazzers made a Latin House record of it, 'Eldorado', which was incredible. It had that pounding House piano – when it was still fresh – and the sound of the crowd roaring Ortega on and on and floating over it all was some sublime Latin diva, singing her heart out, as if communication alone could somehow make a difference. That record gave off enough passion to power the entire national grid. Even now, if it doesn't move you, then check your pulse, you may be dead. The record flopped, of course, since it wasn't meaningless enough for the House mafia and to OneFM its radical meaning was all too clear, but it was still great, still made Sam cry when she was drunk. Sam was very beautiful and very right-on but she'd made my life hell in the end. Never live with a victim, not ever; they win every time. 'I'm doing you a favour,' she'd said when she finally dumped me, and it had taken me years to see just how true that was.

I was better off now, I tried to tell myself, but the truth kept bubbling up to the front of my mind. The truth was that I had no one, I had nothing, not really. A story, maybe. My one consolation . . . but what was a story, in the end? Just a bit of paper, and this bit of paper – the forthcoming big break, *when* it finally came out – was going to take me away from the music work that I still secretly loved, probably take me away from it for ever . . .

I'd cleared the decks for Anna and the big story and now neither seemed to be happening – despite the cash advance I'd already half-spent, despite the kiss that I could still feel on my lips . . . I was going nowhere, fast, without her. I needed some coke. I needed Anna.

26

Every City Has Its Soho

'*Every city has its Soho, London more than most. It's a condition, an addiction, an affliction. It's that one area that manages to be both in the middle of town and on the edge of it – the edge of town being the place where some of the more questionable practices of the modern, and ancient, world are still tolerated (I use the word ancient because the world's oldest trade still struts its funky junkie stuff there – either that or I've got it wrong and there's a helluva lot of young-but-retired 'models' out there and all of them with a genuine burning desire to teach irregular French verbs to passing strangers). All-day drinking, all-night drinking. All-dayers, all-nighters, plus weekends that well and truly end a week the way it should be ended. With a bang, not a wimpy-burger. All bodily needs are catered for in Soho and – what with the drink, the drugs, the sex, the food, the hotels and the markets – you could actually live there. Some madmen do.*

Which is partly why Soho is the place where all the master symphonies are unfinished, where all the classic novels stay great notions – sometimes – and where the Big Town's big players invariably come to foolishly play their lives away. Bigtime. While bigger fools look on.

A place where some fine folk can't ever tread without being photographed or filmed or quoted or misquoted or lied to or spied upon or fêted or hated or laid, slayed and flayed. In other words, made. Soho makes some people, really makes them. The centre of attention, the centre of everything. While others live and die there without ever being noticed at all, by anyone – least of all by the bar staff and the nightclub door-men . . . London's Soho, the biggest, the oldest and – without a doubt – the ugliest and the prettiest on the planet, is bounded by the four circuses of St Giles, Piccadilly, Oxford and Cambridge (there's no escape from Oxbridge and the Oxbridge set, not in London anyhow, and not during those endless summer hols when you're sure to see many a don downing doubles of Jack Daniel's while keeping their blood-shot pupils firmly fixed on their ex-pupils – the heroes of the rowing class – as they prop up the bar and talk Channel 4 contracts).

Within these circuses operate many, many others. A vast array of musicians, night-owls, hustlers, boozers, losers and schmoozers. There are, naturally, all your usual big-top attrac-tions – OTT queens, clowns, showmen and scantily-clad showgirls are all present and incorrect as well as the trapeze, piste and piss·artists. There's blood and sawdust a-plenty too, because Soho, to define it, is the difference between a discus-sion and a fight; the difference between a tart and a good-time girl, the difference between a drinker and an alcoholic. Soho is, to simplify things further, the difference. It is, in English, the only night-time game in town.

And the object of this game without end, of Soho, is to get recognised, and then barred, from as many places as inhu-manly possible. And as often as possible, so you can become a kind of Unfreeman Of The City . . .'

Yeah, I know, it's somewhat overwritten. And in places it's as congested as the traffic that's constantly wrapped around Eros, but never mind, no one'll notice the difference. And those that do will probably love it. There's no accounting for tastelessness. The above ramblings are part of an intro for a *Young Americans' Guide to 1999 London* (Chapter Two: Soho). It's a book that's coming out next year but don't bother to look for my name on it because it's a ghoster. I'm ghost-writing it for A Well-Known Celeb. This Well-Known Celeb is thought of as being something of a wit; I know this because me and an ageing drunk in Gerrard Street write all his witticisms for him. And the Well-Known Celeb, Gawd bless him, pays cash in return for us giving him some prose sincerity. People are said to like his dense, overwritten style (or should that be *our* dense, overwritten style?) but he doesn't write stuff that often. Not because I, he and the Gerry Street drunk don't want to. *Au contraire*, we do, we most definitely do – the Celeb really enjoys ticking the pages and me and the merry Gerry gent could do with the wedge, but the big problem is the Celeb's agent. He doesn't want said Celeb to get 'over-exposed'. So these little ghost things are a rare opportunity. There's lots of discreet competition as there's dozens of starving hacks who'd give their eye-teeth to see their name in hardback (well, someone else's name, actually). And think of all that lovely lolly, which isn't that much when compared with the Celeb's royalty cheques but it's better than a candle-lit night in with the landlord . . . so I can't muck up this re-write. I can't afford to, basically.

I'd made things worse by returning at who-knows-when in the morning and spending the next three hours being a coke-head, i.e. writing crap as I zap-watched all-night TV. I've now re-written the Soho mess above half a dozen times. I'm now trying to stick an ending on it while wondering if I'm still writing anything like the truth about Soho, the inner-city village that's at sleaze with itself. I think it is true generally. Apart from the dons downing Jack Daniel's; that is a blatant exaggeration-stroke-lie. Such folk are far more likely to be tippling their gin-and-tonics in some country pub or quaffing their Quinine in the quads. Most of the rest is a true, if somewhat technicoloured, rendition.

And it is, after all, a big cliché that modern journos wouldn't know the truth if it came up and slapped them in the face. So I'm being true to this lie by slipping in the occasional lie. And even this talk about lies is a lie, because a lot of journos do know the truth, and some even care about it. And it's not just your big names who know that much. Even I know this much – the truth is always that part of the story you're not supposed to use. Either that or the bit you're not legally allowed to use. The public – you and sometimes me – never, therefore, get to see most of this truth stuff. In fact, thinking about it now, it is only hacks – them and sometimes me – who could give you, if they wanted, the whole truth and nothing but. The whole unvarnished, uncircumcised, blow-by-blowjob account of what, or who, has actually been going down. It's a truth that we often exchange, watching other people's dirty linen in private. This gossip circuit has been well-damaged by all the closures – and by all the moves to Wapping and Canary Wharf – but it still exists. In the endless alleys of Soho, in the champagne bars, private drinking dens and Members-Only clubs of the West End, it's still there. You can still get all the dirt, for the price of a few (dozen) drinks.

'*The endless alleys of Soho . . . an inner-city village at sleaze with itself . . .*' That's not bad – yeah, not good, but not too bad either. That just might do for the preamble to the last line. My last line. I'll be down to that soon. My last line of charlie. I swapped some more for some booties. A mate of Chas was holding. So soon I'd be down to my last ever line, and I'd give up. It's said that Freddie Mercury, the Queen queen, was spending fifteen hundred a day on coke at one point. Stuff allegedly bought for himself and friends. I'd never do that – for a start, I couldn't afford to. And I was an all-or-nothing character. I was going for it in a big way. Too much, too soon, too young. I'd kicked things before. I hardly smoked fags now and I hadn't had speed for months . . . so I was definitely going to give up the coke.

27

Am I A Face Like All The Others?

There are several different levels of sex, as you're no doubt aware. Jake once quantified them and came up with nine – count 'em – levels. The first level of this scale was, admittedly, kinda primitive. In fact, Level One is completely dismal sex of an unnatural order and is thus only indulged in by fifth-formers, art students, total strangers, long-distance lorry-drivers and those who have been living together for many years. Both partners are often completely off their faces, skunked as a drunk or even drunk as a skunk if they're traditionalists. But don't get Jake wrong about co-habitees. The latter group of lacklustre lovers can also enjoy a higher level – because that's the thing about getting it on. The same person can move between different levels, sometimes dragging their partner, or a partner, with them.

Level Two is when everyone is not quite so blasted, or bored, and he actually fancies him or her. Note that, *he* fancies him or her. I am afraid, Germaine darling, that it does *have* to be him, because if it's a her and the feeling is not reciprocated then Level Two operations are not going to proceed in any way, shape or form. And if she, and/or he number two, does not lust after their Level Two man in any way at all, then they are doing it because they like the guy or it's a good career move or whatever.

Now if they both fancy each other, then fine, we've humped our way up to Level Three and the three-course sex will be pretty dirty sweet for all concerned. And this means, thinking about it, that you don't have to think about it. Leastways, you don't have to consider the mechanicals too much. It just happens. Just as love laughs at locksmiths, so lust laughs at gear sticks, toilet locks, sleeping-bag zips, the arms of sofas and the fact that your Aunt Sophie is ill in the next room. Level Three also indicates, students of the bleedin' obvious, that we are much, much closer to Level Four, wherein one of the partners, and it can be either at this point, has a real heavy passion for the other. It also means they've already heavily hit Level Five coupling.

Six is when you've got levels two to five already burning inside you *and* – and this is a crucial bit for the very highest Levels – you also love the squeeze in question. It's a bit unsexy, in a way, to admit it, but love can add a certain something. Level Seven is when you love that person *and* it's all mutual. 'Now we are cooking with gas!' as Hungarian professors say. This means that the mains supply is on, the amp is hot and you've got sound coming out of both speakers. And as you've put the amp and speakers far too close together, the moving magnets are gonna produce some serious feedback. This feedback will be one continuous note of pleasure which'll make many of the younger elements dream of Level Eight.

Level Eight is when all the above criterion apply *and* you're actively *in love with them at that moment*. Actively 'in love'. Nothing has to be scripted, it all works with passion and compassion and lust and everything else. You've thrown in everything bar the kitchen sink, and then you've thrown in the kitchen sink. And then you've chucked in the factory that made the sink. And, of course, it's pretty damn hot even if your opposite number isn't actively *in love with you* at that moment. If they are *in luuurve with you at that moment* then you have reached the Full Monty – the legendary Level Nine. Congratulations, you have scaled Everest, spat in the eye of the tiger and conquered the north face of the Eiger. *I think we're alone now.* You are alone now, but alone together, see? The way it was meant to be. Or so Jake claimed, and who was I to disagree with one of Soho's greatest lovers?

I couldn't help wondering what level I'd get to with Anna, if any. If ever.

28

Anna And Me

Anna wriggled her shoulder against me. It was a dazzling bronzed TV advert of a shoulder with an equally perfect, equally bronzed stork-like arm attached to it. She was lying on my bed, on her back, with one naked leg stretched out and the other propped up, her left foot half-tucked under her prone right knee, moving her legs back and forth, shameless as a kitten. There were the most delicate, minute particles of perspiration on the short hairs that curled up where her flat stomach ended, and every little liquid bead was sparkling softly. The light that helped provide the hazy sparkle came from the sunlight filtering through my cheap and faded curtains. This filtered sunlight also made her eyes a shining chocolate-brown colour, as warm, pretty and glossy as some South Sea seashell. And, as I glanced down again, I saw the faint magical light also cast a tiny shadow within her neat tummy button. The latter looked so good that I wanted to cut it out and keep it. Which always feels like a funny feeling; admiring a woman's body after you've shared it with her. Because after the balloon's gone up once or, if you're real lucky, twice, there is simply no lust left. Not for an hour or two, at least. So then you can study a woman's frame with complete objectivity. For once. Not being attracted or repelled by them but just looking, just studying – I know artists are supposed to do that, but do me a favour. They wanted those bodies as much as anyone else. And this one, Anna's, was pretty damn exquisite. In fact, most of them are, in one way or another, if we're being honest, but this one here was also special because of what you couldn't see.

I returned my gaze to Anna's face. She was staring intently as her fingers tugged at one of the ringlets that framed her face. The drag was she was staring intently at me, which I find a bit of a downer sometimes. It was as bad as being on the phone to someone – nowhere to hide.

'You go on staring at my face like that and you're gonna make yourself sick.'

'Away with your nonsense,' she scathed, 'you look fine . . . men are supposed to look a bit rough.'

'Well, in that case, I qualify.'

'And I really like staring at your face.'

'You'll be sick as a dog.'

'And your eyes . . . they're such a deep shade of blue.'

And my eyes *are* blue. Well, the irises are blue, to be medically precise. They usually provide a nice bit of contrast with the bloodshot red that makes up the rest.

'Yeah, I'm a blue-eyed devil. A Saxon from way back, I'm afraid. No doubt about that. Not at all trendy and World Music-like . . . guilty as charged . . .'

'You're fucking loco, you are,' she said in soft, amused exasperation. 'Where do you think I'm from? In the dim and distant past? Racially speaking, I mean.'

She had a strange way of talking. 'Away with your nonsense' is some Scottish phrase. Maybe she picked it up off me after I'd picked it up off Caledonia. And 'dim and distant past' – now there was a grand old English cliché. And 'loco' was from her native Latin . . . her native Latin where? She never had said exactly which country she came from; she'd said 'Latin America'.

'Some hill tribe of the Andes?'

'Nooo . . . I'm mostly Spanish . . . well, of Spanish origin.'

'You are?'

'Yeah. One – just one – of my great grandparents was Indian—'

'An American Indian?'

'Yeah, Latin American Indian. It caused a big scandal back then.'

'I'll bet. I hear that in places like Peru, they still don't mix much. Indians and Spanish descendants.'

'What do you know about Peru?'

'As much as anyone who watches afternoon TV. There's a big stash of coke there. A small war. Lots of furry llamas. And the Andes . . . is that where you're from then? Peru?'

'I saw a picture of her once, an old photo, she looked really beautiful. My mother's grandmother, I mean.'

'Yeah. Where exactly are you from?'

'You ask so many questions.'

'I'm a reporter, lover. Well, kind of. It's what we do.'

'Between drinks . . .'

'Yeah, between drinks. And between times. So where are you from?'

'Are you door-stepping me?' she grinned.

'Always. Where you from?'

'If I told you I'd have to kill you,' she said, trying to keep a straight face before she finally cracked up and roared with laughter.

'No, seriously, where you from?'

'I'll tell you if we live together . . . when we live together.'

'That's a nice thought . . . despite the complications.'

'Yes,' she sighed softly, suddenly looking sad, 'there are some complications.'

There always are complications, I thought. Always. No matter what the situation. Either both of you are complete amateurs which means trouble because no one knows the rules. Or one or both of you are on the rebound from some-one else. Which usually means you're flying around at obtuse angles. You two may be on the same train, yes, but you're walking in different directions. And you connect just long enough to hurt each other. Just long enough to twist the knife. Well, that's the normal way. Sometimes I think it's a miracle any couple stay together long enough to exchange names. Or writs.

And we had complications. Me and Anna. Anna and I. We had complications. Which stopped me telling her about the story. And she didn't seem to mention Sally again, which was nice but, I later found out, all that meant was more compli-cations.

And then there was the similarly unnamed Vee. Anna and I had spent an afternoon way up high, drinking the drink and smoking the smoke before launching into our physical ascent. I'd always known we would get it on, I just hadn't realised how good it would be. Sliding around deliciously on my bed, sliding around on one of Jake's higher levels of passion. Trust is a many-splendoured thing, made precious – like a diamond – by its sheer rarity. There's few men you can trust and even fewer women – just as, for girls, there's few women you can trust and even fewer men. But I trusted Anna.

She'd never once mentioned Vee. Neither of us had, though I did think about him for a second when Anna slipped me a small bag of charlie. A bag for later on, like. Did that bag come from him? Is seven up? So what to do about him? What did she want to do about Vee? What did she want to do about anything?

The live version of Bowie's 'Sweet Thing' was still swirling out of the hi-fi, reaching its epic conclusion, piano notes tin-kling out like broken glass ringing out on marble. To me it sounded as desperate and passionate as we felt. All I'd ever wanted . . . but that song was about faking it, wasn't it? Faking it in a fake world?

'So tell me, gorgeous, what do you actually do?'

Her smile returned. Either she was smiling at the compliment or at the question. Or me – or all three. I did amuse her, if nothing else. A man of words . . .

'What do you actually do? Between times?'

'I always do,' she answered, quoting herself as her chin came up, 'anything I want to . . .'

29

Mingle, Mingle

I went to some press conference but it was a waste of time. The usual yankee pop star trying to be an actor, flying in for the day just to see us humble natives. All the glossy mags were already in there – nowhere for me to squeeze in, in any sense of the word, but I did score a few drinks so don't say the NUJ doesn't ever help us little freelancers – so the next day all the glossies would all have the same 'world exclusive' with the great man (a Scientologist, for pity's sake).

I hadn't scored the real thing for hours, so I took a tug of amyl nitrate. I got that quick heart jolt that soon turns fairly nasty . . . despite being legal, amyl wasn't really anyone's drug of choice – NRG gays aside – although I did recall one of the sound rig guys at The Paradiso who used to refuse all other known stimulants just so he could snort amyl all night. He'd then run around on the lighting rig, completely out of his tree – and that rig was over sixty feet up, hovering directly over a packed dance-floor. And the metal bar he was running on was less than four inches wide.

I ended up in the Rikki Tik. Downstairs. Someone was

babbling at me. Guy with a beret and too many gold teeth. And too many words. Way too many words . . .

'It's incredible man, this guy in Panama, this fuckin' professor, he's invented this chemical that you put in charlie and it cleans it up. Actually *cleans* the charlie, stops it making you paranoid afterwards – and feelin' addicted and shit. Makes it perfect, fuckin' perfect, man. You can fly for days and feel nothin' bad, nothing bad at all, you know what I mean?'

I had heard all this before. From various quarters. But rarely delivered with such manic passion. Which didn't make it any more fun to endure.

'And does it work?' I asked, like an idiot.

'Course it works man, *course* it fuckin' works. It's so fuckin' pure you could give it to your goddamned grandmother, you know what I'm sayin'? The professor guy's makin' a fuckin' fortune. He sold the patent to the Colombian cartels and he's making a fuckin' fortune, boy, a fuckin' fortune! He flies around over Panama City in this 747 and the royalties are beamed up to him by air-waves, e-mail and all that shit, you know what I'm sayin'? He's on the Web, man, the fuckin' Web! Connected up by pirate satellite beamin' in from fifteen fuckin' galaxies away. He plays Doom with his fuckin' mates, man, his fuckin' mates, bets on it! Ten thousand dollars a game! Cash, boy, fuckin' cash! Cash on the fuckin' e-mail nail! You know what I'm sayin'? He's sorted, makin' a fortune, man, a fuckin' fortune!'

'So when are they gonna market this stuff over here?' I asked – another big mistake.

'They already fuckin' are, boy, they already fuckin' are! Yeah! I'm on it now! Can't you tell? Can't you? Can't you?'

He'd lost the plot, lost it big-time. With every other word his foot tapped at mine – while his hand kept touching and re-touching his red raw nostrils. Coked to the gills and beyond. His half-empty glass shook like a washing machine – mainly because his other hand was now gripped around it, knuckles white and flexing.

'Yeah, right, I see what you mean,' I said, mentally backing away from the massive anger that suddenly seemed to flow into him.

'I mean it makes everythin' purer, you know what I mean? Purer and purer, you know what I'm sayin'? You know where I'm fuckin' comin' from? Do you really think you know where this fuckin' cat's head is fuckin' comin' from?'

And every 'fuckin'' was like a punch to the head, as he tensed himself up, his overloaded brain trying to decide whether he was actually going to glass me or merely punch me or what.

'Not really,' I said, cool as fuck, as my real nerves slipped between my knees and on to the floor. *Yes,* I thought, *I know what you're saying, I know where you're coming from, I know where your cat's head is at. It's fucking blown. Your head is blown. You've lost it, matey. Lost it completely. And so I'm going home. I don't wanna score any more today. Not for a few more hours anyway. I can last a bit longer, after seeing you. I just wanna go home. Alone – and alive. So it's ciao bambino, thanks for all the wonderful memories and don't forget to write now . . .*

'Time for another drink, eh Pete, boy?' he said, changing tack. 'Time for another, eh?'

Was that a threat or an invitation – and how the hell had he known my name? Had I told him during some moment of utter madness?

'Nah, I'd love to have another but I've really gotta go.' I tried to stand but he pushed me back down.

'Nah, nah, nah, you gotta have one more, just one more. One more for the fuckin' road, eh? Relax, it's the fuckin' weekend soon, you know what I'm fuckin' sayin'? Relax, boy, relax! You fuckin' sit now. I'll get 'em in . . .'

'No, I'll get 'em in, I owe you one.'

'Do you? Yeah, fuckin' do, doncha? Yeah, go on, get them in, cheers, mate.'

Money, or something it bought, often did the trick. Especially early on. Because money saved on a drink is good money – all money is good money, in fact, as you can always use money to buy charlie. I scrambled to the bar and ordered him a half of something. Under the barman's baleful eye I slapped a couple of coins on the counter.

'You're not having one yourself then?' he asked, eyebrow raised.

'No, I'm going.'

'Bit of a live one, that boy. Mate of yours, is he?'

'He's not really me mate, we've only just met,' I said as I prised myself off the bar-stool, all ready to go. 'He's a little bit too fast for my liking.'

'Well,' snapped the barman, sharp as a knife, 'you know what they say, mate . . . it takes one to know one, eh?'

30

We Interrupt This Broadcast

The phone was still ringing as I came back from the laun-
derette. It hadn't been a good trip. The Irish pensioner
who ran the place had lost a black needle-cord shirt of mine –
£25, down from £60 in World Service last year. I tried to
argue with her but soon realised she was even more abstract
than I was.

'It's the street, the whole street has gone forkin' crazy. The
whole street. My Michael's back in Cork now, you know.'

Yeah, right. What's that got to do with the shirt? I could
have spent hours trying to enter into her philosophy but what
was the point? Some far-out old woman wasn't going to steal
anything. She was so off her nut that she'd probably try and
fry it with chips before eating it. I decided it was time to change
launderettes. Arguing with her was also a waste of precious
time and I was running out of that fast. I thought I'd left my
ansafone off and the thought nagged me because Anna was
going to ring. So I dashed back just in time to hear it ringing.
Ringing and ringing. I ran up the stairs two at a time, damn
near killing myself, to catch it. But it stopped ringing the

second I picked it up. As I knew it would. I also knew, I mean I *knew* that it was Anna who was ringing me. I dialled 1471 for a trace – 'sorry, we do not have the caller's number. Sorry, we do not have—' then slammed it down. Why hadn't I left the ansafone on? Why? It doesn't matter, it doesn't matter, I kept telling myself, she'll ring back. She'd be crazy not to. Or would she be crazy to ring me? Me who had all these debts to offer her. So I sat down to wait. She'll ring back. She *will* ring back. She said she was leaving Vee. This weekend. For me.

The minutes turned into hours as my apprehension grew. Maybe she wouldn't ring. Maybe she couldn't. Maybe Vee had killed her and was, even now, digging her a shallow grave somewhere. Vee. I hadn't really thought about Vee. My main man with two gold inlaid shotguns. How would he react to all this? I seemed to have spent the last few weeks winding him up. I began to wonder, then stopped myself.

My wait ended at seven o'clock. There was a ring. On the doorbell. I don't know about yours, but my doorbell is one of those Scotland Yard-type affairs that could wake the dead. It's wired to the mains and my landlord has probably used it in the past to torture tenants with sensitive hearing. Tenants like me. It went off like a bomb, like it always does, and I nearly hit the ceiling. When I'd got my heart back in my mouth, I wrenched open the window and threw the keys out as I shouted, 'Keys!'

What if it wasn't her? I asked myself as the weighted keyring flew out the window. So? If it's a friend they can buy me a drink, if it's a gang of kids they're welcome to come in and try and steal my hi-fi. What have I got to lose? My most valuable asset was, hopefully, walking up the stairs. I grabbed the remote and switched the TV on. A bit of background. Current affairs. Finger-on-the-pulse stuff. The flat's doorhandle turned as I tried to strike a knowing man-of-the-world pose. Anna. How are you? Fancy seeing you here. Shall we take in a movie? A drink? The bed?

The door opened and I struggled to keep my smile afloat as Vee walked in. Vee! His nose was streaming. Too much of that snow white. He was holding a long case – must be the shot-gun – and he had a face like thunder. I noticed the TV was broadcasting nothing but static. It was a minor detail. *We interrupt this broadcast to bring you more of the same . . .*

'Vee!'

'Pete, how ya going? Heard the bad news?'

I shook my head as I thought, *Yes, I've heard it; in fact, I made it. I tried to take your Anna and now you're going to kill me for it . . . Anna must have confessed all after getting a good kicking . . . God, we were so crazy to think we could have got away with—*

'Anna's bleedin' gone off, ain't she?'

'She's gone off where?' I said, hoping he wouldn't suss that she might just have gone off somewhere to wait for me. Could you read all that into a look? I reversed my prayers and hoped that, now, the phone would not ring.

'Gone off, ain't she? Left a note and gone off. Gone off with her fucking personal trainer.'

'Huh?' *Huh huh huh? Huh?*

'Yeah, can you believe it? Her fat Spanish friend has gone an' all. Said it wouldn't be respectable for her and the nippers to stay. I thought, "My God, woman, you flatter yourself, don't you?" And can you believe Anna, eh? Doing me like that. Doing my fucking head in?'

No, no, I can't, I thought, how could she do me like that? So that's why she had dancing lessons and visits to the gym and all that. So what was I? Some kind of decoy? Maybe Vee was lying . . . but what about the note? And what about the . . .

'Personal trainer?' I mumbled. 'I had no idea.'

'Yeah, Jerry saw 'em. Getting a cab in the West End together. All lovey-dovey.'

Even Jerry wouldn't lie about something like that. Not to Vee anyhow. I honestly hadn't even thought about that possi-bility. Sucker. Men are real amateurs when it comes to love affairs. I began to wonder idly if phrases like 'love affair' were offensive to modern women in London. They probably were. The word 'love' probably was. It certainly offended me at that moment. Never give a sucker an even break. Anna didn't. She knew how to use me and she did. I was just the decoy. A minor diversion.

'Yeah. She must have been planning it for weeks . . . What's she gonna do with a bleedin' personal trainer?'

'Dunno. Train, I s'pose. What are you gonna do with him?' As Vee sighed deeply I looked at his case. It was too short for a shotgun. Unless it was a sawn-off.

'Nothin' . . . I'm gonna do nothin' . . . He's bleedin' run away, ain't he? With her. He can't be reached by phone. Probably gone on holiday. He'll come back in a few weeks, though. Little toe-rag. I should kill him, by rights . . . but, you know, I can't be fucked, I really can't . . . It ain't him, anyway, is it? It's her. Two-timing bitch . . . I mean, fuck me old boots! What's she gonna do with a bleedin' personal trainer? What?'

Yeah, what?

'She certainly had me fooled, I can tell ya.'

He went to the window and, despite my own pain, I felt for him too.

'Yeah. I know what you mean, Vee.'

'Too much, eh?' he said uninterestedly.

'Yeah, she musta fooled me too . . . I had no idea she was gonna do this . . . no idea . . .'

'Yeah. And you usedta speak to her a lot, dincha? I almost thought there was somethin' going on wiv' you two,' he grinned sadly at the folly that only I knew was wisdom.

'You what?' I said, forcing a hollow laugh.

'Nah. Forget it. Jus' shows ya how paranoid I was – mind you, I was right to be, wan' I? What with her and her personal trainer . . . a bleedin' personal trainer. I thought she had more class.'

'Yeah . . .'

'Women, eh? Just when you think you can trust one . . .'

'As Bowie said on that *Young Americans* song, "Take every woman like a sock on the jaw."'

'That ain't the lyric,' he said flatly.

'Huh?'

'I saw it written down once. That ain't the lyric.'

'Oh . . . right . . .'

'I wanna go out,' Vee said, picking the long case up again.

'Yeah, but go where, though?' Maybe he wanted to go round shooting people at random. Let your heart speak at the end of a gun. The American Way.

'I got me cue wiv' me.' He shook the long case gently. 'Let's go shoot some pool.'

'Could do,' I said, still in shock myself.

'Come on, son,' he smiled sadly, 'I need some cheering up.'

I hesitated, thinking, *What if she rings?* But I knew the truth . . . she ain't gonna ring you. Sucker.

'Look, we'll play for dosher, Pete, and I'll even stake yours for you. Whatcha got to lose?'

Yeah, right. What have I got to lose? It's not like anyone's going to ring, not now.

'Yeah, could do, Vee, could do.'

'Come on,' he implored, 'we could go down the Captain's Cabin later, whatcha got to lose?'

'Yeah.'

He was right. What had I got to lose? There was nothing for me here. Not now. Wham! Right out of the blue . . . Vee went to the window and looked out.

'I spent thousands on her, Pete, bleedin' thousands.'

'I know,' I said softly as I gulped down some air to stop my own eyes watering. Big girls don't cry.

'An' she does this to me . . . she left a load of her clothes behind, you know? Said she might send for 'em. I'm gonna drag 'em down Oxfam. What can she say?'

'Nothing.'

'Eggs-zactly. Fucking nothin' . . . Come on, you're s'posed to be cheering me up, ain'tcha?'

I am? Yeah, I s'pose I am. But why me? Why had Vee come to me? Maybe he couldn't use me much any more – post-*Groove* – so now I had the dubious honour to really be his mate. Or maybe no one else was around. Or maybe he sensed that I would miss Anna too. That would make her laugh when I told her. But when would I tell her? I'd never tell her. Because when would I see her again? Never. If Vee was halfway right I'd probably never see her again.

'Vee, take every woman like a car crash. Every one you walk away from is a winner.'

'Yeah, right. Come on then.' He went to the flat door and opened it. I took one more look at the phone that wasn't going to ring and followed Vee out into the hallway. As I glanced back to lock the flat door I caught a glimpse of the TV. It was still on. It was still showing some static nothing. It was nine. I wouldn't be back until . . . well, who knew when? And who gave a damn? I locked the door shut on the affair that might have been. The life that might have been. Big deal. *We interrupt this broadcast to bring you more of the same.*

31

The Triumph Of The West

The Captain's Cabin was like the Beachcomber used to be years ago, when the world was still young. The Beachcomber being a humongous bar that actually had real babbling springs and geysers and portholes and baby crocodiles in a mock-sea and beach . . . And all that in an area around the bar. As the Captain's Cabin still does. Remake remodel remix. The Captain's barmaids all wear those naval caps, blazers, high-heeled sneakers and very little else. And, outside of the girls in the Groucho, they've probably had more propositions of an artistic nature than any other group of females on earth. And still they smile. The Cabin had also been in some of the magazines recently, touted as the kind of place where men with money could, after three bottles of lovely expensive champers, cop off with some good-looking good-time girls – and there were a good few of those draped around the bar. It had once been *the* place to be, but was now more and more frequented by the sons of oil sheikhs, city slickers, hoorays, French aristocrats and failed models. The usual Euro-coke-trash . . . as well as those second-hand car salesmen and quantity surveyors who were prepared to spend a fortune in order to pretend they weren't who they were. It was a place to go.

I'd told Vee, halfway through his last, losing, pool game, that the best way to forget Anna was to get stuck into another relationship as soon as possible. I don't know if I believed it or not myself – I think part of me just wanted him paired off with someone else. Because, that way, if Anna did eventually ring me again, Vee would be out the way. If Anna did ring . . . what a sad bastard I am. I thought it was worth a try anyway. Might even do Vee some good.

There were some girls by the bar who were sitting pertly on the bar-stools. In fact, the way they were sitting allowed you, if you were seated yourself, to see that they were wearing gold and silver undies. Poles, probably, or Czechs. Russians, most likely. All Gorby's ballerinas and gymnasts were strippers and hookers now. Or good-time girls. That was progress. The triumph of the West. The triumph of McDonald's. And such girls, I'm told, went in for that kind of sparkly display out East. Like the hookers in Moscow. Which isn't to say the girls at the bar were hookers exactly, but whatever they did it seemed pretty obvious that they didn't do it for love. Vee was staring at them like no one's business, and I didn't know how to deflect him from that particular target, or even if I should try, when I noticed a couple of Chinese-looking girls at a table diagonally opposite.

They were the usual girl combination, one fairly plain and the other pretty-pretty and both of them all too aware by now of which was which and how crucial it had all become. This is the market. Things are bought and sold. Who's buying?

Vee tossed a bread-stick to one of the baby crocs. It looked quite evil as it wolfed it down in three bites, crunching all the way. What happened when the buggers grew up and got dangerous? Sold them, I supposed. To a zoo or something. Either that or killed them.

I looked at the Oriental duo again. The good thing about the plain one was, it had to be said, her substantial chest, which I figured Vee might go for. Leaving the coast clear for me on the other one, who was quite stunning in her own delicate way. More than stunning. And I only had to feed her some vintage champagne as I honestly described her own face – to her face – and I'd be there, or near as dammit. If I could be bothered. I forced myself to bother – the alternative was manic depression. But I'd need Vee's help and he hadn't even noticed them yet.

'Wanna hear a joke?' he said. 'What do you call a Scouser with a legitimate job? A fucking liar! And whatja call a ten-year-old Scouser? The accused!'

'You're being regionalist again,' I chided him as I stared at the pretty one. This is all so basic. *Do you come here often?*

'Bollocks . . . I keep an open mind,' rambled Vee.

'Yeah, you do keep an open mind,' I said, slipping into a Vee accent, 'you keep it at home, doncha? You don't fuckin' use it.'

'Chill, man, chill,' he cackled as he thought about my sad little joke, 'we could be in with them tarts at the bar. Those ones on the stools.'

'Forget 'em. Russian Mafia tarts . . . haven't you seen the quality stuff, Vee? Haven't you noticed those two over there?'

'Oh them. Yeah, Chinese . . . they're both hot though, ain't they? Fit is not the word.'

He gestured to them with the by-now empty champagne bottle – *Do you want some? Do you come here often?* – then went over to speak to them when they remained seated but interested. Sweet as they looked – especially that one – I didn't much care if he succeeded or not. I didn't know what I wanted. I know I didn't want Vee crying on my shoulder any more. Not when I felt the same way and couldn't even admit it to him. Couldn't tell him about Anna. And the way she acted . . . I thought I could see it now. I thought I'd sussed a part of the female mentality, or one tiny aspect of it. It's like when you glimpse a girl once, at a party or something, and then pull her weeks later. If you later asked that girl to describe you, she honestly wouldn't remember you. But she *had* seen you, had seriously considered you – if only for two or three seconds – and had then wiped you from her memory banks. Girls can do that, they get the eye from a dozen, maybe a hundred guys in any one night and they can just wipe it out. It's history. I've had that from girls I've later dated, even girls I've later lived with. *You weren't really at that club/party/gig, were you Pete? I bet you weren't.* I bet I was. I know I was. Maybe I'm more anonymous than most, but with a mug like mine I don't think so. Anna had wanted me – a little – but I was out when she rang. That simplified everything. And, if the personal trainer wasn't the original target, he certainly was now. Call him. That's it. Live dangerously. What's he really like? Don't know, don't care. Everything is of the moment with some girls – emotionally they act the same way men act physically. Total impulse. She loves you for ever – at this moment. What can you do? Been there, missed that . . .

Vee came back. The Chinese girls were gesturing they would soon be in tow. The sweet one stood up and I could see that she was wearing one of those sky blue Wit & Wisdom skirts, you know the type, so short they have the underwear built in, literally. Ten days ago I'd have given a lot just to look at her. And now? Now even she couldn't take my mind off Anna. I was still musing sadly when Vee's voice burst in, ringing with contemptuous affection.

'I said, Pete, you deaf fucker, this . . . is Jackie.'

'Hi Jackie,' I said, sounding as ironic as the name Jackie would let me.

'And this is Sam.'

'Hi, Sam.' Chinese Sam, as I couldn't help dubbing her in my head, was the fitter of the two so I couldn't help adding, 'I used to live with a girl called Sam . . .'

'Yeah?' said Vee. He knew very little about me, having never really asked.

'Yeah,' I said.

'What was she like? Was she nice?' Chinese Sam had the soft squeak of the public school English–Chinese female. A Roedean gel. Or that's what mum and dad would have liked folk to believe. But, for all her obvious charms, I didn't know if I was too interested; not yet, anyhow.

'My Sam was a pathological liar,' I said forthrightly, 'to be honest with you.'

Vee kicked me, gently, under the table. *Don't blow it, son*, his eyes said, *we're in here.*

'I've ordered the champagne, girls, I've just gotta get Pete to the khazi – the, er, washroom.'

'Can't we come too?' pouted Chinese Sam, stroking under her neck as she looked sincere. She'd probably sussed, maybe from the outset. She knew the score. A polished voice but a real London chick too. Which wasn't that bad a thing to be. So she wanted a line? That wasn't necessarily a crime. That didn't make her dumb. I wanted a line. It wasn't what you took – smack and crack aside – it was how you handled it. Maybe she could handle it. Maybe she was okay.

'No, you can't come wiv' us,' said Vee and their faces dropped but then he added, 'but . . . take this on account.'

And with that he slipped a half-gram bag under the table to them. I thought afterwards that 'on account' line was genius. Sub-conscious genius. On account. Like they already owed us something, like the relationship had already been described. And prescribed. It was a touch mercenary, at this stage, but wasn't everything these days? This is the way it's gonna be. On account. Chinese Sam gave him a big smile. Vee had the stuff, she reasoned, so Vee was the important one, the pretty one. I was the plain one.

The toilet was bright and intimidating, but the attendant was busy with some toff's towel so no one noticed as Vee and myself crammed into one cubicle. Vee pulled the chain like the real pro he was, knowing that the sound of splashing water would cover the sniffing.

'Just one line,' he muttered, 'or we'll never get it together with them two.'

'Yeah, you're right,' I said, transfixed by the sparkling powder as it poured on to the cistern, 'just one or we'll blow it.'

'Blow it? We should be so lucky . . . here goes nothin'.' He finished chopping it up with his Amex card, smeared it into a lazy line and used a rolled-up fiver to sniff it all up in one go. *Chop 'em out! Chop 'em out! So now who's having fun, baby?* He chopped me a line.

'Cheers.' I took his rolled-up fiver and sniffed away.

'Well, another half wouldn't hurt.'

He laid out another line and demolished two-thirds of it in two seconds. I hadn't wanted another line – or even a third of a line – but I knew if he'd taken it away then, at that moment, I would want it. If he'd taken it away, at that moment, I'd have got seriously narked. But he didn't. You don't wave a bottle of Scotch under the nose of a dipso. He knew the form. So I took it. On account, like.

'I wouldn't say this to just anyone, dear boy,' said Vee as he led me from the cubicle, staring at my face, 'but *you* are a dirty slag.'

After a moment of puzzlement, I realised he meant that my over-powdered nose was showing signs of substance abuse.

'Thank you very much, Vee, very kind of you to say so.'

I wiped my nose again as I wondered disinterestedly if this was the prelude to some all-out assault. *You owe me!* It wasn't, as far as I could tell, and then some suit changed the subject by walking into Vee. The latter glared after him, knuckles whitening.

'Forget it, Vee, he's just *something* in the City.'

'Well, he's bleedin' nothing down here. And if he walks into me again he'll be something in fuckin' hospital.'

'Yeah, right. Shall we get back? Get those girls while they're still hot to trot – if they are.'

As we sat down again, Bee Jay, the fortysomething rock star, came in. I'd just heard this funny, well funny-tragic, story about Bee Jay. There was some ageing bluesman he liked and this guy was dying, poverty-stricken, for want of a forty-grand operation. So Bee Jay hears this and decides to be generous. But it takes time when you're a multi-millionaire – he has to meet agents, brokers, PR people to arrange the press conferences, fave pop video directors to shoot the conferences and, of course, he has to check it all out with his all-powerful accountants – and

so, by the time the moneymen have finally given Bee Jay permission to give out the cash, well, it's all too late. The old
bluesman is dead, not waking up this morning. Which proves
my theory about the super-rich. They don't own any money.
They don't own a single penny. Bee Jay doesn't own a single
penny – the money owns *him*. You see? Not that you'd glean
any of the above from your mass media. They all love him too
much, every comeback hailed as some big deal. Big deal. And he
gave great TV – 'Of course I'm not that modest, I haven't got
much to be modest about, have I?' Smirk-smirk, kissy-kissy.

Bee Jay still had his greasy black-grey hair tugged back into
a pony-tail – he bloody would, wouldn't he? – and he also had
a tiny sneer for the entire room. Arrogant prat. He'd recently
gone on some short break to the French Caribbean, taking
along one of those *stand-up is the new rock'n'roll* comedians.
Both Bee Jay and the alleged comedian had taken their
middle-aged road managers with them. And their road managers' wives. And both had then spent the next week
unthinkingly humiliating said road managers. The comedy
man had his running various errands while Bee Jay turned to
his, mid-morning, and said, in front of this guy's embarrassed
wife, 'You're in the way now, I want you to go to the toilet
for an hour, or go for a walk or something.' Which the guy
then did. Good ol' Bee Jay. Heart of gold. Twenty-four-carat,
tax deductible gold. And then I noticed that his companions
were Vee's model friend and her sister. Styla and Silvia, two
lovely girls. Vee turned, saw them and calmly looked away.
They blanked him too. Deliberately. And then, of course, I
finally twigged. This was business. The A & R boyfriend, of
the Model, was just one of many. The Model was Vee's entry
into the whole modelling world. All those catwalk creatures
needing to make the weight. Stay thin, make money. A line of
this and you won't need to eat all day. Or even all weekend.
Of course, it all made sense. And that's why they'd ignored
each other. I knew a couple of models, and they did nothing
stronger than beer – normally someone else's – but maybe
they were the exceptions who proved the rule.

But the thing that disturbed me most about Bee Jay's arrival was the way it had also provoked looks from the Chinese chicks. Jackie had taken just one glance and swung back round to look at Chinese Sam. Just one concerned look. And Chinese Sam had ignored that concern, had tried to look disinterested, had looked, in fact, everywhere but at Bee Jay. And then it hit me – she'd slept with Bee Jay, of course, that was why. A discarded ex. Hence Jackie's worried look. Bee Jay had had her. A real West End Girl was our Chinese Sam. Sharper than a razor and possibly as dangerous. When me and Vee were thirteen we were still playing the occasional game of conkers – at that age she was licking coke off some rock star's stomach. And not just any old rock star. Bloody Bee Jay! Bought and sold. How sickening. Bee Jay, the biggest sell-out of them all, I'd rather she'd have worked her way through a couple of chapters of Hell's Angels than sleep with him. Bee Jay, who had banged around so much that he'd once managed to get crabs in his nasal hairs. And that was from an impeccable source, the same one who'd told me about the top manager who'd filled one of his young boy-band stars with smack and humped him stupid on some transatlantic flight. The same source that had told all about the top rock couple who had shared needles *and* fifteen-year-old boys. Which meant Bee Jay's nasal crabs phenomena was all true. What a prat. Or were we all just jealous of him? No, I really hadn't been jealous of that idiot before. I just hated what he did, or rather didn't, stand for. I wasn't jealous at all – not until tonight. Until the minute I realised he'd had Chinese Sam.

'He's a dozy sod, isn't he?' I knew Vee was talking about me.

'What you saying, sir?' I blustered, trying to brighten up my own dark horizons – I'd been waiting for Anna and now I was still waiting for the *Chronicle* to run the Scallies story. Waiting . . . always waiting . . .

'I said, you're a writer, encha?'

'Yes.'

'He'll write about anything. Long as the price is right.'

He laughed. Bought and sold. I thought he must be thinking that, as he drunkenly rambled on, *Pete's bought and sold. He's not a bad lad but I bought him.*

'He goes to gigs an' that and writes and writes. All the time getting paid by both sides. And getting free drinks . . . most of the time,' he said as if accepting free booze was a major crime. Which I kinda resented – it was the least of my crimes.

'What happens at those things? When the free drink runs out?' asked Jackie, the plain one.

'Being a man of integrity, when the free drink runs out, I leave.'

Jackie smiled but Chinese Sam could only make it to a feeble smirk. She wasn't really looking at me anyway. Her eyes were on Vee. She had twigged, probably from the outset, that Vee was the one with the real money. And the real thing; the cocaine. He was the Bee Jay, not me. It was quite funny, in a sick sort of way. I could tell that Vee wanted Jackie. Jackie, in turn, now wanted me a little, and I myself wanted Chinese Sam. And her? Well, she wanted Bee Jay, of course. And Vee. And his charlie. I was twitching now – the line and a half was reacting with the drink and sending me on great emotional roller-coasters. I fought to keep calm. I wasn't going to see Anna again. Not ever again. Why did it keep coming back? The conviction grew until it was so big it was real. My Anna, living by the dice. Living dangerously. You know you're alive when you're dying – the usual crap that justifies anything and everything. But the poor old personal trainer. He'd better be a pretty dangerous teacher or he'd soon be for the high jump.

I had to talk about something else. How could I get into the conversation? I heard someone babbling about how poignant the record we could hear was. How the melody had some kind of philosophy all its own. Jackie agreed.

'I'm going to do a degree in philosophy, about enlightened thinking,' she mused brightly, 'but I really don't know which course to pick yet—'

'That's the trouble with enlightenment,' I said, 'it's all so confusing, isn't it?'

Jackie smiled at my idiot joke. She was vaguely friendly at least. And clever. I looked away, killing her look. Why was I being so uptight? As if I didn't know. Vee whispered something to Jackie then, trying to help me with Chinese Sam, he prompted me. He was all right, was Vee. He had been a human being once. Which is more than you can say for most human beings.

''Ere, son, what was you saying about Sam? Beforehand? Before we spoke?'

'Huh?' I grunted, while thinking: I've given up on her, Vee, forget it. But thanks for trying, boy, thanks for that.

'You said you was gonna say somethin' to her?'

Oh yeah, I thought, I was indeed. I was going to say she looked like that Chinese actress who's been in all the big movies out there. Superstar. Except that I no longer wanted to say it. It was corny and she despised me anyway. Nearly as much as I now despised her. I looked down at Chinese Sam's blue crocodile-skin clutch bag – did any of the Cabin's baby crocs recognise a relative? – and saw that she had one of those *Cosmo*-type mags poking out – 'Be a postman's patsy! Eighteen exciting orgasms – and all by mail order!' – which was pretty typical. She'd probably spent the afternoon reading how you could be spontaneous to order.

'What were you gonna say to me then, Paul?' Chinese Sam said, waiting to be amused – she even tore her eyes off Vee for a moment. Paul? Paul? Yep, she didn't even get my name right. I looked her in the eye.

'Do you come here often?'

Vee laughed and Jackie smiled nervously, but Chinese Sam – sharp, young-old Sam, Sam the West End Girl – she instantly understood. Understood what I really meant. How offensive I was being. *Do you come here often, tart?* Her amused look died instantly to be replaced by a brittle little grin. *And still they smile.* Why am I annoying her? She's bought and sold. Yeah, but aren't we all? It's not her fault she reminds me of all the girls I've wanted before.

Vee ordered some more champagne as I thought *I have got to get home*. There's a bottle of brandy tucked away there. In my ancient fridge. I could blot it all out with that. All of it. Even Anna. And it's not too bad on your gut. In fact, brandy will settle your stomach. Brandy will settle most things, if you drink enough of it . . .

32

Onward 'Til Dawn

I can hear crying. A soft sobbing like a child's. I focus. I'm wearing my black jeans and nothing else. There's a glass in my left hand. I'm propped up on a bed – not my own – and someone's sitting at the end of the bed. They're crying. It's Jackie, I think. Dress pulled in every direction. Well off the shoulder now. Asking for it, as the yobs would say. But why is she crying? I try and trace the trajectory of the evening but I only get fragments of it. A tape that's been partially wiped. A signal that was breaking up. We'd sunk the Captain's Cabin – put it in Davy Jones's locker – and then what? Couldn't remember . . . fragments . . . a black-out. Too much fire-water. Much too much of everything.

I sit up a bit more. I can see myself in the mirror now. I'm cut between my nose and my left cheek – quick flash of Chinese Sam and Jackie fussing over my face in some kitchen – oh yeah, now it comes back. Before we got that big rusty mini-cab, there was a fight with another cabby. A taxi-driver with a proper cab, a black cab. He had said he wasn't 'taking those Chink whores anywhere'. Stupid old Nazi that he was. As I believe I told him. We had grappled through his open window as he'd driven off. I wasn't being heroic, not at all. More like just another stroppy speed-freak who freaked 'cos *he couldn't get a cab home and he wanted it now!* The driver had obviously got his retaliation in first, looking at my cheek. But that whole incident was weird, in itself, very weird. Most cabbies are decent people – don't smirk, I'm serious – and I've even known one or two that'll give you a lift for nothing. I have, of course, heard of some who won't go south of the river or take blacks. Or punks. Once a cabby explained his practices to me while we argued. He said, 'I bin ripped off fourteen times – fourteen! – and twelve of them times, those who done runners or pulled knives were black lads. And the other two times they was punks. So I don't pick 'em up no more. Black boys. Or punks. Not at all. Now, to me that ain't racist or snobbish or whatever. To me it's just cutting down the odds of losin' dosh. It's just bleedin' common sense, innit?' Never try arguing with a cabby. Arguing with a cabby had been Mistake Number 94 that evening.

What else is there? What else can I remember? Oh God . . . earlier on I had taken a half-gram bag of tink and eaten it after sniffing eight fat lines. After drinking umpteen doubles. I could have died. What a head-banger. It's a minor miracle that my heart-beat isn't flickering more. When was that? Two thirty? What time is it now? Nearly seven. The cut on my face is beginning to sting again – if, indeed, it ever stopped – and I'm feeling red raw and strung-out. I look around. I'm in one of Vee's spare bedrooms; its chintzy curtains make it look like some French brothel – how appropriate – like, in a way, the Captain's Cabin. Bought and sold, bought and sold. But why is Jackie crying? Had I been tactless enough to mention Chinese Sam was the one I was really after? I draped a light arm around her shoulders. She turns – lipstick a smeared mess, panda eye-liner running – and I see her hurt eyes. It *is* Chinese Sam. Shit. So I could have had her, after all. Maybe I did.

I wonder what went wrong. She takes one look at me and starts crying again. What went right? That would seem to be the more appropriate question. The room reeks of cheap sex and expensive perfume. And cigarettes. And there's a faint but real smell of gunfire. Gunfire? Wham bam! Who shot Sam? *Gunfire . . .?*

There's powder smeared all over the dresser. There's even some around Chinese Sam's gleaming nose. She must be in a state, a sharp one like her, forgetting to powder her nose properly . . . why didn't I go home earlier? It would have saved so much shit. I dressed quietly around her, and she eventually straightened her back.

'I'm not a groupie,' she suddenly announced in a voice that was feeble, and breaking, yet somehow determined. I must have said something about her fling with Bee Jay. And I'd probably delivered it with all the gentility a speeding, jealous drunk could muster. The realisation of all this hit me as she repeated herself.

'I'm not a groupie.'

'Yeah, I know,' I said, clearing my throat.

'You can be really horrible, you can. Really horrible.'

'Yeah, I know.'

'I'm not a groupie, you know?'

'Yeah, you're not a groupie.'

'I'm not . . .'

'So I gather . . . look, I'm going now. Going home. Wanna share a cab? What do you wanna do? Do you wanna stay?'

'I'm not a groupie, you know, I'm not . . .'

Propped up at the bottom of the stairs I found a big photo portrait of Anna that had been blasted with shotgun pellets. One of the shotguns was still lying there, broken open, on the couch. Anna's black and white face had almost been obliterated. Of course. Vee had shot it a couple of times. Why hadn't the neighbours called the cops? I couldn't think why they shouldn't. Unless shotgun-blasting of photo portraits was a regular occurrence around here.

I did remember one other thing: how high the girls were; almost out of control. And then how frightened they became. One of them said, 'You're not gonna fire that thing, are you?' Just seconds before Vee let rip with both barrels. It came back to me now. The roar of the shotgun. They're loud when you're outside, and they're even louder in a hallway. In a suburban lounge the blast is deafening. I had recollections of Vee lifting someone's skirt with that gun. It was still smoking and the smoke drifted off, up and around her. It would look great on a catwalk, that effect, or on some *Vogue* magazine cover . . . And then there was the Tequila slammers and more tink and some earnest hugging like we'd been chomping E . . . and then some more drinks . . . and then some more toot . . . and then some more.

There were broken glasses everywhere, CDs scattered on the floor, the lovely carpet was stained with red wine and fag burns. Like there had been an axe-murder on the Axminster. Poor old Vee, this – his one-time palace – looked like it had been the subject of a violent coup. Which was true, in a way. I noticed Vee hadn't shot his forty-inch TV out. He never was a rocker, our Vee. Always was much more of a soulboy. I went to the kitchen. Sitting by the French windows was Jackie, alone. She was slightly shell-shocked, I figured. It would have been understandable. It had been a long hot night. She was nursing a coffee. Rocking back and forth a little. She looked up, nodded a faint acknowledgement that brooked no words. She understood. She didn't excuse Vee . . . or even me. But she did understand, what with those sad eyes and her quiet, unhappy blankness. I nodded back. *And now they don't smile*, I thought, and now, finally, they don't smile. And then I closed the door.

33

Big Time, Big Deal

I t was only after I'd left the cab and been in my flat a full ten minutes that I realised that one of Barry's songs was coming out of the radio. I'd snapped the hi-fi on to give myself enough energy to see me through a shower. I needed to feel clean before I crashed out. Not that I'd sleep, not for an hour or two yet, not with all that wine and cocaine still stuck in my blood, still churning around my spinning head. But a shower might help. Or even a bath. That might slow things down. And then, as I dressed, I started singing along with the radio. And it was Barry. Doing his thing. *Barry!* So he'd cracked it! At last! Broken on through to the other side. One of us actually had! One of us had made it! Legally! A breakfast-time show like this must have an audience of millions; ten or fifteen million. This is big-time, this means a major must have finally opted for him. The boy was going to be worth zillions of dollars. You couldn't have songs played on nationwide radio – songs that were that good – without some kind of wide-scale repercussions. Barry had never heard his stuff on radio before – by the time he gigged Spain, his semi-hit was already off the playlists – and I toyed with the idea of ringing him. But surely he must know? He'd need PR sheets, sleeve notes, parties . . . I could do okay out of it all but – in complete honesty – I was just pleased for the boy. The boy had done good. He'd given me some musical thrills and that was enough. Tracks I'd heard in tiny rooms and home studios were now going to be heard around the UK, then around the world. To be heard by millions, maybe billions of people. I picked up the phone and was about to punch in his number when the signal faded, like Radio Luxembourg used to when you were a kid, then it returned with a voice talking over it. I could hardly contain the rush of excitement. How would the DJ describe the song? Was I the only listener who knew it was over two years old? But the voice was babbling the title awkwardly . . . in Spanish. It wasn't an English station, wasn't OneFM or Virgin. It wasn't even Capital. I looked at the radio's digital read-out. Something on short-wave. I must have tuned into this foreign station when I was stoned, the other night. Some small-town Basque DJ was playing some old stuff. Some recent oldies that had made a few waves in the Basque country. Made waves once upon a time. A few years ago. And Barry's track had been picked for this show, probably picked at random. And although it was only halfway through, they had already faded it out. Now they were playing something else, some Euro-disco that was the big thing of '94, total rubbish. And the DJ was talking over that too. The station then faded some more. Now it was down to a low, distorted hum. I dropped the phone receiver, cancelled the call. What a king-size drag.

Another great dream, another great breakthrough. I felt sympathy, real sympathy, for the boy. The song was good, more than good, it was great. But, the way things were, no one would ever know. Except that, now, I was still on the brink of becoming a serious journo. And then – in fact, very soon – I just might be able to do something about the very crooked shit that went down. In a small way. I might even knock the charlie on the head – being a journo was more of a vocation than being a cokehead . . .

34

The Free Press

I burst into Maurie More's office with his PA and a security guard in close attendance. It was the day – D-Day. The Scallies' world tour was starting and the *Chronicle* hadn't run my story. Hadn't run it. Had *not* run it. I was stunned and angry . . . after all that waiting – and for what?

'What the fuck's going on, Maurie?' I stormed. 'Why isn't the fucking Scallies story out? Why aren't you returning my fuckin' phone calls?'

At this point, the security guard laid a heavy hand on my shoulder.

'All right, sunshine, you've had your fun . . .'

As the guard spoke, Maurie stopped fiddling with the evening's sport layout and looked up.

'It's all right, Harry, you can put him down. He's harmless.'

'No, I'm fuckin' not—'

'It's all right, Harry, really . . .'

'As long as you say so, Mr More . . .'

'No problem,' said Maurie as he turned to me. 'Cool it, laddie, you ain't the first reporter to have had a story spiked.'

'This was more than just a story – this was an exposé, a

major piece, a fuckin' feature, a fuckin' cover, you said so yourself.'

'I know, I know . . . Take a seat, Peter.'

'No—'

'Take a seat . . . please.'

I sighed then sat down, shoving the expensive leather-bound chair back as roughly as I could, creasing up the expensive shag pile.

'So, Maurie . . . what's the story?'

'All the stocks and shares change in the morning. All of 'em. Well, nearly all of 'em. You don't follow the stocks and shares, do you, lad?' he asked, and I shook my head. 'Well, you should . . . you should.'

'What the hell have they got to do with anything?' I asked forcefully.

'Sir Ralph, our glorious leader, has bought fifteen per cent of DPC, your old firm . . . the people who own *Express Music* and *Music Mirror* and—'

'I know who the fuck they are, Maurie.'

'—and we've just been offered some exclusive backstage access on The Scallies tour . . . so what you wrote – fun though it was, well-written though it undoubtedly was – would be awkward for everyone . . . it is, in fact, no longer viable. Not news any more, not at all.'

'You surely mean, not this month?'

'I mean not ever . . . all the people who signed the affidavits have been approached, new statements have been drafted, we own copyright on all the photos. You can't restart it some-where else, Peter, it's over. Dead as a doornail, lad.'

'But for fuck's sake, this is like . . .' I groped for a word, 'this is like . . . business fuckin' censorship! And you, *you* gave me your fuckin' word!'

'Word, nothing!' Maurie suddenly roared. 'You got fuckin' paid, didn't you? Nearly everything that was promised? Didn't you? Eh?'

'Yeah, but—'

'Well, you should be fuckin' grateful for that in this day and

age . . . this isn't the Sixties, Pete. It isn't even the fuckin'
Seventies, or haven't you noticed? Everyone's running scared.
If you're lucky you're stuck in a rut, like thousands are, like I
fuckin' am, stuck in a nice, safe cosy rut and keeping your
head down and watching all the shit fly overhead, there's
nothing you can do about it all . . . nothing!'

I couldn't tell if he was really angry – though he did seem
pretty distracted – or if he was faking it to deflate me. Either
way, I was starting to slow down, the anger ebbing away – I
mean what was the point? You can't fight City Hall – or
Wapping.

'Yeah, Maurie, and what does that speech mean?'

'It means . . .'

'Remember,' I quoted back to him, '"you're a newspaperman now". Does that ring any bells, Maurie?'

'Newspaperman?' he scoffed. 'Fuck off, lad, they don't exist
any more. Not in this building – not in your fuckin' shoes –
not anywhere. How'd you think I feel? The shit I've had to do.
I had pictures of the Serbs beheading people – spiked! Sir
Ralph didn't wanna put the Tories on the spot over appease-
ment. I had an interview with Diana's chambermaid – spiked!
A fuckin' budget scoop, tax figures an' all – spiked! Spiked . . .
shit happens, lad, shit fuckin' happens.'

'Yeah, right.'

'There aren't any fuckin' newspapers any more, lad, didn't
you hear what young Piers said t'other day? We're s'posed to
be *infotainment* sheets now.'

'Truth is our profession.' I smiled bitterly as I quoted the
Chronicle slogan back to him.

'Never believe what you read in the papers, lad . . . Look,'
he said, switching on the sympathy after a long pause, 'it's
just business, my son, nothing personal, no reflection on
you. It's just business. That's the way things are these days,
isn't it? Now you've got most of the money you were
promised, haven't you? Eh? And I'll try and line you up one
or two little items in the very near future. What else can I
do? Have a drink . . .'

'No,' I shook my head.

'Go on. Have a drink, for fuck's sake.'

'No.'

'Go on, just a little one,' he said as he produced a bottle of vodka and two greasy glasses.

'No, really, Maurie . . .'

He poured two anyway and shoved one of the glasses toward me. I pushed it back then, despite myself, I picked it up and drank some, the liquid burning bitterly all the way down.

'So,' I finally asked, 'none of it is ever gonna come out? No one'll ever know?'

'No one'll ever know,' he smiled sadly. 'No one outside this God-forsaken goldfish bowl, will ever know the whole truth 'cept you and me and we can't tell. The cat's in the bag and the bag's in the river.'

'It stinks, Maurie, it stinks.'

'Yeah, it stinks . . . but that's business for you. Everything's for sale now – even the news.'

'Especially the news. And you think I can't take it elsewhere? Not ever?' I asked, trying to exude a hint of menace, clutching at straws.

'Not if you don't wanna be sued to death. If you wanna talk about it then go to a priest or tell your mates or something because . . . it doesn't exist as a news story any more. I'm sorry, Peter, 'cos you're not a bad lad, but there's an end to it. End of story.'

35

The End Of The Working Week

As the Latin House beat faded, the chant came up for the umpteenth time.

'*No pasaran! No pasaran!*' – Spanish for 'they shall not pass' – was being shouted by a cast of thousands as the bongos and congas of Working Week's 'Eldorado' drifted into the mix.

I lay on my sofa, clutching the half-empty brandy bottle as a great wash of emotion swept over me, eclipsed me. All that Latin temperament flowing out of a little CD, the chant of a failed revolution captured forever in digital amber . . . The music stopped then re-started as I reeled from all the double whammies I'd been hit by. The Sam of long ago and then Chinese Sam . . . *Rocks* and *Raw Soul* . . . Anna and then Maurie . . . I phoned Barry but he was too stoned to talk. I was so desperate that night I even tried to call Jake in the States but the number was no longer available – he wasn't coming back, and maybe it didn't matter too much anyway. He hadn't phoned for months. I'd thought we were close, real good mates, after all the time we'd wasted together, painting the town red. Like James Brown and Wilson Pickett, the fastest hustlers alive, pals for ever – or not, as it turned out. And what did it matter? He was just a distant friend, as distant as all my dead dreams. And they hadn't even been my dreams, they were second-hand dreams, someone else's love, someone else's cause. Charlie was a bad boy, charlie had lost me Sally – I was too smashed-blocked to see she was a blinder who just needed a little bit of help but who didn't dare ask for it. And coke had blinded me to Anna's real intentions. And yet, and yet . . . the only ideal, the only lover, the only friend I really had, the only one that was still with me at that moment, was charlie. There was nothing else. Just my old pal Charlie.

As the Latin girl's voice stopped her poignant soaring, the people's chant started again as the tiny shiny disc kept flying relentlessly round and round . . . 'No *pasaran! No pasaran!*' And suddenly I found myself crying, actually crying – but not. There were convulsive great sobs hitting me every few seconds but they weren't proper sobs. They were dry, tearless sobs. I'd like to have felt tears on my face, I'd like to have felt something, but I couldn't. The tears wouldn't come. I was numb, completely numb. I wasn't in prison, because I now had some form of cover. But the cover had arrived too late – the patient was already dead. Dead, like his dreams . . . and the voices kept defiantly pleading, 'No *pasaran! No pasaran! No pasaran . . .*'

36

Get Out Of Denver, Baby

The stars were twinkling beautifully, just like a movie, millions of miles above my head. I stopped staring and forced my gaze back down to earth, back down to the tube train that was grinding to a halt before me. I was in the near-suburbia of North Kilburn. I think I'd gone there to score off Jerry but I wasn't sure. I tried to get a grip on myself as I got on the train. The carriage was empty. The doors closed and we moved off, on to Brondesbury Park or somewhere. I closed my eyes then opened them again – I was at North Kilburn again. North Kilburn – again! It completely freaked me out. Tube trains don't go in reverse, they can't. So I couldn't have been to Brondesbury Park. But I'd seen it, hadn't I? Seen it with my own eyes. What the hell was going on? I panicked and leapt off the train as the doors re-opened. It *was* North Kilburn. I felt on the edge of an abyss, like the ground was opening up beneath my feet. What the hell was happening to me? I touched a bench to be sure it was as real as the platform it was on . . .

'Last train to the West End, last train to London,' shouted the electric voice of the station-master. The train's doors began to jerk shut – I squeezed back on just in time, the tube doors smearing my chinos with a black rubber mark. I sat down, my shirt was as soaked and stressed as my screaming nerves. I swore that – despite everything, despite all the shit that was going down – I would knock the coke on the head. Like tomorrow, like now. Because this was way too much, this was . . .

37

Once Upon A Drug
Deal

I was so out of it, so very well out of it. Completely off my
face. Almost floating. Everything was blurred and slurred.
People's faces looked like they were smeared with Vaseline.
They, and everything else, moved either a little too fast, jerky
like, or in slight slow-motion – like a very arty movie. Things
looked like they were in black and white, too, but I don't
suppose they could have been. I was getting out of a cab in
south London. It was one of those areas that's on the border
of bedlam, like parts of Battersea, Herne Hill, Clapham. You
know what I mean. Big flash houses and nearly safe streets
nestling just a stone's throw from council estates bristling
with guns, crackheads and hookers. The cab had just gone
over a small hump-backed bridge. We were in a high street.
The street-light seemed low and bright but that was nice visu-
ally because they gave out that yellow-bronze light that makes
a street look like a film set. The light that gives everyone a bit
of a tan. I slipped the cabby a tenner and he said something I
couldn't hear.

There was a kind of half-covered shopping mall that had a

clòsed video shop and an open take-away. There was an orange-domed toilet between them and I decided to use it before I went to the house. The house? Oh yeah, I was going to someone's house. It was a party – no, sorry, an 'informal function'. The guy was wealthy, very wealthy. Stupidly wealthy. Wealthier than me. Wealthier than Vee. I wander through the half-open mall like a sleep-walker. I notice a gang of four kids, three hanging back and one big bastard standing near the corner of the take-away. The big one must be twenty-five or more. Unshaven, crumpled but clean shirt, hands in his pockets. A real poseur. They all sneer on cue. No one makes a move though. I get to the toilet, use it, wash my hands and get a few face-blasts of warm air from the drying machine. And I thought, between blasts, why didn't they do me? Why wasn't I more worried?

Now I'm back outside, on the high street. Looking for the house. I can hear shouts and screams a few dozen yards behind me. Not approaching. Not particularly. I can't work out if the gang have decided to take the take-away or if the violence is blocks and blocks away. Whichever it is, it's unsettling. I'm having trouble walking straight. I'm having trouble breathing, to be frank. Fighting is out of the question. Even in self-defence.

There's a constant low rumble going on, a deep almost sub-sonic sound that you feel more than you can hear. Like a tube train passing nearby. Except that this tube train doesn't stop, it goes on and on and on. A couple of cars cruise past, dance beats thundering out of their 200-watt speakers. The sound rides uncomfortably over the bass rumble. For one nano-second I feel like a total stranger to all this. All of it. For one moment I can experience this place as my dad might have done, my dad as he was thirty or forty years ago. Young, respectable and with a tie on even when he was working in the factory. And somehow I'm feeling like him then, seeing all this now. He'd have instantly sussed the atmosphere. The menace. He'd have been stunned by 'Those drums, those bloody drums! What is this? Jungle street? The drummer's refuge?' He'd have been shocked by the boarded-up shops, the obscene graffiti, the bright revealing clothes of the girls, the arrogance of the knife-gangs wandering around unchecked. He had relatives – uncles and great uncles – who'd died in wars. World War Two, Korea. Died for their kids, for a decent society, to make the streets safe.

The streets weren't safe. The kids weren't safe. The kids weren't even all right; they were more dangerous than ever. Like the streets were. The land of checks and balances was now a place of dud cheques and chemical imbalances. And sheer viciousness: you could be stabbed here and the blood would have dried before anyone bothered to call the cops. And they'd take an hour to turn up. *If* they turned up. Your life ebbing away as you read and re-read walls that just said, 'Fuck you! Fuck you!' A land fit for zeroes. *You told us we wuz free, Mister Attlee . . .* They used to say the past is another country, but things have changed since then. Now it'd be more accurate to say the present is another country. It's a big betrayal, and even thinking about it threatens to bring me down. I could almost cry – if I was drunk enough, if I could still cry . . . So I forget it and it's all gone. Snap. Hit the 'off' button – all gone. Erased like all the others. Like the dream it now seems to have been . . .

Keep walking, gulp down the fresh air. I feel okay now. More awake. More optimistic. Forget it all. *Let's get happy.* We are, after all, going to a party. An informal function. I see the house. A long arrangement with three more floors stuck on at one end. Like some avant-garde house from the Seventies. It's a mansion. A big mansion. It could take a dozen bedrooms and lose them and not even notice. I'm inside now, can't remember what I said at the door but somehow I am expected and I am inside. There's a dull buzz of conversation, a few girls in evening dresses, shoulders glowing gracefully. Cocktail glasses are swirled around. Second division, really, by their own standards. Nouveau riche types who weren't that nouveau – or that riche.

People are ignoring the two big TVs that are showing porno

flicks. The same images, over and over again. Gleaming muscles flexing and pumping, big red mouths gasping and pouting. I decide to ignore them too. I can hear someone saying, 'Of course not! I'm not some cheap hustler!' Which is, of course, the cry of every cheap hustler. I can see four or five men I know. They are by the corner cocktail bar, all have drinks. All are music biz characters. Movers and shakers – and their attendant liggers. One is moving some bottles and another is shaking a chrome cocktail-shaker. A mover moving. A shaker shaking. Did I say a chrome shaker? No, no way. It must be silver. Silver or platinum. I'm looking at it now. Holding it in my hand. Its metal cold. And it is silver, there's the little hallmark. I pour myself one.

'How you doing?'

I'm doing all right. Doing well? *Yeah, yeah, yeah.* Eighteen with a bullet. Thirty thousand units shifted. What is it? *Margarita?* Tequila Sunrise? *No, Margarita Sunrise.* Right first time. It is bad here, as bad as the West End. As bad as it gets. People flashing eyes at each other, looking for a kiss, looking for a kiss-off. Blank eyes, predatory. We gave already, we gave it all. There's nothing left. Unless you lend me some . . .

'We'll do some slammers later.'

There's some dreamy ambient hip-hoppy stuff rolling out of the hi-fi. I take a joint as it's passed but no matter how long I hold it, no matter how much I inhale, it doesn't make me chill – I can still hear, just under the ambient trip-hop, the rumble from the streets outside. But the screams seem to have gone.

Want some stuff? Want some gear? Upstairs. I walk up the staircase, wide, curved staircase.

'You could use this in a film. This staircase.'

We did. *Didn't you see it?* The staircase carpets are a nice neat grey, like the room. I can feel my heart quicken. At last. Some cream, toot, tink, snow. Gonna score, gonna score. ABC's remix of 'Look Of Love' started to kick in – or was it Melle Mel's 'White Lines'? It no longer mattered.

We go into some room at the front on the second or third floor. Lots of glass windows but we're too high for anyone to look in. So many windows, in fact, that it's almost like an oval-shaped lighthouse. The top of a lighthouse. *The business end.* There is a goldfish bowl on a table. It is a goldfish bowl and it is full of coke. *Full.* Of coke. The *crème de la crème* with the cream of the cream. The stuff that dreams are made of. It's powder but a bit moist, almost like a paste in places, with lumps in it. *Well fresh.* As fresh as it comes. Fresh off the banana boat. Fresh out of some embassy flight. Corps Diplomatique? *Who cares?* The centre's long gone. It didn't hold . . .

That is amazing. *This is amazing.* To be in a room with that amount. *That amount.* That much stuff in just one house, in just one room, *in just one fucking goldfish bowl!* A God-forsaken goldfish bowl . . . It's chopped out, line after line, chopped and smoothed back and forth. The guy doing it repeats the action like a glass craftsman playing with some especially fine grains of sand. Chopped and smoothed with a platinum Amex card. Platinum – people with cover. *What else could it be?* These are quality people – *We can help you, we can help you.* I'm gonna score, *gonna score, gonna score!*

I'm scoring, I'm scoring. Breathing in the powder, lungs tingling. Numbness spreading across my nose-face. Across my entire face. Can't feel the back of my throat. Can't feel any of my throat. The crystalline powder bleaches out my face then passes through the thin walls of the lungs and out into the body itself, stunning the organs and switching all the red lights to green – a wave of elation hits within less than half a minute. And then there's a second wave. But it seems thinner this time. Thinner and less . . . less fun. I need to take *more.* A second, a third line. Two, three, three and a half. Getting to the brink now. My nose is permanently sore these days. The skin above my top lip is red raw too. Most nights I have to dab Q-tips with Germolene and gently push them into each nostril in turn. To ease the pain. But going without the coke was worse. *Is* worse.

'Have some to take away, matey.'

We can help you, we can help you. Have some. I take a big, pasty lump. Nearly half an ounce. Ten, twelve grams? *You can deal for us, you can deal for us.* I could. I could deal for them. White lines tripped through my head. *D-d-d-don't do it!* But why not? I pocket the stuff, smiling sickly, but the buzzing inside me has already crossed over, crossed over into anxiety, serious anxiety. I look around – no one has any pupils in their eyes. *No one.* They all look like aliens. Androids. I feel a sweat descend on me. Need some more air. I go to the window, it won't open. *Won't open!* Calm down, calm down. Twist the handle that way. This way.

'What is this place? A fucking *prison*?'

Chill, chill. It finally opens. The cold night air floods into my face. A face that can't feel it any more. Too numb. I look down. Breathe deep – but my lungs are numb too, can't feel that either. To the left, I see a van pulling up on the deserted high street. It's a police van – a *police van*! Four cops – no, three – get out. One glances up as my face freezes. But it's just a glance up – is it? Isn't it? Yes – not at us, not at anything. The cops start to give a motorist a hard time. My pulse rate is quickening. The cops finally get back in the van and it rolls, just rolls, forward a bit. Half a block. Then stops – doesn't it? Just out of sight – I'm sure that's its back bumper I can still see. Isn't it? Heart-beat, increasing heart-beat. What's wrong? The sound, that's what's wrong. The sound is what is wrong. I can now hear it again with the window open. The slow thunder sound and, stabbing across the top of it, the shouts and screams. The screams. What *is* going on?

I turn my gaze to the right – heart feels like an alligator now, rolling and thumping and kicking against my rib-cage, how much can it take? I mean, how much? Seriously – and the street is pregnantly empty. Something's gonna happen. Something. I look to the left. Someone joins me leaning out of the window. They speak but it's in slo-mo. *Can't they talk any faster? Talk faster!* I speak, but they don't understand what I'm saying, they go back in. I look right again. There's now a dozen people down there, gathered outside the mansion's front door. I start to count them and by the time I finish it's thirty. Thirty-five. Forty. Heart still thumping hard. In fact, it's thumping harder than ever. Forty-five of 'em down there. Fifty. *Who are they?* Gate-crashers. Must be. Not our lot. They look like club people. They can't be plain clothes. Not that many. Maybe some of them. Maybe not. Maybe. Be calm, be cherry . . . I walk down a flight of stairs, brushing aside a waitress with a tray of drinks. One drink falls, glass shatters.

'Clumsy!'

Why is no one else worried? Can't they tell what's happening here? Are they so out of it that they can't tell? *Are they caning it that much?*

The feeling of impending doom is roaring now. I'm run-walking down the stairs two at a time. Nearly tripping on the fitted carpets. Gotta be careful, can't fall with that cocktail glass still in my hand. Still in my hand? I look down. My tense fingers have long ago snapped the glass off its stem. The stem is stuck in my palm, I'm bleeding, I feel the pain in abstract. Not that bad. Loose edge of skin like cut fruit. I shove the glass on a half-empty bookshelf – pieces of ice slush begin to brush the first editions. *Clumsy!*

'What's he playing at?'

I grab a white cotton serviette and wrap it around the spreading red patch on my hand. My pulse is painfully fast now. How much can one heart take? I've got to move, can't stand still or I'll explode. I trip down the stairs, two, three at a time. Reach the base of the stairs, grab the hand-guide to keep myself upright. The voices of the gate-crashers have got louder and there are uglier, nastier sounds crashing against the big wooden door. The blood has seeped through the white cloth on my hand. A red stain is clearly visible. It just begins to hit me how desperate things are getting. If the mob get in – they're really angry now, they've waited so long – they're gonna go *ape*. They're gonna wreck the place but good. They're gonna hurt people. When they see the blood on my hand, they're gonna seek me out. Like sharks scenting blood. They're too wild, not human any more – that wasn't unexpected, no one makes humans any more, there's no market for 'em, no demand. They were too sentimental.

And what about me? I'm gonna get an extra-special kicking when they get in. A kicking? Let's get real here. They are gonna kill me. I know that. I know that now. *Definitely.* Why hasn't anyone listened? *What are they doing?* Those outside are gonna kill us if they get in. If they get in. If? Don't you mean *when?* A voice from outside shouts louder than the others.

'We've been through six foyers. Six! Looking for this fuckin' dump!' The voice becomes a chorus. 'Let us in! *Let us in!*'

And then the voices turn into thumps. They're trying to kick the door down. The old brown wood is slowly being kicked back on its hinges, millimetre by millimetre. A screw jumps out of one of the door bolt-holders. And another. And another! Someone's noticed! *At last!* At last someone's noticed. A girl in an off-the-shoulder dress is frantically tapping out a number on the phone.

'Police. Get me the police. What's wrong with you? We need the police! *Are you listening? I said, the police!*'

And then I think – the police! I clutch at the lump of coke in my jacket. More than seven grams. Much, much more. He's a *dealer*; Pete's a dealer. Three years minimum. Maybe five. No remission. Gotta get rid of it – but I can't – it's the most I've had for years, it feels like years. Not gonna let go of it. An old friend is by my side.

'Didn't know you were here . . .'

He says nothing but I know what he wants. He wants some cream. My cream. *Mine!* He's holding his hand out. His eyes are all grey – an alien. I shake my head – no way, no way – it's my stuff, no way. *No way. No!* His face turns angry, screwed up. It looks wizened in this light, wizened in his pathetic lust for the stuff. A twentysomething looking fortysomething. Looking older. He clutches at me. An angry android. Do I look that way? Is this a mirror? Suddenly everyone's aware of the impending disaster. Now! *Now when it's too fucking late!* People are running up and down the steps behind me. Toilets are frantically being flushed. But the front door is splintering now! Now! Two guys drag a sideboard in front of the door – that'll hold it for all of twenty seconds! I turn around – my old friend has gone. Girls gather in the hallway. Someone's gone to the kitchen – they come back with a pair of knives. One is blunt – useless. Someone has a gun but it has no live ammo with it – *useless*. Some girls run to a back room then run back to the hall. No way out, *no way out*. Some of them are crying. One takes her earrings off, quietly pockets them. It's a small, calm gesture but it says everything. It says she knows she's gonna get raped. She is gonna get raped. *And she knows it*. Just like I know they're gonna get me too. But good. The sideboard is getting pushed over. Three of the host's friends get behind it but it's too late, *too late*. I back away in horror, floundering into some back room. The back room is full of fur coats, Burberry macs, fleck overcoats. The windows are locked and there are bars behind their locks. Bars behind the bars. What is this? *A fucking prison?* There's a key on a dusty side shelf. It fiddles unhappily in the lock. The screams and shouts are in the mansion now, someone turns the music up to drown them out. Thumps can be heard. Furniture being smashed. The key turns. The bars concertina to one side, they stop – *no! no!* – then go on.

I'm in the big dark garden now, bent double, running low, running desperate, running zig-zag style in case someone's looking. In case someone starts firing. A window is smashed somewhere behind me. Then another. *And another.* A scream rises and then gets choked. The back lawn gently slopes down a few feet. There's a mess of bushes and thick plants. Only four or five feet high. But dense. Really *dense*. Impenetrable. I struggle through. Face scratched, clothing ripped but I struggle through. And scramble to my feet the other side, breathing hard. Two cops are standing by their gleaming wet car. We are face to face. They tell me to stop but, though I'm exhausted,

I try and lurch on past them. One gets me. I didn't even get past his front bumper. He hits me with a low punch. Slams me down on his car bonnet. I can feel the cheap modern steel of the bonnet give a bit. One of them twists my arm. Can't blame him. I asked for it. And I got it. The other cop is gripping his night-stick, staring down at my immobile face. But something in his eyes moves and I know he's not gonna use the stick on me. A decent man. A museum piece. He would let me go. They *will* let me go, they have to let me go. What have I done? There's murder going on in there! *What have I done?* They're going through my pockets now. *The cream!* I forgot to ditch the cream. The cat who got the cream. They've got the cat – and the cat's in the bag and the bag's in the river, and now they get the *cream.* And not the game, this is no game. *Grams and grams.* There's no chance of a caution. No chance. The one who's holding my arm dabs at the cream, tastes it, rubs it against his gums just to make sure – and to get a little high. He keeps rubbing. He wants a big high. Perk of the job, guv'nor. He sees that I've twisted my face round to look at him. He feels guilty. He relieves his guilt in anger, pocketing the coke before smashing his hand down on my ear. I feel that lurching, here-we-go feeling. My face dents the bonnet. Dents it a bit more than before. Blood from my ear trickles down and dilutes my tears.

'There's murder going on in there,' I sound weak, like an ill child pleading for attention.

'We know, kid, we know.'

My nose starts to run. My mouth is watering. Tiny white grains stand out in the saliva that gathers on the bonnet.

'There's murder going on in there, you know? *Murder?*'

'We *know.* We allowed it, we planned it . . . only way to get your loose-cannon dealer these days. Mob rule. Persons unknown, by any means necessary.'

Lead by *agents provocateur*, no doubt. In the *plural*. I think about it, it all makes sense now. A cacophony of sirens gets closer and closer. The horror of it all grows and grows and grows until its mood eclipses everything. Eclipses me. I'm going to die here. I knew it would end in tears – or in tear gas. Here or in prison. I babble fragments of the evening, I babble my life story. The story of the evening. And then it hits me like a blast from a sawn-off – the story of the evening is the story of my life. *Is this all there is?* You work late to get the cash to buy the drugs that help you work late so you can get the cash that buys the drugs . . . is that it? All just *faking*? All just money-making? *We can help you, we can help you . . .*

'What about the girls in there? There's blue murder going on in there.'

'We know, kid, we know . . .'

'I'm a reporter, I'm just here on a drugs story—'

'Yeah, yeah, yeah.'

The mob were outside now, smeared faces covered with blood. A riot. Would all this get in the *Chronicle*? Would it fuck . . . I went down. Backwards. I didn't understand that bit at all. *Wasn't I outside?* As my fear reached its height, a sudden warmth covered me. Is this it? I was out there. But I'm not stoned now. *Is this it?* Everything snaps into focus just before the camera is turned off. A photographer looms out of nowhere – my old surveillance photographer – and explodes a flash in my face. Busted. Freeze frame and fade into oblivion.

Silence. Darkness. No, not darkness, I could see some kind of faint murky light. The light, such as it was, washed over a grey ceiling. My eyes adjusted to the dark as I adjusted to being alive. I was lying in a darkened room. The feeble light was coming through the cheap canvas curtains. I was awake. Alive. And not in hospital. It all came back to me, the frantic phone calls I'd made from the police station, phone calls to Maurie at the *Chronicle* . . . He'd answered in the end. Now that he'd killed me, he didn't mind keeping me alive . . .

I was in my own crumbling flat. In the bedroom. My heart had been thumping like crazy while I'd been asleep but then, as I woke up, it had slowed down. How perverse. And the silence – the silence was not complete silence. I could hear some slow measured breathing. Breathing that was not my own. I turned to look. There was a girl beside me, curled up asleep. Sally. Peaceful and perfect as only a sleeping woman can be.

I'd been off the coke for a few days. It wasn't exactly centuries but it was something. A start. I was bouncing back, cleaning up my act . . . It was a start. After my lost weeks of madness.

I was right to give it all up. It was like a cigar. Some ex-smokers can do cigars just at Christmas and birthdays. And the next day they're still off the fags, no trouble. While others just can't hit and quit, can't do it just twice a year. So they shouldn't do it at all. I couldn't just do it twice a year so I shouldn't do it at all. I wasn't, in fact, doing it. Not now, not any more.

Besides – money and paranoia aside – coke was seriously bad for your health. I'd heard that David Bowie gave up coke, years ago now, after he'd seen a autopsy picture of the brain slice of some coke-using dealer. This dealer had been off his face; wasted, when some killer wasted him. The brain of this coke addict was riddled with holes. Listen up here. These were *not* bullet wounds – he'd actually been shot in the chest – but holes caused by coke. By the use of cocaine. They were holes big enough to put your *fingers* into. Like the holes in a bowling ball. Or a Swiss cheese. A grey slice of mouse-trap. Now that, if you really think about it, was frightening. But not for me. Not frightening for me. Not any more. I was in the clear.

I relaxed. I was away from all that now. Let the rats sniff themselves to death. I was well off out of it. Well out of it . . .

I was such an old pro really, I *knew* I'd come through in the end. I always did . . . in the end. I could sleep easy now. I'd just had a 'mare and now it was over and I was feeling okay.

I even felt cosy, all the lights were on inside my head but they weren't overloading any more, weren't squawking like a pinball machine. No, they were just twinkling softly, silently, like the far-away lights of some much-loved city that was home.

Sally and I would live together. *We* would start again. And we'd work it all out. We would. Sound, sorted, solid. And safe . . . safe . . . safe . . .

38

I Live Alone . . .

I had jumped the gun. I'd told Jerry I was doing another feature on his friend's new singer. Vee wasn't really a friend of Jerry's but so what? This wasn't personal, this was business. It justified me charting the singer. After all, Jerry had done me some favours. He'd even got me into some ligs, over the years. Which must have been where I met him, once. Either there or The Coach.

'It's on Vee's new label, his new one,' Jerry said, staring at his glass of JD. I was supposed to know Vee but I didn't, not really. Vee was a big-shot, that much I did know.

'Don't worry,' he went on, 'Vee's good today, he's cherry, he's cool, down with everyone. I'll get him to sort you out.'

Huh? Before I can say any more, Vee walks in. Medium-tall, dark hair, blue Paul Smith shirt – undone. Jerry goes over and whispers something. They approach.

'Hi, Pete . . . how's it going?'

Sarf London. Vee's eyes sweep around the room, taking it

all in, the empty tables, the lovers necking, the deserted bar. As he does so, we shake hands. I realise he's putting something in my hand. A plastic packet. *I pocket the plastic packet without a second glance.*